THE MASKS OF DARKNESS

An Ackroyd and Thackeray mystery

Recently divorced, Jay Morton returns to her home town of Pendle Bridge with her daughter Kate. She gets a job helping to set up a museum at Pendle House, and while searching for artefacts in the attics she stumbles across some extraordinary masks with malevolent and threatening eyes... Donna once lived at Pendle House when it was a children's home and she remembers the menacing masks, and the depraved men behind them, all too clearly. Donna has returned to Pendle Bridge with only one thought in her mind – it's time that justice was served.

THE MASKS OF DARKNESS

THE MASKS OF DARKNESS

by

Patricia Hall

Magna Large Print Books
Long Preston, North Yorkshire,
BD23 4ND, England.

British Library Cataloguing in Publication Data.

Hall, Patricia
    The masks of darkness.

    A catalogue record of this book is
    available from the British Library

    ISBN   0-7505-2235-6

First published in Great Britain 2004 by Allison & Busby Ltd.

Copyright © 2004 by Patricia Hall

Cover illustration © The Old Tin Dog

Published in Large Print 2004 by arrangement with
Allison & Busby Ltd.

Magna Large Print is an imprint of Library Magna Books Ltd.

Printed and bound in Great Britain by
T.J. (International) Ltd., Cornwall, PL28 8RW

1

She was very afraid that she had left it too late. Twenty years was a long time – anything could have happened in twenty years. Donna's breath quickened as she let her mind edge back towards the horrors of the past. Perhaps they'd been locked up in the end, perhaps they'd put a foot wrong at last and got themselves put away. Not that prison would be sufficient, she thought. She had something more unpleasant in mind than that. But she had wasted so much time and that filled her with anxiety. All those years running, hiding, moving on, keeping in the shadows in case they followed her. Then the faces had come, looming out of the dark, grinning, leering, threatening. And that insidious little voice, childish but insistent, always reminding her of what she would rather forget: that it was her fault, all her fault.

And the first of the hospitals had followed, like day follows night, a great barn of a place, mad men and women, staring and mumbling, nurses who sometimes seemed just as mad, shouting incomprehensibly, erupting into sudden violence and talking, talking, talking and creating confusion. She did not want to talk. The conversations in her head were occupation enough. Then big gaps when they told her time had passed but she had no recollection of it. Her mind wiped clean, the memories only coming back slowly, in dreams and flashbacks at first but later with complete clarity so that when she stepped off the bus at Pendle Bridge she had hesitated, shaken by the golden colour of the stone which she knew used to be black and overwhelmed by the unexpected freshness in the air. In those days it had only been so clear far up on the moorland above the smoky little town.

She didn't mind moving again, she thought, feeling the weight of her suitcase as she picked it up again. She'd hated it the first time, of course, so far, far back in time that it seemed like another world, when she had moved out of the house which was the last place she had been even remotely happy with her mother. She had not understood at the time why they'd had to move, though she'd worked out since that there must have been some problem with the rent or the mortgage. No one had told her and she didn't suppose she'd have understood then anyway. All she'd known was that they had to pack up all their stuff in boxes and suitcases into a white van, bundling the twins together in their pram and pushing them halfway across the town, to move into this new place, in a big block, with windows that didn't open properly and great patches of black mould in the bathroom, like witches' fingers crawling all over the ceiling. She remembered lying on her back in the bath, completely covered by the water except for her nose, imagining they'd come down and get her, those fingers, tickle her maybe, or more likely strangle her. She had hated that place, she thought bitterly. That's where it all began. Even in spite of her father, they'd been

8

happy until then. If they hadn't moved that time perhaps he would never have died like that.

And now she was back and the little town, the stone houses crushed tightly on top of each other between the steep hills, looked curiously the same but so different. She lugged her suitcase up the hill from the bus station to the bed and breakfast place she had booked by phone once she had made the decision to do what she and Archie had planned to do for so long. And now Mags was insisting too, coming to her at night and urging her on. And what Mags wanted she would have to attempt, because it was her fault that Mags was dead. Most of the time the small voice which whispered in her ear was very faint but Donna always knew that what it said was true. She had not, and would never have hurt her friend, but she had not helped her either, when she had most needed help. Those who had hurt her would regret it now she was back but she had led Mags into danger and failed her. Deep down, where it counted, she was to blame.

She took another deep breath of the unfamiliar air, filling her lungs to capacity to get rid of the sour taste of the bus in which she had just spent five hours, and gazed around in some astonishment. The market square was clogged with four-wheel drives squeezed into parking spaces and onto pavements in a mechanised jungle of big beasts. The butcher and baker and cobbler's shops she and Mags had skipped past on their way to cash in their spending money for sweets at Woollies and whatever they could pocket besides had been replaced by a deli and a greengrocer's

9

with aubergines and avocados and fruits she barely recognised on display. The mills she remembered had either disappeared completely or seemed to have been turned into apartments, the chimney stacks pointing cool newly scrubbed fingers at the blue sky, more heavenly than satanic now. And the more she absorbed the transformation the more convinced she became that she was too late, the place she knew had almost vanished and the objects of her passion had most likely vanished with it.

She bought the local paper at the newsagents on the corner of the street where she had booked her room, and once the incurious receptionist on the ground floor had given her a key and she had hauled the suitcase up two flights of narrow stairs, she kicked off her high heels and fell back onto the bed, sweaty inside her smart wool jacket. She leaned back against the pillows to recover her breath and glanced at the headlines and almost stopped breathing, the shock was so great. There he was, smiling out at her from the front page, one of the men whose names she had never known and whose faces, except for that one last time, she had never seen. He was fleshier, his hair thinner, more self-satisfied in expression, if that were possible, but undoubtedly the same man, gone, it seemed, from strength to strength in the intervening years.

'There, I told you we'd find the bastard, Archie,' she whispered. 'I bet he's forgotten our Mags and what he did to her, but we haven't, have we? We'll never forget. Kenny and me and you, we'll remind him. Just you see if we don't.'

Feeling much better, she took off her jacket,

hung it carefully over the back of a chair, and turned to the situations vacant columns.

Jay Morton knelt amongst the packing cases which littered her new home and wondered if she had made a terrible mistake. The house, which had been full of sunshine on the day she had decided to buy it, dust motes from the bare boards dancing in the filtered beams of light, just seemed dark and chilly now, with a faint odour of something musty she could not identify. And the mountain of unpacked belongings did not seem to diminish much even after hours of unwrapping and sorting which took her tramping endlessly from living room to kitchen and up and down the narrow uncarpeted stairs to the two bedrooms off the tiny landing. It was already obvious that this Victorian cottage, empty and echoing and apparently spacious enough when she had committed her precious savings to it, would be barely adequate for herself and her daughter Kate and the possessions they had brought with them from the now abandoned family home in London. The detritus of a marriage, even split two ways with the scrupulous fairness of a 'civilised' divorce, seemed more than this little house could accommodate.

Jay glanced at her watch. Kate had gone to her new school for the first time today, just a short walk down to the corner of Adelaide Street where it joined the main road half a mile or so up the steep hill from the centre of the small Pennine town of Pendle Bridge. They had walked down together at eight forty-five and Kate had graciously allowed herself to be delivered to her new Year 6 class teacher in the modern block at the back of the original gothic school building, but she had refused point blank to be collected at the end of the afternoon.

'Mu-u-um, I'm ten and we only live round the corner,' she'd wailed with all the certainty of youth, flinging her ponytail of dark curls back, her lips a thin line in a pale determined little face. 'I've been coming home from school by myself for ages!' Jay had acquiesced reluctantly, knowing that Kate had no friends here yet to walk home with, but anxious not to cramp her growing independence. So she had left her there with that faint lurch of the heart which accompanied every new demand Kate made, worse now that there was no David to at least try to share the decisions with.

'Straight home, mind,' she said, curbing the urge to give her daughter a hug before she left her. She could feel the sharp eyes of some other early arrivals watching from inside the classroom, only too ready to mock, and the teacher, a Miss Ashcroft, as young and blonde and efficient-looking as Jay felt middle-aged and scruffy, hovered impatiently after their few words of introduction as she waited to escort Kate inside.

It was still only twenty past two, more than an hour before she could reasonably expect Kate home. Jay sighed and ran grubby fingers through her hair, then turned her attention back to the precarious stack of books she had unpacked so far when she was interrupted by the wheeze of the arthritic door-bell which worked on an ancient mechanical screw system she had never encountered before – an original feature, the estate agent had said, straight-faced. She climbed to her feet and opened the green painted front door, with its small inset panel of faded stained glass – also original, the agent had enthused so heartily that Jay had wondered if an outdoor privy would rate a desirable antique label too. She found her brother-in-law Chris Hateley on the doorstep, clutching a luxuriant pot plant to his chest.

'Hi,' she said, surprised. 'I wasn't expecting you.' She wiped her hands on the seat of her jeans and pushed her untidy hair out of her eyes as Chris planted a fleeting kiss on the cheek she reluctantly offered him.

'Sue sent this,' he said, handing her the plant and looking slightly abashed at her less than enthusiastic greeting. 'She thought I could drop it in on my way home, but I was just passing now anyway. Sort of house-warming gift.'

Jay sniffed sceptically. 'I'm beginning to wonder if I'll ever warm to this place,' she said.

'Desirable period residences these, now,' Chris said, glancing around at the barely controlled chaos which filled the living room. 'Prices have gone through the roof. They were virtual slums when we were kids, if you remember that far back. The smelly lad in our class came from Adelaide Street.'

'It's solid enough,' Jay conceded. 'But there's nothing out the back but the old yard refurbished a bit. I'd have liked a garden for Kate. Come in the kitchen and I'll make some coffee. How come you're not at work, anyway? Can you always go visiting at this time of day?' She led the way through the packing cases to the back of the house and put the kettle on.

'I'm on my way back from a meeting out at police headquarters. Was passing the end of the road and thought I'd see how you were getting on,' Chris said, taking one of the stools at the small breakfast table. 'Boss's privilege to take a detour.'

'Bully for you,' Jay said, somewhat sourly. 'It's OK, then, is it, being editor of the *Advertiser*? I always had you marked down for bigger and better things. Fleet Street and all that.' Chris Hateley's jaw tightened almost imperceptibly and he watched her pour water into the cafetiere and slowly push down the plunger with more intensity than the task required, staring at the darkening liquid for a moment before he replied.

'Sharp as ever, Jay?' he said. 'You have to choose, don't you? Big fish, small pool or little fish, big pool. Fleet Street's long gone, anyway, and I'm not sure I'm a big city guy in any case. So when the editorship came up I grabbed it, even though it is only a weekly. And you know Sue. She never much fancied moving away, especially after we had the kids. You were always the independent one and you chose something different...' He hesitated again.

'And look at me now,' Jay finished the sentence for him. 'Back where I bloody well started. Well, the job looked interesting and the house prices are mercifully lower than London, so it all seemed to make perfect sense at the time.' She glanced round at the worktops, still piled high with crockery and glassware waiting to be stacked away and smiled wryly. 'We'll have to see,' she said.

'Well, they sell aubergines and sun-dried

14

tomatoes and six different varieties of olives in Pendle Bridge market now, so you won't feel too much like a foreigner. I even saw foccacia in the baker's last week They call us the Yorkshire Islington now, you know. We've moved onwards and upwards, even up here in t'chilly north.'

'I'm sure you have,' Jay said, with half a smile. 'Though I'm not sure being the Islington of the North is much to write home about. All fur coats and no knickers, that, from what I've seen of it. Anyway, I dare say I'll survive.'

'When do you start the new job?'

'The end of the month,' Jay said.

'Should be interesting, though I must say I was amazed when they got lottery money for it. Without extra cash, all that stuff would be mouldering away indefinitely.'

'I should think some of it will have mouldered already,' Jay said. 'As I understand it when the place was left to the council they just dumped the collections in the attics and made what use they could of the rest of the house. If the stuff's as interesting as they say it is, the council officers who made that decision should be shot.'

'Oh, you know local councils. Penny-pinching one minute, squandering a fortune when it suits them, usually when the councillors own comfort is involved. It's a bit of a come-down, though, isn't it, setting up a little local museum after working in one of the big national places?' Chris was obviously not above getting his own back, Jay thought wryly and she wondered how many old scores he was intending to settle.

'Like you – big fish, small pool. It may turn out

15

more satisfying in the end. But tell me a bit more about Pendle House. Wasn't it a children's home or something when we were kids?' Jay asked.

'That's right. And then when big children's homes went out of fashion they used it as county council offices for a bit and let bits off to the Inland Revenue. Then when Pendle Bridge got its own council back a few years ago they built themselves a smart new office block down by the river and let the whole of the house. When that company collapsed, our esteemed MP had this bright idea of turning it into a museum to boost the tourist trade so they had to find a way of sorting out all the stuff they were left thirty years ago. The Wright family had been squirrelling stuff away for years before the last of them died. But I must say I thought the idea was slightly bizarre. I annoyed old Bernie Grogan by daring to say as much in an editorial.'

'Yes, I met Mr. Bernard Grogan MP at my interview. Very full of himself, he was, I thought. The set-up's not ideal, though, and I told them that. As far as I can see I'll be working surrounded by builders for the first year or so while they modernise the place and sort out what's going where, but of course they don't even know what they've got until I've done a rough inventory. They don't know if they need manuscript rooms, galleries for paintings, display rooms for artefacts. The paperwork that went with the collections seems to have either disappeared entirely or just been dumped in cardboard boxes. Quite honestly, I'm amazed the lottery people were convinced by the plan.'

'Personally I thought the whole lot should have

gone to the county museum.'

'Oh, Grogan wouldn't have wanted that, would he?' Jay said. 'He's passionate about the stuff staying at Pendle House. I can't say I warmed to the man but he certainly knows what he wants and seems to have been pretty successful at finding a way of getting it.'

'Oh, no one warms to Bernie,' Chris said. 'I've known him for years. He was a mate of my father's from when they were both on the council together, but Dad gave up politics when his heart began playing up. He's still on umpteen other committees mind, including the museum, as you know. New Labour wasn't really my dad's scene, or Grogan's for that matter, but by then Bernie had become the local MP so he went along with it all. And to be fair to the man, he works hard for Pendle Bridge.'

'Not a man to cross then, my new boss?' Jay said thoughtfully.

'Not if you can avoid it, no,' Chris agreed. 'But he'll not bother you much. He's away in London most of the week. And give the man his due. This museum scheme may be a bit unusual but if it brings a few tourists in it won't do the town any harm. Stranger things have happened now the old industries have gone. You've got miners down in South Yorkshire showing visitors round the pits they used to work in, for God's sake. How sad is that?'

'So Pendle Bridge will pay me to set up a grand memorial to one of its rapacious mill-owning families. Times certainly change,' Jay said.

'For all of us,' Chris said with a speculative look

17

in his eyes. 'And you? How are you really, Jay? You're not looking too bad on it, considering. But you and David always looked so settled ... I was really surprised when you split up.'

Jay stared into her empty coffee cup and wondered again how a twelve-year marriage which she had believed was rock solid had suddenly splintered like rotten wood, leaving her with an aching void which she had no idea how to fill except with a bitter anger which she feared would corrode her whole being. She had so far been unable to find words for what had happened since the day David Morton came home from work to announce that he had met someone else and wanted a divorce. She had handled him, she thought, with admirable self restraint but she did not even want to attempt an explanation for Chris Hateley, who had once pursued her rather than her sister and whom she had rejected precipitately and no doubt cruelly after she left Pendle Bridge to go to university. In spite of his marriage to her sister, they had kept their distance since.

'These things happen,' she said dismissively, getting up and collecting the coffee cups. Chris was the last person she wanted to discuss her emotional state with. There was far too much history there. 'I must get on. I was hoping that I might have cleared some space in the living room for us to sit down and relax tonight by the time Kate gets home from school, but there's just so much stuff to sort out.' She shrugged dispiritedly. Behind them, as if on cue, the door-bell wheezed again. Saved by the bell, Jay thought as she went to the front door and recognised her daughter's

18

slim outline through the stained glass panel.

Kate greeted her uncle with rather more enthusiasm than her mother had done.

'How was the new school?' Chris asked.

'Oh, it was all right,' Kate said nonchalantly in a way which Jay knew meant that it had not been all right at all.

'Make any friends?' she asked, her voice feeling unusually tight.

'I sat by a girl called Sonja,' Kate said, sounding more uncertain now. 'But she talks a bit funny. She's not English. And then some of the boys said I talk funny too.'

'Don't worry, Katie,' Chris said. 'They'll have you talking like a born and bred little tyke before you know where you are.'

'What's a tyke?' Kate asked.

'A Yorkshire lass. Like your mum.'

'Are you a Yorkshire lass, Mum? I didn't know that,' Kate said as she rooted around amongst the kitchen tins and containers until she found a packet of biscuits. 'I'm starving,' she said, helping herself to three.

'I was just going,' Chris Hateley said. 'But we'll see you soon. Your mum must bring you round to see your cousins at the weekend. OK?'

'OK,' Kate said dismissively. 'Mum, is the telly plugged in now? Can I watch?'

Jay saw Chris out, then switched on the television and Kate settled herself down amongst the packing cases in front of the first of the evening's children's programmes.

'How was your teacher?' Jay asked, gazing at the back of her daughter's dark head with a lump in her throat. Kate glanced round vaguely.

'She's all right,' she said. 'Her assistant's nicer. She's called Debbie. But Mum, did you know that a murderer used to live in this house? The boys at school told me. They said I should look out for ghosts and ghoulies here. They said they wouldn't live in this house, no way, ever. Did a murderer live here, Mum? Is it true?'

'I'm sure it isn't,' Jay said with as much reassurance as she could muster, thinking of the sweetly innocent elderly couple from whom she had bought the house. But Adelaide Street, perched on the side of the steep valley where only a few of the dozen or more tall stone textile mills of her childhood still clung to the banks of the river which rushed down from the high moors, was well over a hundred years old and the house could have been home to any number of murderers for all she knew. She was a confirmed sceptic where anything supernatural was concerned but Kate's question made her wonder again if perhaps she had bought the wrong house. Suddenly the cluttered living room seemed poky rather than cosy and the loss of the afternoon sunshine an insupportable deprivation and she shivered.

'They said he killed a little girl,' Kate chattered on, her mouth full of biscuits and apparently unmoved by what she was saying, but Jay could feel her heart beating faster, even as she told Kate somewhat sharply that the boys were just teasing. If it were true, though, she thought, and even relatively recent, why on earth hadn't Sue and Chris mentioned it to her when she first viewed the place more than three months ago?

20

2

Sue Hateley cut her sister a small slice of choco-late cake, as requested, and herself a considerably larger one, and pushed a plate across the kitchen table to Jay. The sisters were not particularly alike, Sue a natural blonde and always significantly heavier than Jay, with her dark unruly curls who, since she had married, had watched her weight and fitness with more than average devotion.

'To be honest, I'd forgotten all about it,' Sue said. 'It was years ago. It must have happened when you were away at university.'

'Like a lot of other things,' Jay said quietly. 'So who was this murderer then? What did he do, bludgeon his wife to death in the kitchen? Am I going to find bloodstains if I take the tiles up?'

'No, it was nothing like that,' Sue said, through a mouthful of cake. 'It was a young girl from the children's home...'

'Bloody hell, you mean Pendle House?' Jay complained. 'Only where I'm going to work.'

'That's right. If I'd mentioned it at all it might have been because you're going to work up there, not because of Adelaide Street. I'm not sure I ever knew where the lad who did it lived.'

'But a child murder? You couldn't forget that, surely.'

'Well, it wasn't an abduction or anything dram-atic. There was no big search, no tabloid headlines and heaps of flowers and teddy bears and appeals on telly and all that stuff. They found her body the morning after she'd slipped out of the home, I think, and enough people knew she'd been playing around with this older boy for him to be the prime suspect from the start. It was all over very quickly without a great deal of fuss. He confessed quite soon apparently. Of course his mother always claimed the boy was innocent, but Chris looked into it later on when there was some sort of appeal going on and he reckoned the verdict was fair enough. You ought to talk to him about it if you're really interested.'

'I've got to tell Kate something. She's getting all sorts of lurid tales at school.'

'I'm surprised anyone remembers,' Sue said. 'More cake?'

'No thanks,' Jay said moving a thoughtful hand across a stomach which was feeling uncomfortably constrained by the waistband of her jeans. Sue, she thought, had put on a lot more weight since she had last seen her. Perhaps being a housewife was not the option of contentment that it was cracked up to be by the *Daily Mail.*

'It's still quite a tight little community in those streets around the mills,' Jay said. 'There'll almost certainly be people who were living there twenty years ago. I expect murder becomes part of the folk memory. It certainly didn't take long for someone to fill Kate in.'

'The estate agent should have told you,' Sue said. 'You're not upset about it, are you?'

'No, not really, if it's such ancient history – and as long as it doesn't worry Kate. I suppose it explains why the house was quite cheap.'

'Cheap? Well, by London standards, maybe. Personally, I was a bit surprised when you went for one of those cottages down there. I'd have thought you could have got something a bit more spacious. It'll seem really pokey after the London house.'

Jay drew a sharp breath as Sue glanced proprietorially around her light and well appointed kitchen with its gleaming appliances, smaller than the one which Jay had reluctantly left behind in Muswell Hill but light years ahead of the well-worn worktops and chipped tiles at the cottage. There was, she knew, more than a touch of *schadenfreude* in her sister's reaction to what she regarded as a fairly rational decision to buy a house which left her with some financial leeway as she began her new single existence in Pendle Bridge.

'I actually like the cottage,' she said, feigning a cheerfulness she did not really feel. 'It's got a bit more character than some 1930s semi-detached up the hill which would have been a similar sort of price. I like it, and that's why I don't want Kate spooked by this murder thing. She's got enough to put up with after the divorce and the upheaval of moving and changing schools without letting her imagination rip on murder fantasies which have nothing to do with reality. I think I'll ask Chris to look out the old newspaper reports for me, and then I'll know exactly what I'm dealing with.'

'Oh, I'm sure he'll do that,' Sue said, and Jay wondered if she had imagined the hint of malice in her voice. She carried on too quickly for her to be sure, but she hoped not. She really wanted to mend fences with Sue, and perhaps find a closeness with her sister that she knew some of her friends had with theirs, but which had somehow eluded them over the years.

'The other problem is the school, of course,' Sue said. 'Oh, I know St. Peter's got a good Ofsted report, but if you want Kate to take the exam for the High School I should think she'll need some extra coaching to get through. We decided to go private from the start, to be on the safe side.'

'I very much doubt I'll be paying school fees,' Jay said sharply. 'Firstly because I'll not be able to afford it and secondly because I don't believe in it anyway. I'd like her to stay with the friends she makes at primary school. I can't see the point of her commuting halfway across the county for the doubtful privilege of wearing a daft uniform and picking up the idea that she's better than the rest of the kids in the neighbourhood just because her family can fork out a couple of thousand pounds a term, or whatever it costs.'

Sue did not hide her irritation this time.

'It's easy to see you haven't changed much,' she said. 'I thought Cambridge and London might have knocked the bolshie edges off you, but obviously not. I hope you're not going to make Ben and Abbie feel uncomfortable about where they're going to school. We've just heard that Ben's passed for Bradfield Grammar next September and he's over the moon. And Abbie's very happy at the Girls' High School.'

'I'm sure she is, and Ben will be too. But what's wrong with Pendle School all of a sudden? It did us proud. I went to Cambridge, for God's sake.

You could have gone to university if you'd wanted to. What more do you want from a school?'

'I want the very best for my kids. What's so wrong with that? Surely David'll pay for Kate's education if you can't.' Jay could see the resentment in Sue's eyes and she did not answer. Her hopes for some sort of re-establishment of relations with her sister and her family did not look promising this morning, she thought. Over the years their meetings over Christmas dinner while their parents were alive, and even more infrequent encounters in the five years since her father's premature death in a car accident and her mother's somewhat precipitous decision to go to live in France, had become frostier. Sue, she knew had always been jealous of her academic success; years of invidious comparisons by insensitive teachers had taken their toll. And more recently Jay had sensed a hint of jealousy over her affluent London lifestyle as David's architectural practice had burgeoned and she had continued with the career she had only interrupted briefly when Kate was born. Perhaps she was naïve to believe she and her sister could be close again after so long. She determined to track down any old friends who were still in Pendle Bridge who might welcome her home less equivocally than her own flesh and blood.

On her way from her sister's back to the cottage where another session of unappealing unpacking waited, Jay took a detour. Pendle House stood on a ridge above the town, sheltered enough from the open moorland to the north for the tree-filled

25

garden to have become lush and overgrown during the summer months when the building had been empty. The site had been carefully selected by its original owner to give far-reaching views across the steep-sided valley to the more southerly moors which extended almost uninterrupted to Derbyshire. Jay drove in through stone gateposts from which the iron gates had long ago been dismantled, steered cautiously up the mossy drive between overhanging tree branches and sprawling rhododendrons and drew up in front of the house itself.

She was surprised to discover an elderly-looking Ford parked outside and for a moment she sat in the car gazing up at the solid stone structure, with its covered porch and generous bay windows under tall gables, knowing someone must be around but unable to see any signs of life. The house looked unkempt and desolate. The paint was flaking from the ornate weatherboards along the roof-line and two of the downstairs windows had been boarded up where panes of glass had obviously been smashed. The rest of the windows reflected the leaden winter sky, giving no sign of a light to indicate that anyone from the car she had parked alongside had gone inside. As a potential workplace it did not fill her with any enthusiasm and she wondered what had happened to the plans to refurbish which had been explained to her at her interview. Tucking her mobile phone into the pocket of her fleece she got out and locked the car before walking slowly round the building.

At the back was a more modern structure

which she had been told had been put up when the house had been used as a children's home in the 1970s and 80s and used as offices later. It was here, rather than in the mansion itself, that she had been promised office space and secretarial and janitorial assistance to enable her to begin to sort out the dusty treasures which had been consigned to the attics of Pendle House more than thirty years ago. The last of the Wright family to occupy the house had not been a collector himself, as his father and grandfather had been, and when he had died childless and widowed he had left the house and its contents, to the fury of distant but nonetheless rapacious relatives, to the local council to do with as they wished.

Jay picked her way carefully along moss covered pathways through rhododendrons, heavy with buds and dripping with moisture, to the back of the building where the modern extension had been linked to the original stable block, which had itself been converted into offices. She rubbed some of the grime from a couple of the windows and peered in but the rooms were dark and empty, the dusty floors evidently untrodden for months if not years, disturbed only by a bird which must have become trapped and expired in a heap of bones and feathers close to a small fireplace in one of the stable rooms. Nowhere did there seem to have been any effort made to prepare a corner of the site for her use when she started work in two weeks' time.

She did not hear anyone behind her and the voice, when it came, made her jump and her heart race.

'Nah then, this is council property,' the voice said. 'You're bloody trespassing.'

She turned round to face the man who had materialised so suddenly.

'Oh, but I'm not,' she said aggressively, hand on her mobile, but still prepared to flee or fight if either seemed called for. She was reassured somewhat by the unthreatening appearance of a small elderly man in blue overalls with some sort of monogram on the breast pocket and a bunch of keys in his hands.

'How d'you mek that out then?' her interrogator asked. 'I don't know you and I'm t'caretaker here.'

'Then you'll know that work's going to start here soon on sorting out the Wright family's collections. I'm going to be working on that and I just called into see if any progress was being made on the offices we'll need...'

'Oh aye?' the caretaker said, evidently still sceptical. 'You'll have some authority then, for poking about? Miss?'

'Well, not really,' Jay said. She had left her handbag locked in the car. 'And I'm hardly poking about. Just looking really. My name's Jay Morton, Mrs Jay Morton, and I'm going to be in charge of the museum project...' She wondered why the man's bright blue eyes made her feel so ridiculously defensive.

'Aye, well, you can't be too careful these days. There's all sorts of vandals roaming about, and worse. I've had to board up half the windows in t'main house so I reckon it's a miracle someone hasn't come round the back here and made a wreck of these buildings an' all. Little beggars.'

'Kids, you think?' Jay asked, trying to gain some sort of rapport.

'Kids, druggies, squatters, gippos, who knows what they were up to. The police are supposed to take the place in on their patrols but I don't reckon they bother meself.'

'Right,' Jay said, wondering what sort of a workplace Pendle House was going to turn out to be. 'They had a murder here once as well, didn't they. Some girl...'

'That weren't up here,' the caretaker said. 'That were some little lass having it off with an older lad down in t'park. Little slag. Maggie or Mags or summat like that, she were called. They blamed the head for letting them get out o't'house at night, but I don't reckon there's any stopping kids o' that age if they're right determined.'

The caretaker seemed to read the hint of alarm in Jay's eyes.

'It were years ago,' he said dismissively. 'You'll be reet enough working here in t'day time. They reckon they're going to open up this whole block of offices. It'll not just be you up here on your own. There'll be other departments up here an'all. Daft to waste the space, like. Then they'll renovate the house as and when it's needed. That's the plan, any road. The offices aren't in bad nick, as it goes. T'cleaners are coming in next week and furniture the week after. You won't know t'place by t'time you start.'

'Well, good,' Jay said cautiously. 'And the house itself? Is all the stuff in the attics still safe if people have been breaking in?'

29

'Last time I looked. They put in a pretty solid door at the foot o' t'attic stairs years ago when it was a kids home and no one's tampered with that as far as I can see. And the place had alarms. That's how we found the squatters quick enough to get 'em out before too much harm were done. Mind, if some little beggar set the place ablaze your treasures would go up wi' all t'rest. That's what I've been worried about ever since t'last tenants moved out. Leaving t'place empty for months is just asking for trouble, if you ask me. D'you want to have a look at t'house, then?'

Jay could tell that the invitation was begrudged and she did not warm to the idea of trailing around Pendle House with this reluctant guide.

'Don't worry, Mr ... er?'

'Fred,' he said. 'Fred Marston.'

'Don't worry, Fred. I'll not bother now.' She glanced at her watch with spurious anxiety. 'I've got to be somewhere in ten minutes. But I'm sitting in on the interviews next week for a secretary and someone to do all the lifting and carrying, so when I've got the team together perhaps we'll all come up and have a good look round and work out where to start.'

Jay drove away from Pendle House feeling much more anxious than when she had arrived. The idea that some of the town's more recalcitrant youth were gaining access to the place worried her. There was no telling when some intruder might not be tempted to explore the upper floor to which the council had so cavalierly consigned the Wright collections. But more than that, she knew that she had been overconfident in going up to the house alone. It was twenty years since she had lived in Pendle Bridge and she had no doubt that the town had changed for the worse in ways that she could not yet know. Surly as he had been, she knew that she had been lucky that she had been surprised by Fred Marston rather than anyone more threatening.

She parked carefully outside her cottage in the street which had not been designed for anything more substantial than a horse-drawn cart and knew before she had completed the tight manoeuvre that she was being watched from the front window of the cottage next door. She locked the car and heard her neighbour's front door open behind her.

'You came then?' The voice was broad Yorkshire at its most direct but not unkindly.

'I did, Mr. Booth. Did you think I wouldn't?' Jay gave the old man the benefit of one of her broadest smiles. She had met him when she first looked over the cottage with the estate agent and he had insisted on brewing them both a cup of tea which he had carried carefully from next door on a small tray complete with tray cloth.

'I was surprised not to see you when we moved in,' Jay said.

'Aye, well.' The old man's face darkened and Jay realised that he did not look as chipper as the first time they had met. 'I've been in t'hospital for a while. Came home yesterday,' he said.

'I'm sorry to hear that,' Jay said. 'Nothing too serious, I hope?'

'Waterworks,' Booth said and closed his mouth like a trap, obviously not prepared to say more.

'Your little lass like it here, then, does she?'

'She seems to, so far,' Jay said, putting her key into the lock, only too aware that she didn't really know the answer to that question. She was anxious to get on but did not want to appear rude and she guessed, as there was no sign of a Mrs. Booth – first names had not been vouchsafed on the old man's side – that her neighbour lived alone.

'It didn't put you off, then, the folk as used to live theer?'

Jay hesitated with the door ajar, with the unwanted feeling of foreboding catching her breath.

'Mr. and Mrs. Green you mean?' she asked although she knew he didn't.

'No, not them.' Mr. Booth's contempt was profound. 'The Bairstows I'm talking about. My missus never liked them. He were a bit simple, were Kenny, and he frightened my Vera. He were a nice looking lad, mind, but it was obvious he were only sixpence to.'

'Only what?' Jay asked, feeling stupid.

'Only sixpence to't'shilling,' Booth came back with a look of scorn for her slowness. 'I told my Vera he were all reet, he were harmless enough, but then it turned out he weren't harmless at all, didn't it? Never heard the end of that, did I? She never spoke to Grace Bairstow after, didn't Vera. Not a word for t'best part o'sixteen years. I tried to be neighbourly, like, and not take it out on Grace, but Vera wouldn't have owt to do with her. You'd think she'd have moved, wouldn't you, after he were put away? But she hung on to t'bitter end, did Grace, till they had to take her to a home. She had him late, you know, her Kenny. They say that's not a good thing, don't they?'

'So how long...?' Jay asked faintly.

'Can't be more'n eighteen months ago since she sold up and went. And she wouldn't have a word said against Kenny even after all that ruddy time. He were innocent as far as she were concerned, daft old beggar. They should hang them, you know. Think what it's costing us to keep that lad in prison for t'rest of his days. He were only seventeen or eighteen when he went in, fit as a butcher's dog, an'all. Bloody fortune he'll have cost us. So I did wonder if you'd really buy t'house, like. Bit of a rum do, in't'it, living in a house where a murderer lived? I reckon that's what the Greens decided in t'end. They weren't here five minutes before they put it on t'market again. Made a tidy profit, an' all if you paid 'em owt like what they were asking.'

Jay gritted her teeth in irritation. Her neighbour might look decrepit and a likely object for her charitable instincts, but he was obviously as sharp as a razor. She did a quick revision of her plans to offer occasional tea and sympathy.

'Well, I'm sure they had their reasons. She's died, has she, Mrs. Bairstow?'

'Not as I've heard,' Booth said. 'She's still living up at Nab End old folks home. She went a bit doolally in the end, you know. Couldn't remember what day o't'week it were. Nab End's where we all end up round here, you know, for our sins.'

33

3

It took Donna time to get over the strangeness of the new Pendle Bridge. She had enough money in the bank, she knew, to live for several weeks if she was careful while she looked for work and somewhere more permanent to stay than the bed and breakfast she had chosen from the Yellow Pages. She made the most of the greasy cooked breakfasts on offer, skipped lunch and then had an early meal at a café by the bus station where the waitresses seemed not to think it odd that a pale, skinny woman of indeterminate age should eat there every evening. She eked out her resources frugally, spending as little as possible while she scanned the *Advertiser* and the windows of the employment agencies for a job which might provide a reasonable reward for her hard-earned skills. To her surprise she found a cyber-café in Kirkgate where she could word-process her applications, taking great care to adjust the dates to eliminate any reference to the time she had spent in Pendle Bridge as a child. No one would bother to check school details, she thought, and by the time she had gained her quite genuine qualifications the records would be there for anyone who bothered to look. She then delivered the letters by hand to avoid the cost of postage.

And all the time she was absorbing this new town grafted onto the old one she remembered so clearly now she was back. She marvelled at the pricey deli here, the smart shop there for outdoor gear for walkers on the hills, a café bar where once the Fleece pub had expelled its drunks onto the pavement every day at three in the afternoon. She and Mags had watched the men, goggle-eyed, on one of the many days they had skipped school classes, seeing them stagger from public bar to betting shop breathing beer fumes as they stood giggling in the next shop doorway where they were generally planning a new foray into Woollies.

One of the first things she did, at Archie's instigation – wasn't everything at Archie's instigation these days, ever since he'd made his comeback – was to encase her sore feet in her well-worn trainers and jog up the steep hill to Pendle House. She had already realised by now that if she was to continue tramping the steep streets she needed new smart shoes which did not chafe her heels and blister her toes so easily. But that would have to wait until she had a wage packet coming in, she thought. The pull up the hill to the children's home made her breathless and hot and sorry that she had been neglecting her exercise lately, and she stood at the gateway for a moment, between the huge stone pillars, trying to see whatever could be glimpsed beyond the slightly overgrown rhododendrons on each side of the drive. There was no sound of children's voices here now, in fact no sound at all, and no identifying notice on the gate as there had once been, and she guessed that the home had closed. That at least was something to be thankful for, she thought, though it would make her task all the harder. Eventually she steeled herself to ignore her blistered feet and walk up the drive, dead leaves and soft moss underfoot making her approach almost soundless. She drew a sharp breath of shocked recognition as she turned the corner and the big stone double-fronted house stood before her, almost unchanged except for wooden boards nailed over the two downstairs bay windows on each side of the porch.

She glanced up. Above the entrance, between the two bays, was a smaller single window behind which there used to be a narrow bedroom with a double bunk bed. She closed her eyes for a second as she gazed up and was instantly a ten-year-old again, the year she and Mags had been expelled from the six-bed girls dormitory next door and consigned to the little room as a punishment for talking so late into the night and keeping the other girls awake. But they had been delighted by their new isolation and slept, more often than not, wrapped in each other's arms under two duvets in the bottom bunk.

Mags, she thought, tears stinging her eyes suddenly as she remembered the reason she had come back to this place, the place she hated above all others after what had happened. Such fun they'd had together, she and Mags. She had always wondered later why people assumed she hadn't liked the children's home she'd been in – she never told them the name of it, of course, or where it was. London was so big that no one would have known it anyway but she always listened to Archie when he told her to take care, you never knew who was listening. But it hadn't been Pendle House she had run away from that night. She had fled from the bastard who killed Mags, the man who had wrapped his arms round her chest and neck, as he had done many times before, but this time too tightly, too violently, and who had pushed a frantic Donna contemptuously into the mud as he pressed on with what he was doing to her Mags's limp body. And instead of jumping up and fighting back, as she could have done, because she had grown by then, and was tall and strong for her age, she had slithered away through the wet grass and run, leaving her beloved Mags behind.

She brushed the tears away angrily and as she gazed at the window and imagined the bare little room where they had slept together for so long, Mags was there with her again, clutching at her arm, urging her to look round the back.

Donna smiled faintly, taking Mags' hand and walking slowly round to the rear of the building where the more modern block had housed the dining room and kitchen and the dormitories where the boys slept. There had been some alterations there, she noticed, when she peered through the windows and saw that rooms had been converted into smaller spaces which could have been offices. There was no sign of the water butt where they'd drowned the cat that time. And the yard itself had been covered in tarmac at some point, though it was so worn that the cobbles she remembered were beginning to show through again. They used to get greasy in the rain, those cobbles, and once she and Mags had clutched themselves with helpless laughter at an upstairs window when they had seen Mrs P. slip in the rain and sit down heavily with her broad behind in a puddle.

'Do you remember when Mrs P. fell over?' she asked the presence at her side.

'Serve her right, stupid cow,' Mags said. 'D'you remember the cat?'

'I remember the cat,' she said, with satisfaction, recalling its dying struggles, and how even Archie had laughed. Clever girl, he had said. Clever, clever girl.

'D'you remember when you first came and what a naughty girl you were?' Mags asked. Donna could see now that she was wearing her blue summer dress though it looked a bit tight round the arms and ended well above her knees as if she had grown in the years since they had both last been here, but her clothes had not.

'That fat social worker brought me,' Donna said, suddenly cold although a pale sunshine was filtering through the clouds, the first she had seen since she had arrived in Pendle Bridge. 'I went to bed and wouldn't get up. I didn't want to talk to anyone so I didn't, not a word, for weeks and weeks. They kept sending different people to see me, a policeman, prying and nagging me, the fat social worker asking more questions, a doctor who poked me and prodded me and asked if my dad had ever hurt me anywhere and said I should eat more and get some fresh air – as if there'd been any fresh air to get around those stinking flats. And there was some tall woman who looked like a man who said she was a psycho-something-

or-other and asked loads more questions that I couldn't see the point of. Archie said keep quiet, talking will only make everything worse, so I kept quiet for weeks till I nearly lost the use of my tongue. In the end, they got me, of course they did, because they realised I was reading all the time. I used to creep down in the night, down the wide stairs with the moon shining through those churchy windows, with coloured glass making bright patterns on the floor, and I'd nick books from the bookcase in the sitting room. I'd read all day and at night under the bedclothes with a torch, but when they found out they knew that without the books I'd go mad with boredom, so they stopped me and in the end I had to get up and get washed and dressed and go downstairs and do what they said – well, some of the time, any road. And then I met you and everything changed.'

'D'you remember when we got our own room?' Mags' voice was fainter now as if she had moved further away, but Donna did not look round. She knew she was still there.

'At first they gave me that bed in one of the big dormitories, the one nearest the door, but after I got up I said I couldn't sleep in there because the other kids were so noisy in the night – snoring and farting an' that – so I couldn't get off to sleep. Though in fact it was us who was talking half the night by then. So they put us in the little room, in those bunk beds, just you and me. I expect it was because we were the same age, both of us ten in May. You remember?'

'I expect they actually wanted us to be friends,'

Mags said.

'Archie did. And when we went to school we were in the same class.'

'*When* we went to school,' Mags said and laughed and her laugh was the same as it had always been and Donna felt happier than she felt for a long time. They had been happy at Pendle House, she and Mags, for a time at least.

'All those sweets and stuff we used to nick from Woollies, while the lads were playing their silly war games, careering round the house shooting Argies and even watching the news on the telly, cheering the soldiers and Maggie Thatcher. Do you remember, Mags?'

'I remember. And how we used to talk all night because they wouldn't let you read in bed any more. They'd come in and check after they put the lights out. But we used to talk for hours, long after everyone else was asleep. You used to tell me stories that you'd read.'

Donna nodded to herself, smiling.

'D'you remember, I told you about my mum and dad and how it had all ended. I never told anyone else about that. And you told me how you'd come to Pendle House, a long time before me, because your step-dad didn't want you and had been hitting you. And the police came and after that your mum said she didn't want you either so they took you into care. And how we hated all the grown-ups, even my mum who should have come back to get me out of there, but she never did.'

'And in the summer sometimes,' Mags said, her voice dreamy now, so Donna had to strain to hear it, 'in the summer, if it was hot, we'd climb out of the window and sit on the little balcony place on top of the porch. You could see right down the hill from there to the town and watch the lights going on and off and the cars climbing up the other hill, bright white coming down, red going up, like pairs of stars in the blackness. And when it was cold, and the central heating had gone off, sometimes we'd climb into each others' bunks and cuddle up under both the duvets while the pipes clattered and the old house creaked through the night.'

'I remember,' Donna said. 'I'll never forget. It was the best time of my life. We did everything together, we said we'd be sisters forever and live together when we grew up, and would never go anywhere without each other and have nothing to do with boys. That's why I was so furious when they sent me off to be fostered at Mrs Cuddly Clough's and why I had to get back, though I didn't tell *them* that. Always hugging and touching, she was. I hated that. Archie said best not to tell anyone I wanted to be back with you because they'd only send one of us somewhere else out of spite. He's always right, is Archie, though he didn't come to talk to me so often when you and I were together. I think he was jealous really.'

Suddenly she knew she was alone again in the damp dank yard with a chilly finger of wind touching her neck and making her shiver. She half fell against the wall of the house, pressing her forehead against the rough stone, wanting the sharp grit to hurt her more than she hurt inside.

41

Not that it ever worked, she thought, thinking of the jagged scars on her wrists which had been there since she was in her teens.

'I loved you, Mags,' she whispered. 'You remember how after I got back to Pendle, they never tried to get you fostered again, or me, how you threw a wobbly if it was mentioned, and cried and screamed and kicked and threw stuff about, and didn't care if they put you in the segregation room for a bit, and eventually they just gave up. And I just said no, no way, and went to bed and wouldn't get up. The rest of that winter and the summer after, we were really happy at Pendle House, you and me, Mags. We didn't go to school much. Whenever we could we bunked off and if we didn't feel like going to the shops we walked up the hill out of the town onto the moors and had picnics up there with no one around except a few birds and lots of sheep, scuttling away as we scrambled about in the long spiky grass, sometimes with Kenny Bairstow and sometimes on our own. We always got back around the end of school time for our tea, and no one seemed to miss us, and when the summer holidays started we stayed out later and later, lying in the heather for hours till it was nearly dark talking, talking, always talking about what we'd do when we grew up, how many babies we'd have and how we'd look after them properly, without any fathers to mess up our families, just me and you and half a dozen kids. I'm not sure we knew then that you needed men to make the kids. We were quite innocent, for ten-year-olds, I suppose. We knew next to nothing about sex.

Until Laurie came, of course, and then we soon knew far too much.'

Her voice trailed away as the hard stone refused a response and she did not even need to glance over her shoulder to know that Mags was still not there.

'Come on Donna,' Archie said. 'We'll find Kenny, you know we will, and then we'll find the rest of them. You know you can do it.'

Donna pushed herself upright, smoothed her hair and pulled a mirror out of her bag and checked her forehead where the rough stone had made indentations in the skin but had not broken it. The eyes which looked back at her were blue and bright although the face was pale and there were beginning to be lines around her eyes. Crow's feet, she thought they called them. She wouldn't like crows near her face, she thought, with a shudder, remembering bold pigeons in London squares where she had shivered in a sleeping bag years ago.

She was glad she had come up to Pendle House, even though she knew she should not allow herself to get so upset. But being so close to Mags again had clarified her mind and stiffened her resolve. Tomorrow they would look for Kenny's house.

'Can I do it, Archie?' she whispered.

'Of course you can. You're a clever girl, Donna. A clever, clever girl.'

A few days later, half way through Sunday lunch with all the trimmings, Jay pushed the remnants of her food to the side of her plate and flashed an

43

apologetic smile at her sister. Lunch at the Hateleys was not turning out to be a great success although Jay had welcomed the invitation as a chance to escape the narrow confines of the cottage and Kate's growing disillusion, as the loss of her circle of friends in London and her failure immediately to make new ones at St. Peter's began to sink in. But by the end of the main course Jay was already wondering how soon she could extricate herself and Kate and get back to what, to her at least, was beginning to look, if not feel, a little like home. She glanced round the table. Kate herself was sitting beside her cousin Ben, six months older than she was though a head shorter, but still ready enough to whisper and giggle with a girl if the chance offered. The cousins were a dark haired and bubbly pair, not unlike each other, and clearly strengthening a friendship which Jay hoped would make Kate feel a little less isolated in Pendle Bridge.

At the other end of the table Chris Hateley sat next to his father George, a father and son most definitely not alike. Chris was still a slim, taut figure for his age, his fair hair flopping slightly boyishly into his eyes and the expressive hands, one of the things which had first attracted Jay to him all those years ago, moving animatedly as he emphasised a point to George. The older Hateley was a big man, his belly straining against his shirt, and his shoulders against the thick tweed of his jacket. His face was square but heavily jowled and his expression varied between discontented and angry, Jay thought, whether or not he was addressing his son, as now, in a sharp whisper or glancing at the grandchildren she might have expected him to reveal some affection for.

Jay had been hoping to chat to George Hateley and discover a bit more about the trustees' hopes for what she was already thinking of as 'her museum'. But the two men had been carrying on an intense conversation in low voices for most of the meal and Jay could see that Sue was irritated by their refusal to take more than a cursory interest in the rest of the family. Thirteen-year-old Abbie sat between her mother and her aunt and had picked silently and unenthusiastically at her food, eating, as far as Jay could see, very little. Abbie had shot up since Jay had last seen her and turned into a skinny, gangling teenager with only the merest hint of puberty beneath her baggy sweatshirt. There was a distinct look of her father in the pale thin face beneath the same floppy fair hair. She looked neither as happy nor self-confident as her mother had insisted she was. In fact, she looked thoroughly miserable and she wondered what her apparently stable home life and expensive schooling was failing to provide. Perhaps, Jay thought, it was no more than the usual teenaged angst she would have to face with Kate in a few years time. But she felt anxious for her niece.

'Shall I help you clear away?' Jay asked. Sue shrugged ungraciously and began to collect up the plates while Jay picked up the vegetable dishes.

'You've eaten almost nothing,' Sue hissed at Abbie, as she scraped uneaten food angrily onto the top of the pile.

'Not hungry, Mum,' Abbie muttered. 'Can I get

down now? I don't want anything else.'

'I've made an apple crumble. I thought that was your favourite,' Sue said.

'Not today,' the girl replied, sliding past Jay and heading determinedly out of the dining room. Jay wondered whether the baggy top was intended to conceal budding breasts and incipient sexuality or disguise the extreme thinness of her frame. They heard her clattering upstairs and the door of her room slamming shut and Jay caught the glance of anxiety Sue exchanged with Chris, who had watched his daughter's departure grim-faced.

'What is the matter with that girl?' he asked no one in particular.

'She's just a teenager,' his father said. 'They're all t'bloody same. Pity, though. She was a lovely little lass.' He glanced at Kate, who was passing over her empty plate, with a smile. 'You've not lost your appetite then, Katie? That's good.'

While Sue extricated the crumble from the oven Jay returned to her seat and glanced at the two men. She knew that this far north of Muswell Hill different rules prevailed, but she still thought Chris and his father were being unforgivably rude.

'I thought you'd retired from the council now, Mr. Hateley,' she put in sweetly, having gathered that one of the subjects of the intense discussion seemed to be local politics. 'Chris tells me you're not a great fan of the prime minister's.' George Hateley was florid faced at the best of times, and his colour rose at this assault.

'I'd not go as far as to say that,' he said. 'I'm still Bernie Grogan's agent, and there's nowt the sharp young lads can do about that. Whatever daft policies they dream up in London, Bernie's a good man and a bloody good constituency MP.'

'I hadn't met him before my interview,' Jay said non-commitally, unwilling to admit that she had been less than overwhelmed by Grogan's domineering manner as chair of the museum trustees. 'What do you really think of the plans for Pendle House? Do you think we can make it work?'

'I can think of better things to do with the money, if you want my honest opinion,' Hateley said, obviously a man for whom Yorkshire bluntness was an unalloyed virtue. 'But what Bernie wants Bernie generally gets and he seems to have convinced folk in high places it's a good idea.'

'You wouldn't have got lottery money for other things, Dad,' Chris broke in quickly, evidently trying to head off any more discord around the table. 'I think it'll do a lot for tourism round here. There's no reason why Haworth should get all the coach-loads of Americans and Japanese.'

Jay laughed.

'I'm not sure the collections the Wrights stashed away will compete with the Brontës' parsonage, but we'll give it a go,' she said.

'Ill-gotten, most of that stuff, I reckon,' George Hateley said huffily. 'They were a rapacious lot, the Wrights. I can remember when they closed their last mill. Every beggar out, without a penny more than they had to pay them. Unions went mad but there was nowt anyone could do about it.'

'Times change, Dad,' Chris said.

'Have you seen what's stashed away at Pendle

47

House yet, then?' George Hateley asked grudgingly. 'Found anything valuable?'

'Far too early to say,' Jay said. 'They're going in to start bringing the stuff down from the attics a few days before I start work apparently. What worries me is whether it will all be in good condition after being stored for so long. It could be damp up there, or there might have been mice and rats, you just don't know.'

'It was all carefully boxed up as far as I can recall,' the older Hateley said. 'It was scattered all over the house when the council inherited it, and no one had a clue what it was worth or what to do with it when it was decided to turn the place into a children's home. I was a governor of the home. So was Bernie, as it goes, so our interest goes back a long way. We decided the attic rooms needed too much spent on them to be made useful for the kids so they were simply used for storage. But as far as I know the building's been kept in good nick, roof's been looked after, that sort of thing. No point wasting an asset like that by letting it go to wrack and ruin, is there. Bad housekeeping, that. I thought they should have flogged the collections off back then, but no one listened and I think everyone forgot about them after that. It's not as if it were gold and silver or Old Masters, is it? What I saw of it looked like a lot of old tat to me.'

'I'm sure it'll all be fine,' Jay said more confidently than she felt. The sketchy inventories which had been inherited from the Wright family and survived the intervening years were barely detailed enough, from what she had seen of

48

them, to offer a sound basis for the lottery grant but hinted at a treasure trove of mainly ethnographic items which barely existed outside the Pitt Rivers Museum in Oxford. 'I'm really keen to get started,' she said.

'Well, you'll have your work cut out, I dare say,' George Hateley said. 'Settling down, is she, your little lass?' He glanced at Kate who looked back with what Jay thought was surprising coolness. She did not like being spoken about as if she was not there.

'I'm all right, thank you,' she said, answering George herself.

'She'll get that southern accent knocked out of her pretty quickly at St. Peter's,' Hateley said.

'What accent?' Kate asked sharply and the men laughed.

'Don't you worry, Katie,' Chris said. 'You'll soon feel at home, and sound it too, I dare say.'

'I don't know what you mean, Uncle Chris,' Kate said with all the superciliousness she could muster so that even Jay had to smile. George was still looking at her daughter with an intensity that she found slightly uncomfortable and she wondered if he were seriously thrown by these southern cuckoos dropped into his northern nest. He had, she recalled, been quite a welcoming, if somewhat overbearing, figure when she had gone to Chris's home as a love-sick schoolgirl all those years ago. Surely he did not believe that Chris had married the wrong sister after all this time. She knew that Chris had been distraught when she had dumped him in favour of a more charismatic lover she had met at Cambridge, but she had

49

never considered that perhaps his family had been disappointed too. She must have been a more exciting catch than she had ever imagined, she thought, glancing somewhat guiltily at her sister who had returned with the pudding and a jug of custard.

In the end her plans to get away were subverted by Kate who allowed herself to be dragged upstairs by Ben to explore the delights of his computer and it was George Hateley who was the first to depart.

'Your father's wearing well,' Jay said as she sat over coffee with Chris and Sue.

'Well, yes and no. He's fit enough but he's very frustrated that he's pretty well out of politics now,' Chris said. 'Being Bernie Grogan's agent is only really important at election time and it's little more than being his minder and general dogsbody even then, really. All that over lunch was about some scheme the council's got to redevelop the town centre which he dislikes but can't influence any more.'

'So why did he resign if he still wants a finger in the pie?' Jay asked.

'The bright young men didn't want him. It's as simple as that, I think,' Chris said. 'He went through a bad patch when my mother died and threw his weight about in the party once too often. They deselected him and he's never found another council ward willing to take him. What really galls him is that he's quite a few years younger than Bernie Grogan who's still very popular in the town and having a great old time at Westminster, as far as I can see. Dad wouldn't admit it for a second, but he's as jealous as hell about that.'

'So what does he do with his time if he's got all this energy to use up?'

'Interferes in everything he can get his nose into,' Sue said sharply. 'And harasses Chris if he won't provide the publicity he thinks is his due. I don't see what he's got to be so bitter about. As far as I can see he's as active as he ever was.'

'Ah, yes, but he hasn't got the power, Sue, that's what bugs him,' Chris said. 'That's slipped through his fingers and he knows it. Grogan and the smart young councillors have got the power.'

'Yes, it was pretty obvious at my interview that Grogan was the main man,' Jay said. 'Still, I just hope that they all leave me in peace to get on with what I've got to do at Pendle House. I really don't want the trustees interfering up there.'

'Oh, they'll interfere,' Chris said. 'I think you can bank on that.'

It was almost dark by the time Jay parked outside the cottage and chivvied Kate out of the car and through the front door. She was surprised to see the curtains next door twitch as she closed the car door and wondered if the self-styled Mr. Booth was going to monitor her every movement. She had not given a new relationship much thought since David had left, shying away from any consideration of her new and unwanted single status, unwilling to probe the wound for fear she would discover just how deep it really was, but if she did ever find the time or the confidence to acquire a boyfriend in Pendle Bridge she did not think she wanted her next

51

door neighbour watching his comings and goings with a close and no doubt prurient interest. Still, she thought, as she had neither a burglar alarm or a dog, perhaps he was a useful stand-in for the moment. She waved cheerily and the curtain dropped quickly back into place. Nosy old bugger, Jay thought and slammed her front door with unnecessary force.

When she had chivvied Kate to bed she sat alone in the single comfortable armchair she had cleared in the living room, most of which was still cluttered with books and CDs for which she could find no home, and considered the afternoon. Sue, she thought, had looked stressed and she wondered whether it was Abbie's adolescence or Chris himself who was causing her anxiety. As for Chris, she had begun to think that moving into close proximity with her former lover might be more of a mistake than she had anticipated. More than once during the afternoon she had felt her space invaded by her brother-in-law, and she wondered if her sister had noticed that arm brushed a fraction too intimately in the kitchen when they found themselves alone there for a few seconds, the cheek to cheek kiss lasting a little too long as they said goodbye, the look held a little too intensely as he saw her into the car and closed the door for her.

Theirs had been a brief and passionate affair when she had been eighteen and Hateley a year or so older. She had lost her virginity to him in a warm hollow on the moors above the town, and thought of little else but him as she waited for her A level results and her university place. But the obsession passed as quickly as it had flared, and she could think of a million reasons why it should not be rekindled, even if she had the inclination. And in fact, if she was honest with herself, she could no longer remember quite why she had found Chris Hateley so attractive.

It was pitch dark when Jay woke later on that night, her heart thumping, quite sure that something in the cottage was wrong. The bedside clock told her it was just coming up to three but strain her ears as she might she could hear nothing unusual that might have dragged her from a dreamless sleep. She picked up her mobile phone from the bedside table and slipped carefully from beneath the duvet. The uncarpeted floor was bitterly cold but she did not dare hunt for slippers or dressing gown until she had made sure that Kate was safe.

She eased open her bedroom door which creaked in protest but once she was on the landing she could hear Kate's regular breathing coming from the smaller bedroom at the back of the house and she relaxed slightly. Kate had left her door open and after standing for a moment looking down at the child, Jay crossed the room to the window and glanced outside. There were no street lights in the alley between the two rows of terraced houses and the tiny yard beneath the window was in pitch black shadow. But beyond that, in the faint silver moonlight, Jay spotted a sudden shift of grey on grey as someone moved quickly between the houses, heading towards the main road.

Less cautious now, Jay switched on the hall light

and went downstairs, checking the front door, the windows and finally the back door into the yard. Everything was as secure as she had left it, but when she switched on the light in the yard and looked out of the kitchen window, she could see that the gate, which she had closed and locked with a heavy bolt earlier, was now ajar. Dressed only in her thin pyjamas, she shivered with fear as much as cold and glanced at her mobile. She guessed that if she called the police to complain that the gate had been opened, she would get little sympathy and she felt no inclination to rouse Sue and Chris or even her neighbours from their beds. Suddenly the distance she and Kate had travelled in the last months stretched behind her like an unbridgeable gulf and the future loomed ominously, as full of dark shadows as the night outside. There was no going back, she thought, and she was not at all sure how the two of them would go forward.

4

Jay Morton wiped the thick dust off the cardboard box she had found in the loft and hefted it
onto the kitchen table. She had been stowing
boxes of her own possessions under the roof,
crouching under the low beams on boards which
creaked ominously beneath her, torch at times
clenched between her teeth as the only means to
cast a fitful light on the floor which here and there
gave way to lathe and plaster which she knew
would collapse under her weight if she stepped on
it. To her surprise she had spotted a cardboard
box wedged under the eaves. Curious, she had
dragged it out to the hatch and found that it had
been sealed with yellowing Sellotape and was
impossible to open in the half light in which she
was working. Eventually, when the possessions
she could find no storage space for downstairs
were safely stowed, she backed cautiously down
the stepladder and pulled the box down behind
her, cursing the grime and cobwebs which by now
covered her sweatshirt with streaks and smears.

Slightly cleaner after washing at the kitchen
sink, but feeling in urgent need of a shower,
which was something that so far the cottage
could not provide in a bathroom which might
have been state of the art in the 1960s but now
offered only inconvenience without a shred of
retro charm, she took her scissors to the sealed

box which had once apparently held a dozen packs of Persil. She had not known quite what to expect but what she found made her smile with recognition and delight. The box was packed full of records, old LPs and EPs and singles of pop music from the early 1980s, the stuff of her own teenage years. Carefully she lifted the treasures out and discovered underneath four or five posters, all of the same group, obviously the collector's favourite as it had been her own. She spread one out and drew a finger over Debbie Harry's flying blonde hair and exuberant figure, skirt slashed to the hip, mic. clutched high in the air, and recalled the nights she had spent dancing to Blondie, as a sixth former and a student.

'God, we were so young,' she said, feeling the years stretch back to a time of almost forgotten innocence and enthusiasm. 'I wonder what happened to Debbie Harry.' As far as she could recall the band had ridden high on the singer's brittle energy for only a few years before sinking without trace. Harry had already been mature for a pop star, in fact positively in her dotage compared to current teenaged stars, who were lucky if their careers glittered for months rather than years if what Kate said was anything to go by. Or had there been some sort of come-back more recently? She could not quite remember. If there had, this collection certainly did not reflect it. Carefully she sorted through the records, selected the mono-chrome cover of *Parallel Lines* and carried it reverently into the sitting room where an almost unused turntable sat on top of the audio stack in the corner. She put it on with unaccustomed

56

fingers and sat back for a moment to enjoy.

To her intense disappointment the tracks had been almost completely wrecked, and repeated phrases, cacophonous scratches and a jumping stylus made the disc almost unrecognisable. It had, she thought, been played almost to death, and she knew exactly why. Reluctantly she switched the system off, unwilling to face disappointment again from anything else in the collection, and sat for a moment recalling her last years in Pendle Bridge when she and Chris Hateley had been almost inseparable for eighteen months. Blondie had been a part of all that, she thought, and the band was something it might be best not to resurrect even casually after all this time. It might be nostalgic to dance with Debbie Harry again but the emotions the music resurrected were dangerous too. A fragment of one of the lyrics insinuated itself into her mind: *love is so confusing there's no peace of mind.* That certainly turned out to be true, she thought, remembering Chris's devastation when she ended their affair. She shook herself slightly to bring herself back to the here and now.

She had no doubt that the record collection had belonged to Kenny Bairstow and that it had been carefully boxed and hidden away in the loft by his mother, probably distraught at what had happened to her son. Was he her only son? Jay wondered. She shivered. The idea that while she and Chris had been playing Romeo and Juliet in their late teens, a young man who had lived here, in what was now her home, had been pursuing and seducing a loveless child from Pendle House horrified her. She might well have seen Kenny Bairstow around the town, she thought. She could have passed the murdered girl in the street. And she had known nothing. Even if she had already gone away to university when the murder happened, no one, neither Chris, nor Sue, nor her parents, had felt it to be significant enough to mention to her, even in passing. The whole episode, the murder, the arrest, and presumably a trial, had passed her by and even after all this time she felt an overwhelming need to find out more.

She knew it was faintly ridiculous after all this time but she wanted to calm Kate's riotous imagination. And she could not help feeling that her own accidental connection to the murder, through the house where the boy had probably spent most of his life, linked her too closely to the snuffing out of a young life not much longer than Kate's own. She felt a trail of guilt leading right back here to the room in which she was sitting. She shuddered and took the record off the turntable and returned it to its sleeve. She had shared that enthusiasm with Kenny Bairstow, perhaps he too had danced to Blondie at one of the hops she and Chris used to go to in the town's single dance-hall, and she marvelled at how the banal and the horrific could exist in such close proximity. Suddenly Debbie Harry's voice did not seem so attractive any more. It might seem crazy, but she knew she needed to know more, and quickly.

Nab End was another double-fronted Victorian mansion like Pendle House, built to accommodate the large families and unostentatious wealth of the Pendle valley's mill owners more than a century before. But here the front garden had been stripped bare and covered with Tarmac to make a car park, and the back of the house extended to provide extra accommodation for the fifty or so elderly residents whose final home this would almost inevitably prove to be. Jay parked close to the front door. A blustery weekday afternoon was obviously not a popular time for visitors, she thought, as she put her box of musical memorabilia on the floor at her feet and rang the door-bell after finding the front entrance firmly locked. She waited a while before a sleepy looking woman in a pink overall opened the door and warm air hit Jay in the face in a wave that was tainted rather than fresh.

'Sorry to keep you,' the woman said. 'There's only me on this after', and we have to keep t'door locked because some o'them wander.'

She listened with slight surprise to Jay's request to see Grace Bairstow.

'She's likely asleep,' the woman said. 'They usually have a nap after their dinner. Mind, she's a bit restless at the best of times, is Grace, so you might be lucky.'

'I won't keep her long,' Jay said.

'You're not likely to,' the woman said waving her in through the door and locking it again. 'She's not got much conversation, hasn't Grace. Are you from t'probation people, an'all?'

'Sorry?' Jay said, her mind a blank.

'Oh, don't mind me,' the woman said. 'Grace seems to be right popular just now. You're the third visitor she's had this week. I just thought...'

'Probation?'

The woman glanced round slightly furtively and then lowered her voice.

'Well, I don't know for a fact, of course, but I thought it must be summat to do wi' that son of hers. I heard they were thinking of letting him out, but if they think he's got Grace to come home to they'll be sadly mistaken. You'll be a relative, then, will you? Like the young woman who came on Monday, said she were Grace's niece.'

'No, no,' Jay said quickly. 'I just bought the house the Bairstows used to live in and I found this box of stuff in the loft that I think must be theirs, Kenny's maybe, as it goes. But if her memory's poor...'

'Oh, it's not that poor, if it's the past you want to talk about. Like a lot of them, she doesn't know what day it is, or whether it's her dinner or her tea she's eating, but if you talk to her about what happened thirty years ago she's as clear as a bell. If it suits her, like.'

'She might remember stashing this stuff away then.'

'Kenny's stuff, you reckon, do you?' The carer's eyes were avid with curiosity now and Jay felt she had already said too much about someone she had not even met.

'Shall we see if she's awake?' she asked. The woman shrugged irritably and led the way down a corridor which smelt of boiled cabbage and air freshener which did not entirely mask the sharp edge of incontinence beneath its flowery scent. She knocked on a door, opened it and peered inside.

'Are you up and about, Gracie?' she asked. 'There's another lady here to see you, you lucky girl. You'll be getting t'prize for most popular resident this week.'

Jay did not hear any response but the woman pushed the door wide and waved her into a bedroom where a tiny frail figure sat in the single armchair, a blanket over her knees and a look of confusion in her pale blue eyes. She had obviously just woken up.

'This is...?' The woman stopped and looked inquiringly at Jay.

'Mrs. Morton,' Jay said. 'Jay Morton, Mrs. Bairstow. I've just moved into your old house in Adelaide Street.' The old woman's eyes did not appear to register this information and she continued to pick at infinitesimal specks on her blanket and drop them irritably on the floor. Jay edged her way past the carer and properly into the room, parked the box on the bed and pulled out the recording of *Heart of Glass*.

'I found this up in your old loft,' she said. 'I thought it must have been Kenny's.'

She had hit home this time and Grace Bairstow's eyes brightened and filled with tears.

'Kenny,' she said. 'He liked that song. I've not seen our Kenny for a long while, you know, love. They keep saying he's coming to see me soon, but he never does. D'you think he's gone to Australia? He always said he wanted to go to Australia when he grew up.'

A snort of derision from the woman in the doorway drew a flash of anger from Jay.

'I'll be fine now, thank you,' she said sharply.

'I'll bring her tea at four then, shall I?' the carer asked, more as a challenge than an offer. 'You can have a cup yourself for forty pee.'

'Thanks,' Jay said, but she guessed the heavy irony was lost on her audience.

'Are you all right, Grace?' she asked gently when the door had been closed. 'Till they bring you your tea?' Grace struggled to sit more upright in her chair and Jay tucked the blanket more securely over her knees and put the record into her hands.

'D'you remember when Kenny used to listen to Blondie?' she asked. 'Are all these records I found in your loft Kenny's? And posters of Debbie Harry? Do you remember? I thought you might want to keep them for him.'

'Them little lasses used to come round and listen to Kenny's records,' Grace said, her voice firmer now. 'He had his record player in t'front room and they'd all sit on t'settee and listen. I used to buy him the records every time a new one came out. He weren't too good at shopping, you know. He'd get the money all muddled up. But he were right fond o'them two girls, you know. It were all nonsense what they said about him later. He'd never have touched a hair of their heads, wouldn't Kenny. Not a hair of their heads. It were a wicked lie. But they never believed me. He weren't a dirty minded boy, wasn't Kenny. Not ever. They said he'd never really grow up, and he didn't. He grew big, but he didn't grow up.'

'It wasn't just the one little girl he knew, then? The one who died?'

'No. There were two of them. You never saw them apart, them two. Went everywhere together.

62

Mags and Donna, they were called. They'd been pals with our Kenny for years before all that happened.'

'Mags and Donna,' Jay said softly.

'I never saw either of them after,' the old woman said, a tear rolling down her wrinkled cheek. 'They said Donna ran off when Mags were killed. Was killed herself, maybe, and the body hidden. But they never found her. And I never saw her again. He really loved those little lasses, did our Kenny. I don't mean owt wrong in that, whatever they said later in t'court. He were only a little lad himself really, and he liked doing the things they liked doing.'

'What sort of things?' Jay asked wondering how far Grace Bairstow was still deceiving herself about her son after all these years.

'Playing in t'park, going on t'swings, going down in t'woods. They first met Kenny in t'park. We called it that, but really it were just a bit of grass where the lads used to kick a football around and a small patch with three or four swings and a roundabout thing that was too heavy for most o't' kiddies to move.'

'I know where you mean,' Jay said. 'Up the hill from the primary school, from St. Peter's.'

'Aye, that's it. It's still there, though they've put new swings and things in, last time I went up there, and a fence to keep t'dogs out. Mucky things, dogs. Any road, Kenny liked that park. Used to go there with his dad, before he passed on. And the girls used to stop there on their way home from school. Kenny got to know them there. He used to push them on t'swings, he said. They made out he were waiting for them for t'wrong reasons later, the police, but it were just a bit o' fun, just kiddies playing. He'd tell me all about it when he came home. They liked him because he could push them higher than t'other lads.'

'But he was a bit old, wasn't he, to be playing in a children's playground?'

'There were a notice on t'gate that said the swings were for children under fourteen but no one took any notice of Kenny being there. No one ever complained. He were quite small for his age then, not much taller than them lasses when they were eleven or twelve and had begun to shoot up. And he were never any trouble. They said after that he were too rough for them, that they got back up to the home all muddy and their clothes torn, but no one said owt against Kenny at the time. No one complained.'

Grace leaned back in her chair looking tired, the animation which had seized her and briefly lit up the pale, lined face draining away. She closed her eyes.

'Does your niece often come to see you,' Jay asked, thinking that dwelling on the past might not be doing Grace any good.

'Niece? What niece is that?' Grace asked.

'Your carer said you were having a lot of visitors this week. Your niece came...'

'Someone came,' Grace said, her voice sinking to mere mumbling now. 'I don't know who she were. I don't have a niece. Another young woman, asking questions about Kenny. People keep coming. Who are you, any road? I don't know you.'

'I bought your house in Adelaide Street. I found

Kenny's records in the loft.' She handed the old woman Kenny's disc again. 'You remember Blondie.'

'Oh, aye,' Grace said. 'Blondie. He really liked Blondie, did our Kenny. And those girls did, an'all. Played them records over and over again in my house, they did. Over and over. Took the radio out wi'them when they went down in t'woods for a picnic even.'

'You mean down Threshfield,' Jay said, remembering the narrow wooded valley with a stream at the bottom where she and Sue had gone for walks when they were growing up, a secret valley filled in spring with the smell of bluebells and wild garlic, stepping stones over the rushing peaty water which provided endless hours of entertainment with just the hint of fear of falling into the dark pools where minnows and sticklebacks lurked.

'Aye, Threshfield woods, that's where they used to go,' Grace said. 'When they were a bit bigger. He liked the woods, did Kenny. Built fires for their picnics, roasted 'taters in t'ashes. Liked finding frogs and toads and always brought me some wild flowers back an' all. Bluebells. Lots of bluebells, and then them big daisies later on, and them buttercups that grow near t'water. Then the little blonde one fell into t'stream one day and cut her head. There was blood everywhere and he made a bandage with his t-shirt. He wasn't as daft as everyone thought sometimes, wasn't Kenny. He carried her all t'way home, right up the hill and over t'stile and past the cricket ground – must be a mile or more. And I washed her head where

65

she'd cut it, and called Pendle House on t'tele-phone to tell them what had happened.'

'I shouldn't imagine they were very pleased,' Jay said.

'Some woman came down in a car, right furious because the girls had been bunking off school, summat like that. Said they shouldn't be playing with our Kenny, they weren't to play with him no more.' Grace stopped and her face seemed to set like stone.

'And did they?' Jay asked. Grace sat very still, eyes closed, her fingers picking again at the blanket for a long time before she answered.

'It's a long time ago,' she said. 'I don't remember everything that happened. But I don't think I saw them girls again. And then they came for Kenny. Later that was. A lot later. And said he'd been interfering with them, and had killed one of them and the other one was missing. They never found her, you know? Never. Donna, she was called. But my Kenny never interfered with her, or with Mags. Never. He wouldn't know how.'

Jay looked out of the window at the bleak winter garden at the back of Nab End. Time had not softened the catastrophe which had overwhelmed Grace Bairstow all those years ago, because for her it was the present which had dimmed and the past which had leapt into sharp relief. Officials, if that was what Grace's recent visitors had been, would find little to help them plan a future for her son here where Grace was still locked in a battle to save him that had been lost long ago. She wondered what Kenny was saying now about his conviction. If they were seriously considering releasing him, she thought, he had probably admitted his guilt years ago. She had a feeling that parole was indefinitely delayed if prisoners did not take responsibility for their crimes. She just hoped that if he were released, he did not come seeking out his old home, and she shivered slightly, though the room was oppressively warm.

'Would you like to keep Kenny's records and things?' she asked.

'Keep what, love?' Grace said, blank again. 'I don't know where our Kenny is. He's been away a long time.'

'The Blondie records I found at your old house,' Jay said, with a sigh. 'Kenny's records.'

'Oh aye, he'll be coming soon. When he gets back from Australia. You leave them here, love, and I'll see he gets them.'

After Kate had finally taken herself reluctantly upstairs to bed that evening, Jay turned off the television and flung herself back into the corner of the sofa with a heavy sigh. Her visit to Nab End had depressed her, she thought, and done nothing to relieve her fear that Kenny Bairstow would turn up unannounced on her new doorstep if he were to be released from jail. And Kate had done nothing to soothe her anxieties either when she had come in from school soon after Jay herself had got home. She had flounced through the front door, looking pale and anxious and closely followed by a small, thin child whom she had introduced as her friend Sonja. Sonja, dressed in clothes of muddy colours and an old-fashioned style, turned out to speak little English and to smell faintly of garlic, none of which facts were likely to endear her to her classmates at St. Peter's, Jay thought. She wondered if the friendship she seemed to have struck up with Kate, in spite of the language difficulties, was a case of the two most unpopular kids in the class clinging together for support. She did not underestimate the local children's capacity for suspicion of anyone different from themselves. London might have transformed itself into a rainbow nation but up here in Yorkshire she knew that questions of race and nationality were more problematic.

'Does Sonja's mother know she's come here instead of going straight home?' Kate asked her daughter anxiously as the two girls dropped their school-bags in the hall and Sonja followed Kate into the kitchen to help themselves to milk and biscuits, which the visitor ate with more enthusiasm than Jay found entirely comfortable.

'Her mum's taken her little brother to the doctors,' Kate said. 'I said you wouldn't mind if she came here.' Kate's words were confident enough but Jay picked up the tension in her voice.

'No, of course I don't mind,' Jay had said, too quickly. 'Does she live close?'

'Fanny Street,' Sonja said slowly and distinctly. 'I live in Fanny Street.'

Jay controlled the smile which flickered at the corner of her mouth, aware that neither of the children shared the joke, and wishing that the mill owner who had built the rows of cottages had perhaps not chosen to name the streets after his children quite so inclusively.

'Just round the corner,' Jay had said. 'Are you going to watch television then? I'm doing some unpacking upstairs this afternoon.' The stepladder was still propped up on the landing so that she could dispose of yet more of their possessions in the loft.

'We do not have television at our house,' Sonja had said solemnly and followed Kate into the living room where they were soon absorbed.

At five thirty Sonja, an unusually self-possessed but silent child, announced that she would go home now, and Kate watched her walk down the street in the rain and turn into Fanny Street without a backward glance.

'Where does Sonja's family come from?' she asked Kate.

'Somewhere funny,' Kate said absently. 'Ko-so-vo? Is that right?'

'Could be,' Jay said, wondering how permanent Sonja's stay would be.

'She's very clever,' Kate said absently. 'She gets all her maths right. And I'm teaching her ten new English words every day.'

'Good for you,' Jay said.

After they had eaten and Kate had done her homework, Jay chased her to bed as soon as she decently could. The day had unsettled her even more than the events of the previous night, and she took extra care to make sure that the gate to the backyard was firmly bolted at top and bottom and the kitchen door was securely locked before she could even think of beginning to relax. Living without another adult in the house, she thought, was more unsettling than she had anticipated.

She had never felt so insecure while she and Kate had lived alone in London after the break-up, but she supposed that was because the house had been the long familiar one to which she and David had delightedly brought Kate home from hospital and where she had friends and neighbours always within easy reach. Here she had exchanged little more than polite greetings with the neighbours, apart from Mr. Booth, who would be an unlikely champion in a crisis.

She watched television desultorily for a while and then picked up the phone and dialled her sister's number. Her brother-in-law replied.

'Do you want Sue?' Chris Hateley asked. 'She's just popped out to pick Abbie up from a friend's house. She won't be long.'

'No, it was you I wanted,' Jay said, wondering why her tongue seemed so reluctant to frame those particular words. 'I was wondering if you knew whether this man Kenny Bairstow who used to live in this house has been freed from prison – or if he's likely to be?'

There was a silence on the other end of the line.

'Not as far as I know,' Chris said eventually. 'You're not seriously worried about that old case, are you? I'm sure you've no reason to be. If they do let him out they'll keep a close eye on him. Life prisoners are only let out on licence, you know.'

'D'you remember listening to Blondie?' Jay said, changing the subject. 'D'you remember how crazy we were about them? I found this collection of old records in the loft here and it turns out Kenny Bairstow was crazy about them too. It just seems so weird to think of him obsessed with Debbie Harry at the same time as we were... I feel very odd about it, Chris, as if something's come back to haunt me.'

The silence again.

'It won't be Kenny who comes back to haunt you, will it?' he said.

This time it was Jay who drew a sharp breath, almost as if she had been stung, and she took her time considering exactly what Chris meant. She decided to ignore him, for now anyway.

'Did he really kill that girl?' she asked. 'Sue said you did some digging around when he appealed.'

'Oh, he did it all right,' Chris said. 'His solicitor was making a great fuss about the case and I did think at first that there'd been some great miscarriage of justice, backward boy bullied by the police, all that stuff. Hoped I could make a reputation for myself by proving he didn't do it, if you really want to know. But the more I looked into it the more convinced I was that he must have been guilty. The police said it was open and shut right from the beginning: he had the motive – sex – the means – he was twice as big and heavy as the girl, and the opportunity. Not even his mother claimed he had a real alibi, apart from her, that is. And he confessed. It really was open and shut.'

'What about the other girl? The one who disappeared?'

'The police thought either he'd killed her as well, and hidden the body, or, more likely, she was there, they'd both gone to the park to meet Kenny like they always did everything together, and then it got out of hand and she ran away. She was never traced.'

'Surely she'd have been the witness everyone needed, to be sure what happened,' Jay objected. 'Didn't they look for her?'

'The police looked for her, as far as I know. But she never turned up. It's not unusual, is it, with kids like that, children in care. Sometimes they run off and just vanish. They can be very mixed up emotionally. All sorts of things go wrong. They end up on the streets. As far as I can remember, her mother had killed her father before she was taken into care.'

'How awful,' Jay whispered, almost to herself.

'She's probably dead by now,' Chris said.

'Can I look at your newspaper cuttings about the case?'

'Yes, if you want to,' Chris said. 'Why don't you pop into the office tomorrow and I'll show you what's in the archives. But seriously, Jay, I don't think it's anything you need to worry about. Kenny Bairstow's not going to come back to pursue you.' There was that odd emphasis again and Jay did not think that she was mistaken this time. If anyone was coming back to pursue her, Chris thought it would be him and that was a complication she did not want at all.

'I'll see how I'm fixed,' she said, hoping her voice sounded as frozen as she felt inside. 'I've quite a lot to do tomorrow.'

'Whenever,' Chris said. 'I'll see you then.'

5

In the end Jay decided almost as soon as Kate had left for school the next morning that she needed to know more about Kenny Bairstow. She had slept uneasily that night, waking more than once, tense and uncertain, her ears straining for any unusual noise. When she finally heard her alarm in the grey early daylight she went straight into Kate's room with her dressing gown clutched around her shoulders, to find her daughter sleeping peacefully, only the top of her head visible beneath the duvet. And when she looked out of the window the yard at the back of the house was as tranquil as when she had last inspected it before going to bed, the gate securely locked, the alley between the houses deserted. But the niggling doubts remained and by half-past nine she had driven down the steep hill into the town centre and parked at the back of the main supermarket.

The offices of the weekly *Pendle Bridge Advertiser* lay behind a simple shop front window in one of the steep and narrow thoroughfares which made up the commercial heart of the town. Jay glanced at the display of wedding photographs in the window and smiled. Nothing much had changed here, she thought, and felt again the sense of surprise that Chris Hateley had been content to spend his working life in their home town recording the hatchings, matchings and dispatchings of such a small community.

The editor came down into the reception area himself when Jay had explained her mission to the young woman behind the counter. He looked tired and strained, Jay thought and, raw from her own break-up, she wondered whether her sister's marriage was as secure as she seemed to think it was. She did not believe she had imagined Chris's tentative attempts to revive a relationship long dead and, on her side at least, far beyond resurrection.

'You promised I could browse in your archives,' she said. 'I might as well get on with it now. I won't have the time once I start work.'

'Are you sure you're not making too much of this?' Chris asked. For a moment Jay was tempted to tell him about the unlatched gate in the night but was reluctant to offer him any handle on her own uncertain emotions. She might need help, she thought, but not from Chris. He watched her for a moment and she found his expression unreadable. Then he shrugged and gave her one of the tentative smiles which had melted her to the core all those years ago.

'Come on then. I'll show you where we keep the back copies. You'll find it a dusty exercise going back twenty years, I'm afraid. We started putting them on microfiche about ten years ago, but the eighties copies are still mouldering away in racks.'

'I'm used to handling mouldering old artefacts,' Jay said. 'It's what I get paid for.'

'Right,' Chris said, leading the way into the back of the building and down a corridor. 'This is what we call our library, though it's a bit of a joke really. We can't afford to keep a proper archive, just the back copies of the paper and a few box files of council minutes and official stuff like that.'

He opened the door and switched on the light to reveal a large room offering almost no natural light through its grimy windows, lined with racks on which unwieldy bound copies of the *Advertiser* lay in untidy heaps.

'I did look up the relevant dates for you,' he said. He fished a sheet of paper out of his inside pocket. 'The murder happened in May 1982, the trial was at the crown court in Bradfield about ten months later, and then there was an appeal in 1985. That failed and I don't think we've heard anything about Kenny Bairstow since. The murder was a big story for us, of course, but the nationals didn't take much interest. The arrest was too quick for it to build up a head of steam nationally. It was right at the height of the Falklands war, too, and they had other things on their minds.'

'Sue said you did some investigating yourself...'

'I did, later on,' Chris said. 'Mrs Bairstow was very persistent after Kenny was convicted. She wrote endless letters to the *Advertiser*, and to all the papers, as far away as Leeds. She went on and on about him being innocent, about him being bullied by the police, about him not being capable of rape, about him being still a little boy, though by this time he was a big heavy lad, not tall, admittedly, but running to fat. Anyway, I began to think I could make a name for myself by doing a bit of investigative reporting and uncovering a major miscarriage of justice. I talked to everyone involved I think, while they were waiting for the appeal to be allowed, but I couldn't find anything.

He had confessed, after all, even though he withdrew the confession later. The trial judge wasn't convinced by that and nor was I in the end. A lot of the evidence might have been circumstantial, but he knew those girls, had played around with them for the best part of three years. What clinched it for me was something the doctor who did the postmortem said. He said he couldn't be sure, so he hadn't been asked to mention it in evidence, but he thought that the dead girl was sexually experienced before that night. She wasn't a virgin. She'd been sleeping around, and if not with Kenny then who?'

'How old was she again?' Jay asked, horrified.

'Thirteen when she died,' Chris said.

'And Kenny was capable?'

'According to the medical evidence, Kenny was perfectly capable. His mother had been living in a dream world with her fantasies about him still being a little boy. They found soft porn magazines in his bedroom.'

Jay shuddered slightly, knowing that Kenny's bedroom was now Kate's. The thought of her sleeping where this boy had probably abused himself filled her with revulsion. Then she sighed, thinking of Grace Bairstow, waiting in her old people's home for Kenny to come to see her, confident still of his innocence, as any mother might be. She guessed that whatever your children did there was still an irreducible place in the mind where they were still your innocent babies, a place which perhaps nothing which came later could touch. But she was not Kenny's mother and the more she learned about him the more she regretted buying his former home.

'Are you really worried about him being released?' Chris said. 'They keep a close eye on lifers, you know. I'm sure if you got in touch with the right people they'd make sure he was kept well out of your way.'

'I don't know what I'm worried about,' Jay said, running a hand through her hair wearily. 'I just feel I need to know a bit more about what happened as I'm living in the Bairstow's house. I just wish someone had told me what had gone on there *before* I bought it, not after.'

'Yes, well, I feel a bit bad about that but I honestly didn't realise it was their house. But the estate agent should have been more upfront. Or the sellers.'

'You're joking,' Jay said sourly. 'Anyway, you can just leave me to browse through these dusty heaps.'

'Fine,' Chris said. 'If it'll make you feel better.'

'It might,' Jay said.

But it didn't. She made a few desultory notes as she leafed through the yellowed pages of the 1982 *Advertiser* but as she read the reports of the trial evidence and particularly the judge's summing up, she was left with the indelible feeling that Chris Hateley was right and that Kenny Bairstow had been fairly convicted on the basis of the evidence. She left the *Advertiser's* offices without making contact with Chris again. She felt hot, dusty and slightly sick and as she made her way back towards the car park, she castigated herself for over-reacting. She had never regarded herself as a nervous person and she guessed that the fact that she was, to all intents and purposes, solely responsible now for Kate's welfare, was fuelling her response to the Bairstow affair. She shouldn't have to put up with this alone, she thought irritably, and a wave of fury at the way David had split up the family almost overwhelmed her. She knew her friends, and quite probably her sister, took the conventional view: it takes two to split a marriage. But however long she agonised over the part she might have played she could think of nothing which might have provoked David's affair: they had not been quarrelling, they had still, she thought, been good together in bed, there were no outside tensions that she was aware of to throw their twelve-year relationship off course. It had come out of a clear blue sky and she was still reeling.

She stopped at a café and ordered a coffee to steady her nerves, and while it was cooling she looked at the sketchy notes she had made in the *Advertiser's* library. One of the names she had jotted down was that of Granville Stott, Kenny Bairstow's solicitor and, she recalled from the legal transactions which had followed her father's death, her own family's as well. She would, she thought, make one more attempt to discover a bit more about Kenny and the murdered girl. If anyone should know the truth and confirm that justice had been done, she thought, it would be the man who had defended Kenny.

It proved more difficult to track down Granville Stott than Jay had anticipated when she dropped into the offices of Stott, Macadam and Ahmed on her way back to the car park. The older Mr.

Stott had retired eighteen months ago, she was told by the receptionist who guarded the entrance to the partners' offices at the top of a steep and narrow staircase in one of the tall stone buildings which backed onto the river in the only level street in Pendle Bridge. And the receptionist did not think that Mr. Stott would want his retirement interrupted by clients these days, or even, when Jay explained her past connection with the firm, by the children of clients. When Jay became more insistent the woman reluctantly agreed to telephone her former boss and seek his opinion on the matter and with pursed lips eventually conceded that Mr. Stott senior would be happy to renew Jay's acquaintance if she could call at his home that afternoon at two.

Jay had done a quick calculation and reckoned that she could just make it out to Shipcar, a moorland village about ten miles to the north, and be back in time for Kate's return from school. She was acutely aware that the network of friends she had relied on in London to help out in an emergency while she juggled work and child-care simply did not exist yet here, and wondered if it ever would. But against the slight risk of not getting back in time she had to set the fact that tomorrow she was due at the town hall to interview six applicants for the post of her assistant and another six who wanted the job of porter, handyman and general dogsbody for the new museum. Her new job was closing in on her fast and she did not want it to start under the shadow of Kenny Bairstow.

She drove fast up the twisting lane which led

from the centre of the town onto the open moors above and then put her foot down on the snaking road which crossed the rolling hills. It was possible to see for miles in all directions across the dun-coloured winter landscape, where cloud shadows raced across the sheep pastures broken up only by the darker traces of meandering streams and bogs and an occasional dilapidated dry stone wall. There was no human habitation in sight up here on the crest of the Pennines, and it was not until the road began to drop again into the valley of the Maze, where she could see a cluster of cottages, that she passed an isolated farmstead, separated from the road by a rutted and waterlogged track. At last she spotted the handful of buildings which made up the village of Shipcar, little more than a hamlet of low stone farm cottages and converted barns set around a village green. The green was muddy and desolate in this weather, with an old-fashioned red phone box and a signpost at the fork in the road from Pendle Bridge indicating that one leg plunged downhill towards Eckersley and the twisted upward branch wound its way over the highest of the windswept tops into Lancashire.

Jay parked on the edge of the green, got out of the car and found her breath almost snatched from her body by the sharp wind which was sweeping down from the north. She pulled up the collar of her jacket and crossed the road. Each of the huddled cottages was identifiable by name rather than number and after passing Mooredge, Long Barn and World's End she identified Shipcar Lodge, a slightly larger double fronted house with mullioned windows and a stone tiled roof, distinguished from its neighbours mainly by the fact that it boasted a narrow strip of front garden behind a stone wall accessed by a white painted wooden gate. Almost reluctantly she opened the gate and rang the door-bell.

Granville Stott opened the door himself and Jay was shocked at the change in him. She recalled a substantial man, neatly turned out and soberly dark suited, when she and Sue had accompanied their mother to his office to discuss her father's will, of which Stott was executor. The figure who faced her now was only a shrunken shadow of his former self, rake thin, stooping, his hair turned from iron grey to white and barely covering his scalp, his face haggard and the eyes sunk into dark sockets. He must be not much over seventy but he was, she guessed as she shook the trembling hand he held out to her, quite seriously ill. She wondered why he had agreed to see her at all.

Stott led her into a comfortable sitting room to the right of the front door, where a tray with milk, sugar and teacups for two stood on the coffee table.

'Will you take tea, Mrs. Morton?' he asked. 'My wife had to go out but she left everything ready.'

'Thank you,' Jay said and while Stott busied himself in the kitchen she took the chance to glance around the room, taking in the good quality, if old fashioned furnishings, the books and magazines littered everywhere and, by the picture window which gave a panoramic view of the moors and hills beyond the trim back garden, a powerful pair of binoculars. Stott caught her gaze as he came back into the room carrying a teapot and smiled faintly.

'I've always been a birdwatcher,' he said. 'When I retired we moved out here and I hoped I'd be able to spend a lot of time up there on the moors.' He sat down heavily and Jay caught a spasm of pain in his features which he quickly suppressed. 'It didn't turn out quite like that,' he went on as he poured the tea and passed her milk and sugar. 'You never know, do you? Now tell me. How is your mother? Did her move to France work out as she had hoped?'

'Yes it did,' Jay said. 'She was always a sun-lover and she and my father spent most of their holidays in Provence. She's very happy there and of course the whole family is only too pleased to go and visit, so she's getting the best of both worlds.'

'A happy retirement then?' Stott said, unable to suppress the note of envy which simply confirmed what was obvious, that his own was not turning out nearly so well.

'So what can I do for you, Mrs. Morton?' he asked. 'I told the office I didn't want to be bothered with visitors. In fact someone was trying to find me only a week or so ago, and I told them I really didn't want to be disturbed. But when they said it was you... I was always a great admirer of your father, you know. A good man, who was taken far too soon.'

'Yes,' Jay said, as emotion threatened to overwhelm her for a second. She swallowed hard and hesitantly told Stott her worries about the house in Adelaide Street and her fear that Kenny Bairstow might return to Pendle Bridge and intrude in some way on the new life she was trying to build for herself and Kate. Stott listened gravely and sighed but did not speak for a moment, as if he was trying to gaze into some dark place that he had not visited for a long time.

'I suppose I want to know if he was guilty, Mr. Stott,' Jay said. 'For my peace of mind, and because I have a daughter almost as old as the girl who was killed. Living in that house brings it too close for comfort, if you see what I mean.'

Stott got up painfully from his chair and stood for a moment gazing out at the view from his window at the moors, where it was obvious he was now too frail to walk far, but still he did not speak.

'I suppose I'm being idiotic, wanting certainty where there probably isn't any,' Jay said quickly, wanting to fill the silence.

'No, it's not that,' Stott said at last. 'You're a mother and have every right to be concerned for your child. What makes me hesitate is that I don't really know what to say to you. Solicitors don't necessarily know the truth in these cases any more than anyone else does, you know. Kenny Bairstow didn't confess to me in private or even offer any very coherent explanation of what had happened in his own defence. When it got to court, he told the jury what he had told me: that he was at home and went to bed as usual. His mother said he was at home and went to bed as usual. But as the prosecution said over and over again, they would say that, wouldn't they? And under police questioning the day the body was found he had confessed, agreed that he frequently met the girls in secret, not just the victim, Margaret Emmet, but the other one as well – what was she called? Donna something.'

'Donna Latham,' Jay said. 'She's never turned up again, has she?'

'No, no, she either died that night as well, or else she ran away and has taken care never to be found. A dreadful thing in itself, don't you think?'

Jay nodded.

'So, as to Kenny. I thought at the time the police had behaved very badly. He was a backward boy, a mental age of about ten or eleven the psychologists said, and he had no one with him while he was being questioned, not his mother, not a social worker, not a solicitor. Quite irregular. I didn't see him until long after he'd confessed, and I simply told him to withdraw that statement. It wasn't worth the paper it was written on, in my judgement, and Kenny's barrister and I were outraged when the judge ruled it admissible. We hoped the appeal court would overturn the verdict but...' He shrugged wearily.

'Kenny Bairstow has been on my conscience for twenty years,' he said. 'I did what I could when the editor of the *Advertiser,* Chris... Ah, he's your sister's husband, isn't he? So you'll have talked to him. But when he was investigating, before the appeal, he thought he was onto something with the pornographic magazines they made so much of at the trial. The prosecution sprang those on us at the last minute, and Hateley thought he could show that Kenny hadn't bought them at the local shop. The newsagent couldn't recall the boy ever buying anything of that sort and he wasn't capable of going far to seek out that sort of stuff. But that idea seemed to run into the sand in the end and I think Chris concluded we were wasting our time. I've always suspected that Les Green, who led the murder inquiry, was not above bullying the boy in the initial interview, or even fabricating a bit of corroborative evidence if he felt it was needed, but DCI Green died ten years ago, so there's no chance of ever getting an admission out of him.'

'But you don't think he was guilty, do you?' Jay said quietly. Stott turned from the window again to face her squarely.

'I never thought Kenny was guilty,' he said. 'I thought he was a convenient scapegoat although whose convenience he served I have no idea. But I failed to find anything to cast doubt on all that circumstantial evidence. There were no DNA tests then, of course.'

'These days, that would prove it one way or another in a case of rape, I suppose?'

'Yes, these things are much more clear cut now,' Stott said. 'Forensic science has advanced by leaps and bounds.'

'Would they have kept the evidence they found then?'

'For twenty years? I doubt it,' Stott said. 'The verdict was guilty and the police would regard the case as closed. I'm sorry, I'm not being much help to you, Mrs. Morton. I can't give you the reassurance you want, I'm afraid.'

'Well, I think the fact that you have doubts is pretty reassuring,' Jay said.

'Although it means that Margaret Emmet's murderer is still at large?'

'Yes, there's that,' Jay conceded. 'But if he is, he's

unlikely to come snooping around Kenny Bairstow's house, is he? That's all that really bothers me.'

But after she had made her farewells to Granville Stott and was driving back over the moors to Pendle Bridge she wondered if that was strictly true. She recalled Grace Bairstow's blind faith in her son's innocence, those blue eyes, so blank when trying to comprehend the here and now, but bright with faith when summoning up the events of twenty years before. And now the boy's solicitor seemed certain that justice had not been done and seemed tormented by that certainty as he apparently approached the end of his own life. She sighed. Perhaps Chris was right and these people were just deceiving themselves. And she felt little optimism that she could unravel the mystery after all these years when so many had tried and failed.

She drove home quickly and parked outside her house with the usual complex manoeuvring in the narrow street. As she collected up her bag and mobile phone she noticed without too much surprise that her neighbour was peering out of his front door, an expectant look on his face.

'Afternoon, Mr. Booth,' she said without much enthusiasm, glancing at her watch. She had not much time to spare before Kate arrived home from school and she was hoping to read through the application forms ready for tomorrow's interviews at the Town Hall.

'Somebody were looking for you earlier,' her neighbour said, a note of accusation in his voice.

'Oh yes?' Jay said absently as she juggled her keys to find the right one for the front door.

'Woman, it were. Caught her peering through t'letter box when no one answered t'door.'

'Really?' Jay said, her attention caught now. 'Did she say what she wanted?'

'Shot off, she did, when I told her you were out,' Booth said scornfully. 'Said she thought the Bairstows still lived there, then buggered off. Everyone's in a hurry, these days, always rushing. I told her they'd gone away and you lived there now but I don't reckon she heard me. Too busy to listen, you young folk.'

'I'm sure you're right,' Jay said, as she pushed open the front door. Her neighbour hovered, and she knew he was desperate to talk, but she felt tired and irritable and disinclined to humour him. Guiltily she closed the door firmly behind her and dropped her bag on the sofa with a groan. She had enough on her plate with her new job and a daughter to bring up alone, she thought, trying to justify her rudeness, without playing good Samaritan to lonely neighbours. The message light was flashing on her answerphone and she was surprised to find four messages recorded, but when she played them back one by one she found that after each request to leave a message there was nothing but the hissing of white noise on the tape.

'Damn and blast,' she said to herself, erasing them all and banging the receiver down too hard. 'Who's playing games with the phone?' Perhaps, she thought, it was the same person who had been peering through her letterbox earlier, and the small nagging doubt at the back of her mind crystallised into worry. Perhaps her anxiety about living in the Bairstows' house was not so far fetched after all, but maybe it was not Kenny Bairstow, still safely confined, seeking her out she needed to worry about but someone seeking Kenny.

Distracted, she found it difficult to concentrate on her paperwork, and Kate arrived home with Sonja before she had finished.

'How was school?' Jay asked, but neither girl seemed eager to talk, and when they had settled down in front of the television she tried to turn her mind back to her work. It was not until much later in the evening when she went into the kitchen to make herself a drink before bed that she noticed the marks on the window. She switched on the light in the backyard and illuminated from that side of the glass it was clear that someone had pressed their face against the glass and left a distinct impression of mouth and nose and the smeared print of what might have been a hand. Jay drew a sharp breath and peered out at her back gate on which the bolt seemed as tightly closed as when she had last checked it. She knew that it would take someone pretty athletic to climb into the yard and for a second panic clutched at her stomach as she absorbed the implications of that. She scanned the yard again but unless someone was hiding in the small stone outhouse that had once housed the family privy, she could see nothing untoward. Could she really call the police to look at a smear on a window pane, she wondered, anticipating the scorn with which such a request might be greeted. David, she thought, with more desperation than she had felt for the last six months, where are you when I need you?

6

'Wait,' Archie said. 'Keep calm. We'll find them.' How many times had Archie said that over the years, Donna wondered, easing her tights up her thighs. And he'd usually been right. Don't go in with fists flying, as she'd been prone to do as a child, wait, think, plan instead, and the revenge is all the sweeter. Wasn't he right that time at that horrible freezing cold farm up on the moors when they had tried to get her adopted?

She pulled on her trousers and zipped them up, passing a hand over the taut muscles of her stomach. She had learned a lot of things since she had left Pendle Bridge so suddenly twenty years ago, things she barely believed she could ever have learned, but one of the easiest had been how to keep fit. In the hospital that time, she'd spent so many hours in the gym that they'd rationed her in the end, alarmed, she thought, by the way her body was building muscle to replace the skinny cadaverous form with which she had come in off the streets.

She sat down again on the edge of the bed, suddenly transported back to another damp and chilly room with a window that rattled and buckled in the Pennine gales where they had made her sleep alone, with only Archie for company when he bothered to show up. She remembered her blind rage when she was told that she was to be fostered.

No warning, she thought, no asking would she like it, or what did she think about it? Nothing. The fat social worker just told her to get packed up, she'd got a new mum and dad for her, and off they went in her car one day to this farmhouse up on the moors, miles from anywhere. She'd really like it, she had promised, but when Donna asked what happened if she didn't, she had no answer.

Donna was murmuring to herself now as the memories flooded back. Like Wuthering Heights, it was, though she didn't know that then because she hadn't read the book, a sort of farm, scruffy fields on the edge of a brook and then hundreds of sheep out on the fells beyond. It was midwinter and the wind cut down those hills like a knife most of the time. It howled, just like in the films. She had never known wind could really howl. Not just howl, but wail like a child sometimes, and scream like a banshee. She was never warm in that house, actually really warm, like you get sitting on a radiator or in front of a fire. Even in bed she usually wore a sweater. She bit her lip as remembered emotion almost overwhelmed her.

In other ways, she thought, it had been too warm. Mrs. Clough turned out to be a big, smothering sort of person, always touching. The memory made her shudder suddenly. She had never liked touching much when she was a kid, even from her own mother, and certainly not from this new woman who was always pressing her to call her mum. She had never called her anything at all, Donna thought with satisfaction. She was used to giving her own kids cuddles and all that stuff, even though they were lads and older than Donna.

She could see they hated it too. She couldn't be doing with all that. She remembered keeping out of her way as much as she could. Mrs. effing Cuddly Clough. She had hated her and began to torment her: tip extra salt into the boiling pans, kick away the clothes prop in the yard so the billowing sheets fell in the mud.

She pulled out a white shirt from her suitcase and slipped it on, buttoning it up critically in front of the small, dirt-flecked mirror over the chest of drawers, then pulling on her single smart jacket and deciding that she would probably do. She glanced at her watch and realised, as she usually did, that she was far too early for her appointment, and sat down on the bed again, her mind flicking back to the farm on the moors where the only con-solation she'd found had been with the farmer himself. Mrs. Clough, she thought, had always been pestering her to help in the house, with the washing up or the ironing because she was a girl, wasn't she, she said, and that's what girls did. And if she went to her room to read the two Clough lads came and teased her, wanting her to play football with them, but she had hated that too. She had always ended up flat on her face in the mud or with huge bruises on her shins.

But then she remembered that, probably in desperation, Mrs. Cuddly had eventually given her some wellington boots and let her run off and follow Mr. Clough about when he was out in the yard, so she could watch him load up the feed for the ewes and check them in the fields close to the farm. They were pregnant most of them, and he'd been so gentle with them, not rough like he was in the house. They used to remind her of her mother and the twins and the new baby they'd been going to have when everything had fallen apart, and she remembered how angry those memories had made her, almost as angry as that last day when she'd swung the heavy lamp at her father's head and missed and her mother had taken it off her and done the job herself.

She had quite liked the sheep in some ways. They didn't talk or get too close and seemed contented enough in a woolly sort of way. Once or twice when she had been really miserable she had gone and cuddled up to them where they were lying against the stone walls to keep out of the wind. They were a bit smelly but warm and she had felt safe there and sometimes Archie would come. In the end though, Mr. Clough came out and found her and shouted about her being a daft lummox and gave her a clout round the ear and she had decided then that she wasn't stopping there much longer. And she'd gritted her teeth and thought that he wasn't her dad, though if he carried on like that she might wish him dead too.

She had hated that village school as well, she thought. Of course it had only been tiny, a couple of dozen kids, and they all knew each other, and didn't exactly welcome strangers. In fact they hated them. She remembered how they had interrogated her, how they had wanted to know why she was living with Mrs. Clough and where she'd come from really and was she foreign because she talked funny. And how she hadn't wanted to tell them any of that and how she thought they talked funny with their broad country vowels that had made her snigger, so she just stayed in the classroom and read all the books there were to read to keep out of the way of the rest of them.

It had taken her no time at all to decide that she wanted to go back to Mags and Pendle House. She knew very well that kids got sent back there from families that couldn't cope with them. She remembered them returning sometimes, clutching their suitcases, all uptight and defiant, trying not to cry, so she knew she didn't have to stay at the Cloughs if she couldn't stand it. At least people at Pendle left her and Mags alone. Mrs. Clough just laughed and told her she didn't know how lucky she was when she said that, so she decided she had to try another way.

She glanced at her watch again. There was still time to spare. It would not take long to walk down to the town centre for her interview. She took off her jacket again and swung her legs up onto the bed. Relax, she thought, you need to be relaxed to do yourself justice. She shut her eyes and the image of the fat social worker loomed in front of her. She had spent her eleventh birthday at the farmhouse and the social worker had come round, all smiles, with a postal order for her official birthday present. Mrs. Clough pocketed that, as far as she could remember. No doubt she thought it would pay for the cake she'd made with eleven candles that they had made her blow out. And there were soggy sandwiches and jelly, she recalled, and the boys thought it was all a great joke and burst balloons behind her back to make her jump. They were called Steve and Joe, and they were always laughing at her. After tea, she had been desperate enough to follow the fat social worker back to the car and ask if she could go back to Pendle House, but she had just smiled and told her that she was far better off where she was. 'He hits me, Mr. Clough,' she had said and the social worker had looked a bit more bothered then and asked if she'd been a naughty girl and she had said no, so she went back into the house and she could hear her talking to old man Clough, but when she came out she just smiled again and got into the car and drove away.

She had decided to try harder then, talk to Archie about it and be a bit cleverer maybe. Next time the social worker came she made sure she had a nasty burn on her arm from the big old stove thing Mrs. Clough was always shovelling coal into in the kitchen. Donna shuddered even now as she recalled holding her arm against the stove until she nearly screamed. She had never showed the burn to Mrs. Clough, but she showed it to the fat social worker as soon as she arrived. It had gone all blistered and yellow by then, and she told her one of the lads had pushed her against the stove. She hadn't actually said it was deliberate but she had hoped that was what she would think. The fat social worker had looked a bit shocked this time and her lips went all tight and she and Mrs. Clough went into the sitting room for a talk with the door shut and she had sat on the kitchen table swinging her legs and hoping that she'd take her back to Pendle House in her car right then. She didn't of course. But Mrs. C had taken her down the doctor's in the village the next day and the nurse put a dressing on her arm.

Archie had kept telling her to run away but it was a cold winter that year. There was snow on the ground for months after Christmas and Mr. Clough had to dig the sheep out of the drifts once or twice and she had seen the stiff bodies of the dead ones and she knew she might end up the same way if she ran off in that weather. So she had stayed and tried to work out with Archie something that was bad enough to get her sent back to Pendle House, no messing. She knew now that smacking and getting burnt on the stove thing wasn't bad enough and anyway she had rather gone off the idea of hurting herself again. The burn took a long time to heal and left a red mark for months afterwards. But then she remembered a girl called Sally at Pendle who said that she was there because of stroking. And they had all laughed at that because most of them were there because of getting thumped or having parents who'd left or something really serious like what happened with her own mum and dad. But Sally said stroking could be really serious too, especially if it was a man or a big boy who stroked you and especially if it was in certain places. And they wanted you to stroke them back.

So that's how in the end she got back to Pendle House. The next time the fat social worker turned up she told her Steve had been stroking her where he shouldn't. And asking her to stroke him. The social worker went very white and quiet then and shut herself in the sitting room with Mr. and Mrs. Clough and when they came out Mrs. Cuddly wasn't very cuddly any more. She was very red and had been crying and Mr. Clough marched out of the house into the fields to see to the sheep without saying anything at all. The fat social worker took her upstairs then and helped her pack all her stuff and put her straight in the car while she talked to Mrs. Clough again. The boys were out that day somewhere so she never saw Steve again. A couple of days later a policewoman had turned up at Pendle House to see her, and asked her all over again what had happened, but some of the questions she couldn't answer. She had known what a willy was but she had no idea what erect meant so she had never imagined that her story had made much sense or that Steve's denials would not be believed in the end. It had served its purpose though, and that's all she had cared about then. Welcome home, Mags had said. Job done, Archie had said. Clever, clever girl.

Donna swung her legs off the bed and put her jacket back on, checked her bag and folded her coat carefully over her arm. At least she knew now what had happened to Kenny, though his mother had been vague about where he was being held but quite sure that he would be coming home soon. She had come out of Nab End consumed by a blind fury that she had walked off on her way back into town. How could they have thought Kenny had done it, she muttered to herself again. But never mind, she thought. If she achieved what she was planning, the truth would come out and Kenny, gentle, kind Kenny would be free. That would be a bonus she had not known she could expect and one well worth the sacrifice of giving up her London job and coming back north again for the first time in all these years. And with a bit of luck, now she knew the score, she could make sure Kenny's house was ready and waiting when he needed it. That, at least, was something she was sure she could fix.

'Come on, Mags,' she whispered. 'We're getting closer. And Kenny needs us.'

Jay Morton was surprised the next morning to discover Bernard Grogan MP deep in conversation with Chris Hateley's father George when she arrived in the small committee room at the town hall which had been set aside for the appointment interviews for her staff. She had applied her make-up particularly carefully that morning, aware that she had slept badly, waking a couple of times to strain her ears for threatening noises which did not come. She guessed that dark circles under her eyes might not inspire confidence in the trustees of the new museum whom she expected to form the interview panel. She had been told that Grogan would be at Westminster and was slightly surprised to find that he considered the morning's business in Pendle Bridge more important.

'Good morning,' she said brightly, aware that the two men's eyes were raking her black trouser suit, her red silk blouse and high heeled boots and, in Grogan's case, hovering a moment or two too long on her breasts. 'Do we know if everyone on the shortlist is turning up?' A third figure she had not noticed at first turned his attention from the sets of documents he was sorting into individual piles on the polished table and nodded a response.

'We've got four coming for the secretarial post

and a couple for the porter's job. Both of them are already working for the council so it would be a case of seconding them to Pendle House for the duration.' The man was small and precise and jerked his head like an alert and slightly disapproving bird. His tone made it sound as though the duration might be brief.

Jay turned to the two older men and gave them a smile which she hoped did not appear as uncertain as it felt.

'Are you planning to sit in on the interviews, Mr. Grogan?' she asked.

'No, I just popped in to make sure everything was going smoothly,' Grogan said. 'I'm sure George here can cope, can't you, George?'

Hateley scowled at this but nodded.

'I dare say we'll manage, won't we, Jay?'

'I did just wonder, my dear, looking at your shortlists, how far you were hoping to get hold of people who know summat about museum work?' Grogan went on, ignoring any tension he had ignited. 'There's no experience of that kind here that I can see.'

'It's not really necessary,' Jay said. 'Later on, when I've completed the initial cataloguing and we move on to actually establishing the museum I'm sure I'll need some professional assistance, as we discussed at my interview. But in the initial stages I need someone to help me move the stuff about and an assistant to deal with the paperwork and help with the cataloguing. There's nothing particularly expert in what they'll have to do.'

'Well, if you're happy...' Grogan said. 'Are you settling in all right? I hear you bought the Bairstows' house in Adelaide Street. That brought back a few memories, eh George? Not haunted by that evil little toe-rag, is it?'

Jay shook her head, wondering how Bernard Grogan had uncovered that piece of information. She had had no contact with the man since her interview and appointment four months ago when she had still been living in London.

'It's fine,' she said. 'I don't believe in ghosts.'

'Aye, well, it's some time since Grace Bairstow moved out,' George Hateley said. 'She's gone a bit doolally, as I heard it.'

'She's in the old people's home up at Nab End,' Jay said. 'I took her some stuff of her son's that I'd found in the loft, but she didn't seem to know what was really going on with Kenny or even where he was. She's very confused, though she remembered clearly enough how Kenny used to play with the two girls from Pendle House. And she's still convinced he didn't do it.'

'Batty as a fruitcake,' Grogan said dismissively. 'She used to write to me every other week after he was first sent down, asking for appeals and inquiries and God knows what else.'

'I suppose she would,' Jay said. 'It must be very hard to accept that your son has done something as awful as that.'

'Aye, well, there wasn't much doubt in that case,' Grogan said. 'For myself, I'd hang 'em all, though my party doesn't agree. Right, George?'

'Right, Bernard. Open and shut, that case,' George Hateley added for good measure.

Jay turned away, not wanting to get into a debate on that score, and glanced at the papers on the table. She was disappointed to see that the application from the prospective assistant she had most favoured – a woman of about her own age with a solid record of administrative jobs before she had taken time out to have children – was no longer there.

'What happened to Judy Spencer?' she asked the clerk, who was still fussing over the seating arrangements.

'Withdrew,' he said crisply. 'Got offered something else, as far as I can remember.'

'You've got some solid enough candidates there, Mrs. Morton,' Grogan said. 'Right, George?'

'Oh, aye,' Hateley said. 'Pretty solid, I'd say, Bernie.' Jay wondered if his entire function in life was to agree wholeheartedly with whatever Grogan said.

The clerk turned to George Hateley and the two colleagues, a wispy lady trustee who Jay recalled as an entirely silent presence at her own interview, and a young manager from the council's human resources department, who had now joined him.

'Are you ready to start, Mr. Hateley?'

Hateley nodded and ushered his colleagues to the three seats behind the broad oak table, leaving Jay to take the seat at the end. She shrugged slightly and half-smiled, recognising her place in the scheme of things. Bernard Grogan, she realised, had left while she had been riffling through the applicants' details, without any acknowledgement to anyone. The appointment of a porter and odd-job-man was quickly settled when the caretaker she had met at Pendle House, Fred Marston, turned up as one of the candidates and George

Hateley suggested that he combine his occasional caretaking duties with general factotum for the new museum, based there full-time. Jay did not demur. It seemed a sensible enough arrangement.

But when they had interviewed the four women candidates for the post of her assistant she quickly became uncomfortable as the interviewers' discussion began. It was clear that the candidate she preferred, a slight, fair-haired woman called Margaret Davies, smartly dressed in a black trouser suit, with a rather intense manner but a solid record of admin jobs in London, had not endeared herself to George Hateley. He seemed to lean to Pam Bentley, a more stolid woman of much the same age but more cheerfully clad in blue, a widow who had also just returned to Pendle Bridge after spending some time in the south. Neither of the other candidates seemed to have enough experience to cope with a job which, as Jay kept emphasising in her questioning, would require a fair amount of flexibility.

'What I really need is someone who can show some initiative,' she said. 'This isn't going to be a normal secretarial job. To some extent we're going to have to make it up as we go along. When I get to grips with the collections I'm going to have to create a filing system which works.'

'I'm sure Mrs. Bentley can cope,' Hateley said. 'Your Ms. Davies looked a bit of a flibbertygibbet to me. One of those nervous types, all enthusiasm for a bit and then fading before they've been round the course for the first time. She'd give us a couple of months and then be off somewhere else, I shouldn't wonder.'

'She seemed quite sure this was where she wanted to settle,' Jay objected. 'And she's a solid record of previous jobs.'

'Not married, though. Probably got some boyfriend local – she'll be off if it comes to nowt.'

Jay bit her lip, outraged at this sort of speculation but wary of antagonising Hateley too much. He was such a traditionalist, she thought, that he could as well have taken against Margaret Davies's trouser suit as anything else. But the whole future of the project, she knew, depended on the support of the trustees and the council and she was only too aware that there were more than a few doubters amongst those local worthies. She had to admit that there was not much to choose between the two candidates in terms of qualifications. George was looking at her without much warmth.

'If we can't agree we'll have to take a vote on it, but it would be better if we were unanimous,' he said.

'All right,' Jay agreed reluctantly. 'I dare say I can cope with Pam Bentley if you all feel so strongly about it. She seems pleasant enough, and well qualified.'

'That's settled then,' Hateley said, snapping his folder of papers shut. 'I'll take care of the letters going out, and ask Mrs. Bentley to report to you at Pendle House a week on Monday, Jay. That suit you?'

Jay nodded, and remained seated while the three other members of the panel filed out. She had been stitched up, she thought, and wondered why she had expected anything different. As she collected her papers together the clerk who had been there earlier came back into the room.

'I hear you gave the job to Pam Bentley,' he said as he began to tidy up the table. 'Your choice, was she?'

Jay pulled a wry face.

'She'll be fine, I expect,' she said. 'But I would have preferred the other woman, the one who'd been working in London. Do you know Mrs. Bentley? She seems to have been away for years...'

The clerk pursed his lips and shrugged.

'Not personally,' he said. 'But she was local, wasn't she, originally. I'd be surprised if someone didn't know her.'

'So that's what it was all about, then, was it? I thought as much. What is she? Bernie Grogan's second cousin?'

The clerk gave a thin smile.

'I couldn't possibly comment, Mrs. Morton. I'm just surprised you're surprised, when you're related to George Hateley yourself. You should know how these things work.'

'But...' Jay began and then stopped. It had never crossed her mind that she might have got her job because of her connections in Pendle Bridge, but she could see that might be an assumption some people would make. Surely George wouldn't have pulled strings on her behalf, she thought angrily. And then an even more appalling thought struck her. Perhaps it was not George who had got her the job but, more indirectly, his son, who certainly might have reasons of his own to make sure she came back home. Oh shit, she thought. Her new start was turning out to be more convoluted than she had ever imagined.

7

The door to the attic stairs at Pendle House opened with less protest than Jay had expected, although the narrow wooden staircase behind it was covered in a thick layer of dust which did not look as if it had been disturbed for years. She glanced upwards into the dim light at the top of the stairwell and wondered if her snap Monday morning decision to make a start on examining the treasures which allegedly lay in the rooms above was a wise one.

After two weeks in the town, the Adelaide Street cottage was tidy and moderately homely and she and Kate had slipped into a routine of sorts. She was always home when Kate, usually accompanied by the Kosovan girl Sonya, came home from school. She was aware that neither of the girls was particularly happy and had promised herself a discussion with their teacher before she started work properly. But at least at the cottage they seemed relaxed enough with their milk and biscuits and television programmes and Sonya's English was obviously improving under Kate's serious application to her idea of teaching her ten new words a day. Occasionally they disappeared to Kate's bedroom to use her computer. But on the dot of half past five every afternoon, Sonya reappeared and declared that she had to go home, slipping quietly out of the house without a backward glance.

There had been no further indications that anyone was trying to gain access to the house, although once or twice Jay had again picked up the telephone only to be greeted by the hiss of white noise. It was just one of those things that happened, she tried to convince herself without total success. But by and large she had begun to sleep more easily in her bed.

Her third Monday in Pendle Bridge had dawned bright, with a sharp frost, and she had felt sufficiently relaxed after Kate had gone to school for her thoughts to turn to work. She rang the council offices and arranged to meet Fred Marston at Pendle House with the keys. When she got there she found the area at the back busy with contractors vans and several people bustling about cleaning the offices and delivering some of the furniture and equipment she and her new assistant would need. Encouraged, she waited impatiently on the front steps of the main building for Fred to turn up in his council van. He arrived in a surly mood and wasted no time in explaining his displeasure.

'They're going to take my van away when I'm based up here full-time,' he grumbled. 'Say I won't need it. Can you do owt about it? There's bound to be times when I need to go down to t'town offices or fetch and carry stuff for you. Stands to reason.'

'I'll have a word with the trustees,' she had said, although without great confidence that the discussions would be very fruitful. 'There's a computer technician round the back looking to

105

set up for us. Can you make sure the place is properly secure tonight? We don't want expensive stuff disappearing as soon as it's arrived.'

'There's no alarms at the back there,' Marston said, his expression sour. 'Can't guarantee the tearaways won't be back, can I? Not overnight.'

'I'll talk to the trustees about alarms as well,' she promised. But privately she told herself that when she got deep into cataloguing, she would make sure to take backup copies of everything home with her at night. She couldn't protect Pendle House totally from thieves and vandals but she could at least protect her data.

Marston had led her up the broad shallow staircase in the main part of the house, past tall stained glass windows on the half landing, across the broad main landing, where all the doors were closed and the light was dim, and then through a door into a small subsidiary stairwell where the back stairs descended to the kitchen area below and a locked door cut off the stairs leading upwards. He handed Jay a mortise key with a nod.

'No one's been up there for years,' he said. 'There's seven or eight small rooms, servants bedrooms they'll have been once, I expect. Any road, they packed all t'stuff into tea chests and put it up there for safe-keeping, though if you ask me most of them will have rotted away by now. Do you want me to come up with you? I'd best get out t'back and see what them beggars are doing in t'offices with their computers and wiring and stuff. I've told them which room I want for my workshop but you can't trust any bugger to get owt right these days.'

106

'No, I'm only going to open a few of the chests and have a quick look for now,' Jay said. 'If I need anything carried down later I'll give you a shout.'

Marston had marched away and left her at the foot of the attic stairs. Slightly to her surprise she found that the light-switch inside the door worked and the faint illumination of a single bulb on the landing above saw her safely to the top. Ahead of her a narrow corridor stretched the length of the house with four closed doors on each side. The floor of bare wooden boards was covered with the same thick dust as the staircase although it was just possible to see traces of footprints beneath the top layer. Someone had been up here at some time since the Wright collections were stacked away, she thought, and she hoped it had not been Fred Marston's ubiquitous tearaways or children who had lived in the main part of the house below. Either could have proved terminally destructive if they had gained access to fragile artefacts.

She knew from the sketchy catalogues that the last of the Wright family had bequeathed to the council that the family had accumulated several separate collections, one of Celtic and Roman remains culled from the local area, where a Roman road heading to York skirted the valley, and from the moors around it which were pitted with treacherous bell pits where the Romans had mined for minerals. The Celtic tribes had not given in to the invaders readily in parts of York-shire and the treasures included weapons and fragments of armour from battles long forgotten. There was also a collection of ethnographic items, mainly from the Far East and, although not described in any detail, a collection of masks which had excited her interest, although where they came from she had no idea.

She worked her way down the corridor systematically, feeling excited now she had got so close to the objects which had attracted her to this job when she first saw it advertised. Each door opened onto a small room with small gothic windows tucked under the eaves and grimed with years of dirt. Most of the electric lights worked, but the bulbs were low-powered – someone's means of economising in years gone by, she assumed – and the tea chests were firmly tacked shut and apparently unscathed by their long incarceration. She would, she decided reluctantly, need tools to get into any of them, which meant trudging downstairs again and seeking Fred Marston's help. But at the far end of the corridor, in the last room on the left, she drew a sharp breath when her eyes grew accustomed to the gloom and she saw what was inside. Two of the stacked chests had been opened and some of the contents were strewn on the floor. To her horror the object of the interference appeared to be the masks which interested her most. Carefully, she picked up two African pieces carved out of dark wood, wiped off the dust with a tissue and examined them for damage. They appeared to be untouched, as were a chalk white Japanese Noh mask and a red intricately carved monster which she knew came from somewhere else in the Far East although she could not immediately say where. But the ones which interested her most were two brightly coloured masks of intricate design, one a bold representation of a bird, the raven which played an important part in native American ritual, the other a barely human and totally malign face with a skull attached to its forehead, probably an executioner. She knew instantly where these masks came from and knew they were rare if they were as old as they looked. There were many modern versions produced as works of art or as cheap souvenirs for tourists, but these, she felt instinctively and from experience, were original and possibly quite old. She gazed at the blank eye-sockets for a moment and shivered slightly.

She had always been fascinated by masks, these most unnerving accoutrements of ancient rituals, some of them bloody in the extreme, and she realised that in this collection she had objects worthy of display in any museum. She carefully placed the masks which had been removed from the chests back amongst the crumpled news-papers in which they had been packed. If children had unwrapped them, she thought, as seemed most likely, they had probably scared themselves silly in the process. That would explain why they had been flung to the floor to gather dust before the children fled. It was cold up here under the roof and a sudden draught made her glance over her shoulder with a feeling she was not alone. Her initial excitement had drained away now and she felt inexplicably depressed amongst all this silent dust and decay. Somewhere below the old house creaked and made her jump.

'Come on,' she said to herself sharply. 'You'll be

seeing ghosts next.' But she knew that it wasn't the supernatural which had turned her mood so suddenly, more a sense of waste as she crouched at the top of a house full of abandoned treasures and, she suspected, the forgotten hopes and desperate fears of abandoned children. Pendle House, she decided, was a melancholy place and it might be difficult to fill it with life again.

As she packed the last mask away and tried to fit the lid of the tea chest back on, she was startled to hear a voice calling her name. Turning off the light and closing the door carefully behind her she went to the top of the stairs.

'Mrs. Morton?' the voice called from below.

'I'm coming down,' Jay responded.

At the foot of the stairs she was met by a heavy, grey haired woman wrapped in a brown winter coat and scarf, anxious eyes in a pale face watching her without a hint of a smile as she negotiated the last of the narrow steps.

'You've made a start up there then,' the women commented in response to the query in Jay's eyes. 'I'm Mary Petherbridge. I used to work here when this was a children's home. I'm retired now, but I heard they were opening the old place up again and I was passing so I popped in...' Mary Petherbridge's voice trailed off into an awkward silence.

'There's not much to see,' Jay said cheerfully. 'As you can see, the house has been pretty well cleared out except for the stuff up there in the attics.'

'All right, is it? All that stuff?'

'Shouldn't it be?' Jay asked carefully, wondering what was worrying this tense woman, whose fingers were twisting themselves into an agitated knot of anxiety around the end of her scarf.

'I was worried about it,' she said. 'I knew some of those little devils went up there to the attics sometimes. I could never catch them and I could never see that they'd done any damage, but I was never sure. God knows what mischief they got up to.'

'Well, it's good of you to tell me, but I can't see anything amiss so far. Most of the stuff seems to be well packed up, as it must have been since it was put up there,' Jay said. She hesitated. As far as she could see no harm had come to the masks that had been disturbed and she decided not to mention them. 'I won't really be able to tell until I've started unpacking everything properly. You were lucky to find me here today. I don't officially start work until next week but curiosity got the better of me.'

'I found Fred Marston round the back,' Mary Petherbridge said. 'He told me where you were.'

'Well, it's nice to meet you, Mrs Petherbridge,' Jay said edging her way across the broad landing towards the main staircase in the hope that the other woman would follow.

'Miss,' the woman said sharply.

'Sorry,' Jay said. 'This place must have been quite a responsibility when it was full of kids. The house seems to have survived that period pretty well, considering.'

'We had the girls in this part, the lads out in the annexe. Not that the lasses are much less trouble but at least they don't kick footballs around their rooms and smash the windows every other day.'

'You know the place really well, then?' Jay asked, her curiosity fully aroused now.

'I ran the place, as you call it, for ten years,' Mary Petherbridge said sharply. 'I was the head of Pendle House.'

'I'm sorry, I didn't realise,' Jay said, glancing at the closed, pasty face of her companion. Her time at Pendle House obviously did not bring back happy memories.

The two of them walked slowly side-by-side down the wide shallow staircase and into the echoing main hall, with its black and white tiled floor and elaborate cornices.

'Were you here when the girl was murdered?' Jay asked quietly. 'Was she one of yours? Quite inadvertently I seem to have bought the house in Adelaide Street where her murderer lived.' Mary Petherbridge's lips tightened even more at that and she did not answer for a moment. Jay glanced at her curiously and was startled to see that the pale, lined face had acquired two fierce spots of colour on the thin cheeks.

'Mags,' she said, in a fierce whisper, apparently consumed by an inner fury that took Jay aback. 'Margaret Emmet. You've heard about her, then. A little whore she was. And the other one, the one who ran off, Donna Latham. I can't say I was surprised at what happened.' She wrenched open the glass panelled door leading into the vestibule but hesitated for a moment with a hand on the heavy handle of the main doors. 'They made my life a misery, those two. They killed my cat, you know? Crept down in the night and drowned it in the water butt at the back. They thought I didn't know. But I did, though I could never prove it was them. It sounds a terrible thing to say, but I was glad to see the back of them, both of them. I wouldn't wish anyone dead, but I was glad when they'd both gone.'

'You thought they were both involved with Kenny Bairstow then?'

'Kenny Bairstow, Laurie Wishaw, who knows who else? I told you, they were little tarts, the pair of them. Never went to school, nicked stuff here, and down in the town I dare say, ran wild. I couldn't do a thing with them, if you want to know the truth. I know they used to go up into those attics, though I never managed to catch them at it. Laurie was too cunning for that.'

'Laurie?' Jay asked. 'One of the boys living here?'

'One of my staff,' Mary Petherbridge said bitterly. 'There's always one bad apple, isn't there? Well, Laurie was ours. I *knew* he was fiddling with the girls, but I could never catch him at it. I got rid of him in the end, but I could never prove anything. But I just *knew*. I caught the girls up in the attics one day and they told me that Laurie had said it was all right. I guessed that's where he was taking them. There were sweet packets in one of the rooms, and crisps on the floor. Encouraging mice.'

Jay shuddered, thinking of the scattered masks. Perhaps it was the murdered girl and her friend who had unpacked them and quite possibly terrified themselves when faced with the horrific images.

113

'But you never caught him?'

'I didn't always sleep here. We had a rota for night duty so four days out of seven I was able to get home in the evenings and come back on duty the next morning. Once or twice I came back in later on when Laurie was on night duty but I never found anything amiss. I began to wonder if I was imagining it.'

'You didn't think of calling in the police?' Jay asked, horrified.

'None of the kids had complained. I mentioned it informally, no names, to the chair of the governors and he said I needed evidence. We couldn't do anything without evidence. Trouble was, I knew Mags and Donna were evil manipulative little cows. You get a nose for these things when you work with children as long as I did. You could never believe a word they said, basically.'

'So was this Laurie a suspect when Mags was killed? You told the police what you suspected.'

'I told the police to talk to him for the reasons I said, but I don't know whether they ever did. It was an open and shut case with the other lad in the end, wasn't it? Kenny Bairstow confessed and it was all over very quickly. And Kenny had been seeing the two girls, running around all over the place with the pair of them, it turned out. There was plenty of evidence for that and nothing to implicate Pendle House in what had been going on. They said I should have known what Mags and Donna had been up to, but you send them off to school in the morning and assume they're going, don't you? The school never let me know they were bunking off. Glad to be shut of them,

114

I dare say, if they were as much trouble there as they were here. The only time I knew they'd been bunking off with Kenny Bairstow was one time Margaret cut her head open and had to go to hospital for stitches. I told them to stay away from him after that but I don't suppose they did. As for Laurie, I'd nothing concrete to go on, just suspicions, and I didn't want the place closed down around my ears, did I? It would be my job on the line as well as Laurie Wishaw, if anything unpleasant had come out and I hadn't taken any action about it, or passed on my suspicions officially, like. I just bided my time and got rid of Laurie when I found him nicking the petty cash.'

'Is Laurie still in Pendle Bridge?' Jay asked, wondering why she was being expected to feel sympathy for this woman who had so obviously failed in her duty to the children in her care.

'Oh no, Laurie Wishaw's dead,' Mary Pether-bridge said, not bothering to hide her satisfaction. 'He fell under a tube train in London a couple of years ago. Fell, or was pushed, or jumped maybe, for all I know. There was a bit in the local rag because his family still live up here somewhere. I was so pleased I cut it out and kept it for a while, though I was sorry no one would be coming to get him in one of these investigations the police do now about what went on in children's homes. I'd like to have seen him in gaol for what he got up to. In those days no one would have believed the kids, especially those two little madams. They'd have thought they were making it up. And in their case they might have been right.'

'You think he'd have carried on? In other
115

homes, I mean?' Jay asked, horrified.

'They always do, don't they, men like that? They get a taste for it.'

Jay bit her lip to control her outrage at what the woman was telling her. It was all so long ago, she thought, the man dead and the victims scattered. But this woman had suspected the truth and done nothing except protect her own back until tragedy overtook the two girls. She felt sick at the thought. She opened the door and took a deep breath of fresh air.

'Did you ever hear any more of the other girl? The one who vanished? Do you think she was murdered too?' she asked, driven by some need to know the worst.

'I always thought the two of them would have been together that night,' Mary Petherbridge said. 'They were always together. My guess was always that when Donna saw she couldn't help Mags she ran. She'll have fallen into that black hole runaways fall into – life on the street, prostitution, drugs, prison, Aids. She's most likely dead long ago, Donna Latham. It happens all the time. You can count the successes on one hand when you look after kids in care. It almost always ends in tears.' The woman shrugged and her eyes were cold and her face drawn, as if she had looked into too many dark places and had too many hopes dashed. 'You can't let yourself get close to them,' she said, as if in mitigation. 'You'd go mad if you did.'

'I have to go, Mrs. Petherbridge,' Jay said quickly.

'It's been nice meeting you,' the older woman

116

said. Jay did not return the compliment. She almost ran to her car and sat for a moment clutching the steering wheel like a lifebelt before driving back towards home and stopping outside Kate's school. Her daughter was in the playground deep in conversation with Sonya, apparently perfectly content. The girls did not see her and when the whistle went for the end of playtime she watched the two of them drift back indoors hand in hand. 'Keep her safe' Jay whispered to a God she did not believe in as she drove the short distance home. But she knew that was a task which was hers alone and it was beginning to terrify her.

Donna got home that evening feeling well satisfied with her day. She had another job interview coming up, and her evening jog around the streets had brought an unexpected bonus. Heading home by way of Adelaide Street, where she regularly kept an eye on what she still called Kenny's house, she had seen something which surprised her. The door had been ajar as she approached, but the figure she saw coming out had not been the woman she now knew lived there. It was her next-door-neighbour who cautiously peered outside before stepping onto the pavement, closing the door carefully behind himself and stepping back through his own front door.

Donna had hesitated. 'The cunning old beggar,' she said to Archie. 'He's got a key.' Slowly she resumed the regular rhythm of her run, while she digested this surprising piece of information and wondered how she could turn it to her advantage. 'I think we'll pay that old boy a visit,' she said eventually. 'He might be a useful friend, he might.'

'Clever girl, Donna,' Archie had muttered, as breathless as she was by the time they arrived back at the B&B. 'Clever girl,' he said again as she prepared herself a mug of cocoa and got ready for bed.

Donna had come to regard falling asleep as merely opening a door into another world. There had been times when they had knocked her out with strong sleeping pills but these had dulled her perceptions so much the next morning that she soon learned to flush them down the lavatory and take her chances in the lottery of dreams and nightmares which her unconscious produced. Occasionally her overnight adventures were benign, usually when she found herself cuddled up under the duvet with Mags, reliving the happy times she had spent with her friend, running wild around the town and the woods and moors. But since she had come back to Yorkshire it was the horrors of life at Pendle House which came back to torment her.

The dream she feared most, which woke her screaming and sweating in the middle of the night and left her drained and exhausted the next morning, was the one where the detail was more vivid in the dark than she had ever been able to recall when she had been pushed into trying to remember it in cold daylight by those insistent hospital voices. You must come to terms with what happened, they used to say, but she had always resisted them, pushing the memories deeper and deeper into the recesses of her mind, circling around them like her fingers had once circled around a suppurating sore on the arm she had slit with a razor blade that had eventually had her scooped up off the street feverish and semi-conscious to be dropped into yet another hospital ward. She had only just been coherent enough that time to remember that she was not Donna any more: Donna was dead and buried with her past, left behind in Pendle with Mags, poor Mags, the one who did what they wanted, the one who complied, the one who was so unspeakably betrayed.

That worst of dreams had come back more insistently since she had come back to Pendle Bridge, as if her return had in some way thrust her physically back all those years to the time she had been brought to Pendle House, helpless and speechless with shock. The bed at the B&B was comfortable enough, the duvet thick enough to keep out even the chilliest Pennine night air, but she found no rest and woke dark eyed and shivering to dress and attend to her toilet and plod on through her job hunting and occasional interviews like a zombie. It was no wonder, she thought, in her more lucid moments, that she had so far not found employment in spite of her hard-won qualifications and experience. Her parents, long dead, trampled through her sleep, the old quarrels raw and raucous as cat fights, her role alternately trying to pacify one or protect the other, and towards the end, care for the twin babies which neither parent seemed capable of tending.

I was only eight, *eight* years old, she shouted out loud, as she woke for the third morning in a row exhausted by the endless rerun of the old conflict. The odd thing was that in the morning light she could still remember happier times, when the twins were born and they lived in a proper house with a bit of garden at the back where she used to play with Archie. She remembered building little mud houses out of the soil, with roads paved with tiny stones she had collected, pebbledash she thought they called it, and a mud school and a park with real daisies in the flower beds, all neat, with toy cars and a zebra crossing on the main road for the kids to get to school or go to the shops. She remembered that so clearly, that little world they had created, she and Archie. But that was for daylight: she never dreamed of that at all.

And of course her father had hated their games, kicking the buildings over with his cowboy boots, telling her to keep herself clean, wash her face, get the dirt out of her finger-nails or he'd leather her. Even at that age she knew that what he wanted was a pretty girl, a docile child, a Barbie doll he could cuddle and pet when he was in the mood and who most certainly never answered back. She was not that and could never be that and he was always threatening to leather her. But he didn't often do it. It was her mum he leathered. And she often dreamed of that.

The memory she feared most, though, played itself out in the damp-sodden flat they had fled to suddenly and without any explanation that Donna could ever recall. The twins were crawling

120

then, getting under everyone's feet. And her father was drinking all the time. Even at that age she'd learned to recognise the smell of him when he came in from the pub, sweet and sharp at the same time, and the way he lurched about, the way her mother put the twins to bed and shut the door on them so that he couldn't hear them crying. But she couldn't put me to bed, of course, Donna thought bitterly. She was too old to be hidden away by then like she used to be hidden when she was younger and her father went on the rampage.

Though when she could she hid herself, shut her bedroom door tight and blocked her ears to the yelling and shouting, talking to Archie, who always turned up in times of trouble, or reading a book. She wasn't allowed to watch the telly when her mother warned her that Daddy was in a mood, so she read an awful lot of books. Telly was too noisy, it would only provoke him, her mother said. Like the twins crying provoked him. And worst of all her mother provoked him. She didn't have to say anything even. She seemed to provoke him just by being there, by being the mother of these three children he couldn't look after or support, just by standing there with her pale, sad eyes. He'd hit her then and throw her across the room and try to strangle her with those long strings of beads she always wore and tear lumps of her hair out. She took to wearing long hippy skirts and she wouldn't go out at all if the bruises were too bad.

Donna remembered being kept home from school to go to the shops for her mother on the bad days, in case anyone saw where he'd hurt her. She knew that her mother had tried her best to make it up to the children. She knew that she loved them all to bits and tried to protect them. But in the end she had hated all this effort to keep her safe almost as much as she hated her father. Sometimes she had felt as if she was suffocating in that flat. She wanted to get out and run till she couldn't run any more.

But the dream that had her sitting bolt upright in bed, her heart thumping so hard she thought it would burst, was worse than all that, far worse. It thrust her back, panic stricken and filled with dread, to the day she had failed to kill her father. That day that had been so hot and stifling in the overcrowded flat that she had thought the smell of cooking and dirty nappies would choke her. She had never known the date but she knew it must have been during the school holidays because she didn't remember going to school that day. She remembered sitting on her bed wearing just her knickers and reading, with her head right up against the window which would only tilt out a few inches so you had to get yourself really close to it to get any air at all. She was reading a bit and looking out a bit at the lads playing football in the concrete play area down below when she saw him coming home, swaying across the car park with a carrier bag in one hand. That would have been his supplies for the next couple of hours, until he fell asleep on the settee. One of the lads must have said something because he took a run at them and they scattered, laughing as he lost his balance and stumbled and almost fell.

She had stayed in her room then, listening to him as he came in, just at the moment one of the twins started crying, and then that started the other one off. It was usually Emmy who started first. She was smaller and more miserable than Samantha. 'That'll get him going,' Archie had whispered. 'Shut up,' she had said. 'Tell me a story.' So he did. But it didn't work. What with the twins howling and her father shouting she had put her hands over her ears and it still didn't keep the noise out and she heard the old woman from upstairs hammering on the floor to get them to shut up as well.

Then her mother had screamed so loudly that the hairs on the back of her neck stood up and she felt sick. She had slid off the bed and opened the bedroom door a crack and could see her father standing over her. She was on the floor curled up with her hands over her head and he was kicking her again and again. 'You'll kill it, you'll kill it,' she said and Donna knew then what she hadn't taken in before: that her mother's spreading waist meant that she was pregnant again.

Everything happened in a blur then. She ran into the room and tried to pull her father off, but he had pushed her away and she fell across the settee and onto the little table in the corner of the room where there was a lamp, a sort of statue thing made of metal, quite heavy. She had picked it up without really thinking and swung it in an arc at her father and of course it missed his head and caught him just below the shoulder, because she wasn't tall enough to do what she really wanted to do which was smash his skull in. He pushed her away again, like swatting an irritating insect and she dropped the lamp and swore at him, using words she didn't know she knew and her parents certainly didn't know she knew.

Before she could get her balance again and return to the attack her mother had struggled to her feet somehow and grabbed the lamp herself and swung it at him, connecting with his forehead with a sort of soft thump. He fell down then. There was no blood but Donna knew he was dead although her mother made a big fuss about making him comfortable and getting an ambulance, but all Donna could hear as she stood stock still in the middle of the room, unable to speak, hardly able to breath, was Emmy and then Samantha starting up again and more banging on the floor from upstairs.

That was the end of her family, Donna thought bitterly. The ambulance came, and the police and some fat woman who said she was a social worker and smelled of mints took her away, kicking and screaming, and she never saw her mother or the twins again. They said they had taken her mother to a hospital but there never seemed to have been another baby, so she guessed there had been a miscarriage. They never told her much more than that, although months later, when she'd already been in the children's home for what seemed like ages, they did tell her the twins were going to be adopted and she cried herself to sleep that night.

She'd never cried before that. Archie thought it was better not to let anyone see you cry because it just made them angry. He still said to her sometimes, 'Donna should have killed him. It would have been better if Donna had killed him. Your mum could have looked after the twins then.' And she said, 'I know, Archie. You're right. It's my fault. It's all my fault.' 'Donna's fault,' he said. 'It's Donna's fault. Donna's fault. Wicked, wicked Donna.'

That was what the other voice said too, the little voice which came later, which was still saying the same thing even after all these years. And it was right, of course. It should have been like it so often was in the dream, the dream which was so much more bloody than the reality had been. It should have been her hitting her father on the head, again and again and again, with blood spattering everywhere, so her mother and the twins could have lived happily ever after. She had failed, she thought, but she would not fail again.

8

'You must find it very pokey after the house in London,' Sue said waspishly as she followed her sister into the kitchen and watched her make coffee. It was Friday afternoon, Jay's last free weekday before she started work at Pendle House, and Sue had come round that morning ostensibly to take her shopping at the out-of-town mall which had opened recently just outside Bradfield a half hour's drive away but, Jay thought, more likely to poke around her new home and find fault.

'It's a bit on the cosy side,' Jay conceded as she pushed bags containing her modest purchases out of the way and spooned coffee into the cafetiere. 'But we can always move to something more spacious if the job works out and the money runs to it. I didn't want to mortgage myself up to the neck right at the start. We'll see how it goes.' She was irritated by her sister's almost prurient interest in her affairs but reluctant to provoke a row. She had enough on her plate at the moment with all the unknowns of a new job to face and the continuing feeling that all was not well with the new house for reasons far removed from its modest size. There had been no more nocturnal visitors as far as she knew but the silent phone calls continued, to the extent that she jumped and went cold with anxiety now every time it rang.

'Surely David's making a decent contribution for Kate?' Sue persisted.

'Not as decent as he might have made a few years ago,' Jay said, a shade wearily. 'The property boom in London's over now and architects have been hard hit. He was doing a lot of work for City types with more money than they knew what to do with, lavish extensions to Hampstead mansions, swimming pool complexes, billiard rooms, saunas and gyms, you've no idea how the rich live these days. But now a lot of them have lost their million quid bonuses if not their actual jobs and they're cutting back hard.'

'Poor old David,' Sue said unsympathetically.

Jay poured the hot water into the cafetiere and bit her tongue. It was impossible to explain to Sue that she did not want David's money any more, that she actually preferred to be independent after such a gross betrayal and to cut herself off completely from her husband's new relationship and its no doubt substantial financial demands. Many women in her situation, she knew, wanted revenge and the easiest way to gain that was to screw their errant husband and his new family for every penny they could get. But that seemed to her to be demeaning. She had always worked and earned a reasonable salary. She would accept a contribution to Kate's upbringing. But she would not engage in a bitter war with David so long as she and her daughter could live in modest comfort and pay their way. She did not expect her sister to understand. From being a small child Sue had always wanted things and lots of them. She smiled, recalling her sister's obsessive collecting of dolls of all shapes and sizes when they were small and her fury when Jay, in a rage during some quarrel she could barely remember, had tipped half a dozen of the mannikin family out of the bedroom window into the pouring rain, ruining their pink dresses and fluorescent blonde hair. Now, as far as she could see, it was shoes that Sue collected with an almost religious fervour.

Sue, it seemed, was not ready to give up her nagging yet.

'You'll change your tune when you find Pendle School isn't good enough and want to pay fees for Kate,' she said, her children's education obviously as much an obsession as Jay had been used to amongst her friends in Muswell Hill. The fact that children's success or failure depended more on their parents than on their schooling seemed to have passed her sister by, Jay thought. She hoped Kate might prove the point at Pendle School by doing as well there as she had done herself.

'We'll see,' she said, pressing down the plunger on the cafetiere with more force than it required. 'I'm surprised you can manage fees for two of them with only one salary coming in.' She saw no reason why her sister should get away with all this niggling unscathed. Sue flushed.

'The other grandparents have been very generous,' she said.

'Ah,' Jay said, and left it at that. She knew that Chris Hateley's father was, for all his socialist rhetoric, not short of a bob or two, as they said in these parts. He had had a successful career running a small engineering firm which he had inherited from his own father and eventually sold to a larger company a few years before. She had guessed that he had done well out of the deal, but did not realise that Chris and Sue had benefited so directly from his new-found affluence.

'So, does Kate want to come and sleep over tonight?' Sue asked, evidently wanting a quick change of subject now. Jay glanced at her watch.

'Yes, she's looking forward to it,' she said. 'She'll be back soon. I told her not to bring her friend home with her tonight, so you'd be here to take her off as soon as she's packed her overnight things. I could do with an evening on my own to sort out a few things here.'

'She's making friends then, is she?' Sue asked.

'Yes, of course she is,' Jay snapped and then felt foolishly defensive. 'But it's nice for her to have her cousins on hand as well. She and Ben seem to get on well.'

Sue shrugged and took the cup of coffee which Jay handed her, glancing round her sister's unreconstructed kitchen again with critical eyes. Jay knew she was recalling the London house which she had once so obviously envied.

'You need to strip this room out and start again,' she said flatly. A sharp reply was on the tip of Jay's tongue when the door-bell rang and she hurried to let Kate in. Her daughter looked flushed, as if she had been running, and went straight to the fridge to get herself a glass of milk without acknowledging her aunt's presence.

'Why are you so hot?' Jay asked.

'I ran all the way home,' Kate said. 'They said in school we had to go straight home because yesterday someone in a car stopped two of the Year Two girls and offered them a lift. I've got a letter about it in my bag.'

Jay's heart lurched as she tried to take on board every mother's nightmare.

'Kate,' she said, her voice hoarse as she was unable to conceal her horror.

'It's all right, Mum, you know I'd never get in a car with anyone I didn't know.' She fished in her schoolbag and handed Jay a crumpled piece of paper. 'Nothing happened,' she said dismissively. 'We all know we mustn't get in cars.' She seemed blissfully unaware that some murdered children, and even young women, had not been given much choice.

'You mustn't go near cars,' Jay said fiercely. 'If anyone opens a door and speaks to you, just run.'

'OK, OK,' Kate said. She opened the back door. 'I'm just going outside to look at my frogspawn,' she said loftily, slamming the door behind her.

Sue sipped her coffee before glancing at Jay with pursed lips.

'She can be a little madam, can't she? I've not seen her in that mood before. Why don't you just take her to school and collect her if you're worried? I don't let mine go on their own. I take them to the door and pick them up again.'

'You'll be driving miles a day when Ben starts at secondary school,' Jay said. 'It's crazy. St. Peter's is only two minutes down the road. She has to learn to be independent some time, especially when I start work. One of the benefits of living here is to escape the tyranny of the

130

school run. I've been there, done that, and don't want to do it any more.'

Sue opened her mouth to respond but was interrupted by a piercing scream from outside. The two women moved to the back door as one and flung it open to find Kate standing in the middle of the small paved yard with her mouth still wide open and a look of horror in her eyes. She screamed again and again and a next door window was flung up and Jay was aware of Mr. Booth peering out.

'What is it, what is it?' Jay said seizing her daughter in a fierce hug and feeling her trembling beneath her school sweatshirt. Kate seemed unable to speak but she pointed to where two plastic buckets stood side by side next to the stone outhouse, one of which contained her frog-spawn and another, which had been left there empty but had collected a pint or so of rain water during the recent downpours. It was the second bucket Kate was pointing at with a shaking hand and as she moved closer she could see what had horrified her. Floating stiff and lifeless in the rainwater were three identical grey, pink-legged, long-tailed mice.

'Ugh,' Sue said. 'How on earth did they get there?'

Jay glanced at the wooden gate which separated the yard from the alley at the back of the terrace to confirm that the bolts were as tightly closed as she had left them that morning before she went out shopping with Sue. The mice, she knew, had not been there then, but the gate was still securely locked.

'It's the three blind mice,' Kate said, hysteria catching her throat again as she clung to her mother's waist. 'Someone's coming to cut off their tails.'

'No, no,' Jay said, unable to soothe the still shuddering, sobbing child. 'They must have fallen in somehow. It was an accident, pet. It's a big dangerous world for little mice. It must have been an accident.' But somehow she did not believe it.

Later that evening, after Kate, still pale and shaken, had allowed herself to be taken off by her aunt to spend the night with her cousins, and after Jay had carefully tipped three small corpses out of the bucket and into a plastic bag for disposal, she went round the cottage checking the locks on all the doors and windows. Silent phone calls, and even intruders from the back alley she could cope with, but this outrage, evidently aimed at Kate rather than her, was insupportable. She did not expect the police to take her very seriously if she complained about three drowned mice in her back yard, but she was beginning to feel seriously threatened. She would go to the police station tomorrow before Sue brought Kate home at lunchtime and lodge a complaint.

After supper she tried to settle down to sort out a collection of books she planned to take with her to her new office on Monday, in particular books she had not consulted recently on masks of all kinds. She was quite convinced that if all went as planned the collection of masks she had seen at

Pendle House would provide a dazzling focal point for the museum she was intending to set up. But she found it hard to concentrate. She could understand Kate's hysterical reaction to the disconcerting find in the yard, as the image of three tiny bodies with blank lifeless eyes and delicate pink feet floating in crystal clear water kept drifting between her and the pages she was trying to read. Could a cat have dropped them in the bucket, she wondered. Or could they really have fallen in, and if so how had they climbed up the steep and shiny sides of the bucket to the lip from which they must have toppled over? The more she thought about it the more she was convinced that there had been human involvement in the drowning and that it was intended to have the effect on her and Kate which it had in fact caused. She shivered slightly and went to check the doors for the third time since supper. She was, she concluded, being stalked and the effect was profoundly unsettling.

When the phone rang she jumped, heart racing, and stood beside the apparatus to let it click into answer-phone mode, picking it up only when she recognised Chris Hateley's voice. She heard him with more relief than she wanted to acknowledge to herself.

'I thought for a minute you weren't there,' Chris said. 'D'you fancy a drink? There's someone I'd like you to meet. Someone who can tell you more than you really want to know about Kenny Bairstow and the murder you're getting so agitated about.'

'Who's that then?' Jay asked, distinctly

unwilling to stir from home, especially at the behest of her brother-in-law.

'One of the cops who was involved in the investigation,' Chris said. 'Les Green, the DCI who led the investigation, is long dead, but Peter Shipley was a DC here then. He's a DCI himself now. He'll put you right about Bairstow if anyone can.'

'Does he want to talk to me?' Jay asked doubtfully, although she could see the advantage of a quiet chat with a policeman for far more urgent reasons than a twenty year old murder.

'I was going to meet him for a drink tonight anyway,' Chris said. 'He won't mind if you join us. He's an old mate of mine.'

Thirty minutes later Jay, feeling somewhat flustered by a rapid change into well-fitting trousers and a soft cashmere sweater in her favourite blue, augmented by some urgently needed restoration work on her face to hide the dark circles which she seemed to have developed under her eyes over the last week or so, was standing in the doorway of the Drover's Rest, a popular pub on the hilly road out of town. She spotted Chris and his companion before they saw her and made her way through the crowded Friday night tables to join them.

When Chris had gone to the bar to get her a drink she slipped off her coat and sat back to take stock of Peter Shipley as he sized her up with similar and scarcely veiled curiosity. He was a stocky man, liable, she thought, to run to fat if he wasn't careful, dark hair receding slightly, a crumpled face, with what she guessed might be a permanent appearance of tiredness, a mouth that looked as if it seldom broke into a smile and blue eyes that were chilly and appraising.

'I'd no idea Chris had a sister-in-law like you,' he said at length, after taking a draught of his pint. Jay offered only a tentative smile, not sure whether a compliment was intended. Shipley's voice had not lost the local accent and she had been very aware since she had come back home that hers had disappeared, making her an obvious offcomer.

'I've been away from Pendle Bridge for a long time,' she said.

'And how do you find it now you're back?' Shipley asked. 'Changed, I expect?'

'Slightly threatening,' Jay said flatly. 'No one bothered to tell me I was buying a house where a child murderer had lived. I have to confess I find that a bit unnerving.'

'Ah, Kenny Bairstow,' Shipley said. 'Chris said you were interested in him. I see why now, if you're living in his house.'

'They tell me he's coming out of gaol soon,' Jay said. 'It's not unreasonable to be a bit worried about that, is it?'

At that moment Chris came back and put a gin and tonic in front of her.

'I think Jay's getting a bit paranoid about Kenny Bairstow,' he said to Shipley, picking up on the conversation immediately. 'I thought maybe you could reassure her that he's not likely to come round threatening her when they let him out.'

'Someone's already coming round making

themselves a nuisance,' Jay said sharply, disliking Chris's patronising tone. 'I think I may have a stalker.'

'Well, that's not Kenny Bairstow,' Shipley said, looking slightly more interested now. 'He's safely tucked up in an open prison in Suffolk somewhere. They may be letting him out on town visits but he'll be closely supervised and he won't get this far. Anyway, he was always pathetic rather than dangerous, I thought. He let something get out of hand and hadn't got the self control to stop it, that was my opinion of Bairstow at the time. A bit of pressure and he was in floods of tears before we'd hardly started interviewing him.'

'You're sure he did it, are you?' Jay said. 'His mother doesn't think so and I met a woman called Mary Petherbridge who used to run Pendle House when it happened and she reckoned those two girls were fooling around with one of the staff. I reckon she thinks he was the killer. Laurie Wishart? Was that the name?'

'Laurence Wishaw,' Shipley said curtly. 'Aye, I remember him. And Mary Petherbridge going on about him. Obsessed, she was. But there wasn't a shred of evidence linking him to the murder. Funny woman, Mary Petherbridge. You'd think if we'd got a confession from someone outside the children's home she'd have been happy enough with that. At least it let her off the hook a bit when it came to allocating blame, but I remember her going on and on at my boss about this Laurie character. Les interviewed him in the end, I think, just to be on the safe side, but there was nowt in it. Any road, quite apart from the

136

confession, the other lad had the means, the motive and the opportunity – he'd been going round with those two lasses for years and maybe he'd been having sex with them all along or maybe it was just that night the urge got too much for him. Whatever. He killed one of them and frightened the other one so badly no one ever saw her again. Ran like a frightened rabbit, did Donna Latham. Perhaps he raped her too. We're not likely to ever find out now, are we? Kenny Bairstow isn't going to tell us owt at this stage, I don't suppose. He's said nowt while he's been in prison, I understand. Denied it to the end, and has had his parole delayed as a consequence. He could have been out years ago.'

'Miss Petherbridge was very odd about the girls,' Jay said. 'It was almost as if she blamed them for what happened. She obviously didn't like them, said they were evil. And Kenny was backward, wasn't he?'

'What are you suggesting?' Shipley protested, evidently angry now. 'That two thirteen-year-old girls led a hulking great lump like Kenny Bairstow astray? That they were asking for it? Come on, that's not very politically correct. Even twenty years ago Bairstow's defence wouldn't have got away with that.' Slightly to Jay's surprise, Shipley looked genuinely shocked.

'But there was no DNA testing then, was there?' Jay asked, knowing she was pushing her luck. 'You couldn't prove who raped her?' Shipley's face hardened.

'You think we got the wrong man, don't you?' he asked. 'After all this bloody time, you think we

137

got the wrong man. You've only been back in Pendle ten minutes and you're telling me that?'

'Come on, Jay,' Chris, who had been listening to the conversation with a worried expression, broke in. 'I told you. I went through all this years ago when Bairstow appealed against his sentence. The defence couldn't offer anything significant in court. The jury only took two hours to convict. He'd confessed, remember, and the judge allowed it to stand. And I know Peter here, and I knew his boss at the time, well enough to know they wouldn't have bullied him into it, though the defence suggested that.'

'His solicitor still thinks they did,' Jay said provocatively and was not very surprised when Peter Shipley flushed deep red.

'Bollocks,' he said. 'Straight as a die, was Les Green. Taught me everything I know.'

'It's not me you need to convince,' Jay said. 'I really just took an interest because of the house and the risk to Kate if he comes back when they let him out. But I soon found out that it's not just his mother who thinks he didn't do it. And I'm bound to wonder if there's a connection between what happened then and the odd things that have been happening since I moved in. The previous owners moved out very quickly, so perhaps they found the house uncomfortable too. Perhaps they were harassed. Or perhaps I'm putting two and two together and making half a dozen?'

'Dead right you are,' Peter Shipley said flatly.

'Well, I'm sorry,' Jay said. 'It would have been nice if someone had told me a bit about this house I bought *before* I bought it, then I maybe

138

wouldn't have signed the contract and I wouldn't be having all this hassle. Kate was absolutely terrified this afternoon by what she found in the back yard. Really nasty, it was.'

Shipley nodded and shrugged, his face closed, and Jay could see that he was impervious to further argument about what he obviously considered ancient history.

'Well, I'm sorry too,' he said. 'Kenny Bairstow's case was a long time ago so maybe we'd better leave it at that. You'd better tell me about this stalker of yours. That sounds like a much more immediate problem than Kenny's likely to be. I'll let you know when he comes out, any road, so's you know when he's free. But he's a lifer. He'll be supervised, so you don't need to worry about him.'

'Thanks,' Jay said. 'So let me tell you about Kate's three drowned mice, which I must say I found very weird indeed. And the rest.'

Peter Shipley listened politely enough to her catalogue of complaints but Jay could see that he was not impressed by her interpretation of them.

'You've not actually had any overt threats to you or your daughter then?'

'No one ever speaks on the phone,' she said. 'There's not even heavy breathing. Just silence or hissing white noise.'

'Well, I think you should ask BT to monitor your calls for a while,' Shipley said. 'It could just be a technical fault. Most phone pests say something. As for the rest, if they're climbing over the back wall, it's probably just kids having a laugh. Why don't you get a dog? That would

139

give you a bit of added protection.'

'I can't leave a dog in the house all day once I start work,' Jay said.

'A decent alarm system then,' Shipley said dismissively. 'If you do get anything really threatening, either on the phone or by letter, come into the station and have a word with our community protection people, but I don't think they'd regard three dead mice as really threatening. A bit scary for your daughter to find, I grant you, but I guess they just fell into the bucket and couldn't get out again.'

'You're probably right,' Jay said unenthusiastically. Kate's screams still echoed in her head. She finished her drink and glanced at Chris.

'I've got some work to finish at home,' she said.

'I'll follow you home in my car and have a look round the back for you, just in case,' Chris offered and Jay did not demur. She had hoped that talking to a policeman would be reassuring but Peter Shipley had been much too dismissive for that.

Back in Adelaide Street she squeezed into her usual parking slot and Chris manoeuvred his bigger car into another space further down the narrow street. She waited for him in the open doorway and they stood for a moment surveying the long terraces where many of the windows were already in darkness soon after ten and the rest had thick curtains firmly drawn against the outside world.

'It's very quiet round here at night,' Chris said.

'A lot of elderly people around,' Jay said.

'Well, I think Peter's right. You should get an

alarm system put in if you're nervous. Sensible thing to do anyway. Pendle Bridge has its share of young tearaways, you know. Come on. I'll check all your windows for you if you're going to be here alone tonight.'

While Chris set about his impromptu security check, Jay put the kettle on in the kitchen and tidied up. She was standing at the sink when she sensed rather than heard Chris come up behind her and to her surprise felt his arms slide around her waist. She pulled herself away sharply and took herself to the other side of the kitchen table, feeling foolishly flustered.

'Sorry,' Chris said. 'Seeing you there took me back, you know? It's astonishing how little you've changed. You've not put on weight...'

'Like Sue, you mean?' Jay said sharply. 'Come on Chris, don't let's mess about. I'm not about to shaft my sister by playing games with you, you know. Pendle Bridge is a career move for me, not an opportunity to break up your family.'

Chris shrugged slightly.

'It wouldn't take much breaking up, sweetie,' he said. 'Sue and I are not – how shall I put it – close any more. I think that's why Abbie's being such a little cow at the moment. She probably knows something's wrong.'

'I'm sorry,' Jay said, surprised at Chris's frankness yet somehow not quite surprised about what he was telling her. She had sensed the tension at the Hateley's house. She poured two mugs of coffee and they sat on opposite sides of the table sipping them and saying little. She might not have changed much in twenty years but Chris looked older, fine lines of discontent rather than laughter around the eyes and mouth and fair hair which was fading into translucence rather than greying. The mouth which she had once kissed so passionately had taken on a petulant twist, she thought. What had she seen in him? She no longer knew, but when he caught her eye again she flushed slightly. His eyes, pale and enigmatic, had always fascinated her and maybe they still did. But he made no further move until he announced that he must be going. She followed him to the door but before she could open it for him he had turned quickly, taken hold of her and kissed her on the lips. For several seconds she resisted, trying to push him away but as his tongue insinuated itself into her mouth she felt her resolve slacken and she responded in kind. In the end it was Chris who pushed her away and opened the door, with an expression of satisfaction in his eyes.

'I knew you still fancied me,' he whispered.

'No,' Jay said. 'I don't ... I won't...'

'We'll see,' Chris said and slipped out of the house without looking back. Jay closed the door and leant her head against the woodwork and groaned. This mustn't happen, she thought, but she knew from that single kiss that somewhere deep inside her, where no moral compass seemed to guide her, she wanted it to happen. 'Oh hell and damnation,' she said.

Alone in her narrow B&B bed, just like so many of the institutional beds she had slept in over the years, Donna curled herself into an even tighter ball under the duvet as the man in the mask approached. She could hear that he was laughing although the face was white and featureless, a perfect oval with a down-turned mouth of bright red and eye sockets that were like pits of darkness, giving no glimpse of the real eyes inside although she knew that the man could see her very well, just as he always could.

'Donna,' he said. 'Sweet little Donna. Come to Uncle. You know you've been a naughty girl again, don't you? You know you must be punished, don't you? You know how much we enjoy that, don't you?'

Donna screamed, her mouth wide and gaping until she stuffed the foul smelling duvet into it, as she had done all those years ago to stop herself crying out. And suddenly the mask was whirling, spinning on its axis, with other grotesque shapes beside it, the bright bird was there, and the evil black skull, and more and more of the terrifying images she had become so familiar with as she felt herself falling into a deep pit with the masks, detached now from their owners, twisting down into the darkness with her.

'It was all your fault,' she heard that small insidious voice whisper, the one which had kept itself to itself for a long time but was beginning to speak again. 'It was all your fault.' Donna screamed again although she knew that no one could hear her. No one had ever heard her. No one had ever come to help. Laurie had tempted them at first with promises of midnight feasts but once he had done what he wanted with them he did not bother again with the bars of chocolate and the packets of crisps. He told them to come and they came because if they didn't, he said, he would tell and they would be in terrible trouble with Mrs. P., they would be sent away and locked up, they would be torn away from each other and never see each other again. They were wicked girls, dirty girls, and the men who came, the men in the masks, were just doing what all men did. They could not be blamed. Only Donna and Mags could be blamed and would suffer for it all, now and for ever, if he decided to tell Mrs. P.

Wicked girl, wicked girl, the voice had said, shouting at her from outside windows and inside cupboards, interrupting the television programmes and making her tremble with terror. Long after she had left Pendle Bridge the voice had followed her as she drifted from squat to hostel, from city doorway to cardboard boxes in the park. Wicked girl, Donna, it was all your fault, it had insisted until one day a policeman, who had generally looked away from the huddled drifters with whom she slept, had found her raving and delivered her to hospital, drugged, emaciated and semi-conscious, an infected arm threatening her life. Or that was what they had told her later. She did not know whether it was true or just another of the lies people told.

'Archie?' Donna mumbled, waking suddenly and sitting up, shaking violently and spitting feathers from the duvet out of her mouth. 'Are you there, Archie?' But Archie was not there. And nor, that night, was Mags when she needed her. She was in her little rented room in Pendle Bridge, she remembered, as the nightmare receded, still alone, still jobless, no closer to finding Kenny or pinning down her quarry. After scouring telephone directories and the local paper, she had not succeeded in discovering where he lived, and he seldom seemed to visit his office which was well-protected by a taciturn assistant. He must, she thought, spend some of his time away from Pendle Bridge for his work. If only she had known then what he did she might have had more chance of catching him unawares elsewhere than she seemed to have here. But she had had no idea then and no idea when she had come back to Pendle, just that fleeting image of a face which he had turned in her direction as his mask had slipped. The irony was not lost on her, but if she had bumped into him in the street, as she had bumped into Laurie that time, it would not have been enough with him. She wanted the rest of them and needed him to lead her in the right direction. The birdman was not enough on his own. She wanted every single mask torn off, every single one of them made to suffer. Her ambition was limitless, her patience endless. She had waited a long time and she wanted them all, every one of the devils who had devoured her childhood and destroyed Mags. She was prepared to wait, to be patient, to seek out the murderer and all his friends. Wicked girls would burn in hell, Laurie used to say. Wicked girls would be sent away by themselves and never be allowed to meet again. She smiled faintly, hoping that Laurie himself was now sizzling fiercely on the devil's spit. It wouldn't be long now before the rest of them joined him. She would see to that.

145

9

DCI Peter Shipley's breath was whipped away by a bitter north-easterly as he stepped out of his car and put his foot through the thin ice in the rutted track.

'Damn and blast,' he muttered, feeling the water penetrate his sock. He stood for a moment looking at the row of cottages to which he had been called as soon as he had arrived at his warmly welcoming and fuggy office this winter morning. The cottages huddled in the lee of a spur of moorland a couple of miles from the town centre: a terrace of small, stone-tiled houses facing the escarpment across the rutted lane and backing onto a strip of scruffy fields where a few sheep and ponies huddled together for warmth. A spring, which had once no doubt provided the only water supply for the inhabitants, trickled down icicle encrusted rocks into a stone basin and then overflowed onto the track. Above the cluster of police cars, the sparkling heavily frosted heather swept away to the open moors. With his breath forming clouds around his head, Shipley approached the young uniformed constable who was standing guard at the gateway to No.6 Holbeck Lane, and nodded.

'By 'eck, it's bloody brass monkeys out here,' he said. 'What've we got then, lad?'

'A right mess, by t'look of it,' the constable said.

'Brought your breakfast up, have you?' Shipley asked solicitously, glancing round the narrow front garden for signs of the PC's weakness.

'No, sir,' the younger man said, flushing slightly. 'Not a pretty sight, though.'

'Who's in there?' Shipley asked, glancing at the other cars blocking the narrow lane.

'My sergeant, SOCOs and the police surgeon so far, sir.'

'Right, I'd best have a quick look then and ruin my day,' Shipley said without enthusiasm.

He tapped on the half open cottage door and was met by an officer in plastic suit and boots who handed a similar outfit to the DCI.

'Not much space in here, I'm afraid.' Shipley nodded and struggled into the protective suit. Until the SOCOs had finished their meticulous examination of a crime scene he was here on sufferance.

'I'll not be long,' he said.

The place smelled of death, all the more strongly perhaps because the cottage, as far as Shipley could see it at first, spoke only of a houseproud owner: the flagged hall floor had been polished, the rugs were bright and clean and the sitting room to the left where the door was half open was chintzy and comfortable, with every surface adorned with pottery and brass-ware. This was a woman's house, Shipley thought as he made his way down the narrow hallway to the room at the back where he could see his overalled colleagues had congregated. It was, as he expected, the kitchen and as he put his head round the door the smell of blood and worse

147

intensified and he flinched slightly at what he saw and took a deep breath. One of the figures pushed past the others who were examining a huddled shape on the floor between the kitchen table and the sink.

'Do we know who it is?' Shipley asked the local sergeant.

'No formal ID,' the sergeant said. 'We can't bring anyone in here to look at her in this state. But if it's the owner of the house then it's a Mary Petherbridge. Retired teacher, the next-door-neighbour says. Postman called at seven thirty and found the front door open. Poor bugger was a gibbering wreck when I got here. I sent him home for now. Told him we'd talk to him later.'

Shipley's face gave nothing away but he registered the name with a sense of shock which gripped his stomach for a second. He hoped it was only a coincidence that after almost twenty years of putting Mary Petherbridge and her inglorious career at Pendle House out of his mind he had found himself reminded of her in the pub down the road just a few days ago. He nodded at the sergeant and inched his way further into the crowded kitchen where even through the huddle of professionals he could see the bloody evidence of what must have been a fierce final struggle for life. The smell was much stronger here, the metallic smell of spilled blood and the sweeter smell of incipient decay. The police surgeon got to his feet and nodded at Shipley as he gazed down at the body of an elderly woman in a quilted pink dressing gown. Her throat had been cut so that the head hung at an unnatural angle but before that she must have struggled mightily with her assailant, sustaining cuts to her hands and arms which had almost severed the fingers of her right hand. There was blood everywhere, dried to a rusty brown now but splashed unmistakably all over the floor, the worktops and even the walls. And beneath the gaping edges of the dressing gown Shipley could see more wounds which had stained large areas of the fleecy material and had gone deep enough to expose the bone beneath the breast.

'Jesus, he made a mess of her,' he said, his mouth dry.

'Been lying here some time,' the doctor said. 'Days, I'd say. Maybe a week. The PM should give an indication.'

Shipley glanced around and located the sergeant again. He nodded for him to follow and led him into the sitting room where the only sign of the tragedy was a thin film of dust which, now he looked closely, he could see had begun to settle on the polished wood surfaces of half a dozen occasional tables and a fine mahogany sideboard, and the pottery and knick-knacks Mary Petherbridge had so lovingly displayed there.

'Any sign of forced entry?' he asked.

'Not that I've seen, sir,' the sergeant said. 'Postman said the front door was ajar but it hadn't been forced that I could see. There's no real sign of a burglary. The cottage is neat and tidy apart from the kitchen. Her handbag's in the bedroom with fifty pounds in the purse...'

'Not robbery then,' Shipley said almost to himself. The sergeant was young and bright and eager to make an impression.

'The kettle was full,' he said. 'And a cup ready with instant coffee in it. Looks like she was making herself a drink, either just got up or just on her way to bed. Most of the lights were on but that could have been either way if she was an early riser. It doesn't get light at the moment till about seven thirty.'

'But how long could she have been lying there with the front door open? Surely not long?'

'Postman said he hadn't been up here for a week,' the sergeant said. 'The neighbours might not have noticed. There's an elderly woman next door, probably doesn't get out much in the cold weather. The door might have moved a bit in the wind.' Shipley went back out into the hall and pulled the door to and fro a few times. To close it completely took a sharp push to click the Yale lock into place.

'You might be right,' he said. 'It could have been open for days. We'll have to see what forensic evidence turns up. In the meantime I'm going back to the office. Tell the SOCO team to let me know when they've finished, will you? In the meantime I'll set a major incident inquiry in train. I had some contact with Mary Petherbridge years ago in connection with another murder inquiry. It's bloody ironic she should end up like this.'

'A connection, maybe?' the bright sergeant offered.

'I doubt it, after twenty years.' Shipley dismissed the suggestion sharply. But he wondered whether it could be mere coincidence that he had been reminded so recently of the dead woman's existence by that attractive sister-in-law of Chris Hateley's. He pulled the cottage door closed behind him and lit a cigarette in cupped hands, lost in thought. He drew the smoke deep into his lungs. The opportunity to talk to Jay Morton again, on the grounds that she had talked to Mary Petherbridge recently, was not unwelcome. In fact he positively looked forward to it.

Pam Bentley's sharp intake of breath surprised Jay when she unwrapped the first of the masks she had brought down from the Pendle House attics.

'They are a bit scary, some of these,' she said mildly, disguising the excitement she felt as she took her first close look in full daylight at the treasures she had chosen to examine first, surprised that Pam should have reacted so sharply. The massive bird head, decorated in bold patterns of blue and black and red and white, gazed at them with malevolent eyes through a fringe of coarse ginger hair.

'It's enough to give you nightmares,' Pam said. 'I've always had a horror of birds. The idea of getting them tangled in your hair gives me the creeps. What on earth sort of bird is it anyway?'

'Could be a raven or an eagle, or something mythical, a thunder-bird, or a cannibal bird. I'll have to do my homework on these. I've only ever seen pictures of them before.'

'Good God,' Pam said with obvious distaste. 'It's horrendous. Where does it come from?'

'It's native North American. Lord knows how the Wrights got hold of these but there are

151

dozens of them up there, apparently originals not tourist replicas or modern art, as far as I can judge. I'll have to get an expert to look at them. They were used in rituals and ceremonies mainly by tribes on the North East coast of the US and Canada.' She carefully unwrapped another head from its protective paper and flinched slightly herself: a human head this time, with long black hair but green-faced, with distorted red lips, black brows and six or seven sharp spines protruding from the lips and around the nose, a seriously threatening vision.

'I remember reading about this fellow,' she said. 'He almost drowns but survives as a madman to live on sea creatures and these are the spines of sea urchins...'

'Is that human hair?' Pam asked, reaching out a tentative finger to touch the dark mane.

'Could well be,' Jay said cheerfully. 'They used human and horse hair, and sometimes straw. And here's another bird, look. More like an eagle, I think.' She ran an appreciative finger along the smooth carved wood of a curving beak, minimally decorated and elegant, each feather of the head distinct. 'Beautiful,' she said.

Pam shuddered slightly.

'I wouldn't go that far.'

'Well, pretty unusual anyway,' Jay said. 'They'll give the museum some distinction at least.'

'If you say so,' Pam conceded. 'I reckon they'll need an 18 certificate if you don't want kids scared half to death.'

Jay glanced at her companion curiously.

'Do you have children?' she asked, not able to

remember from the CV she had read before Pam Bentley's appointment.

'No, we never got round to it before my husband died,' she said, her face closed, not inviting further questions.

'Well, kids have their down-side,' Jay said, thinking of the mutinous daughter she had dropped off at school that morning. 'But at least it means you won't be clock watching in the afternoons like me. You don't mind staying till four thirty, do you?'

'No problem,' Pam Bentley said. She glanced round the office, still cluttered and barely habitable, making Jay think that she had been premature to rush into Pendle House and retrieve some of her potential exhibits almost as soon as she had taken off her coat. She wrapped the masks up again and stowed them in the cardboard box she had used to carry them over from the house to the offices in the stable block.

'Never mind these now,' she said. 'Let's get this place organised, shall we?'

Jay had not been as excited as she had expected she would be when she finally arrived at Pendle House for her first day in charge of the embryonic museum. She had spent a difficult weekend with Kate who still seemed tense and sulky after her encounter with the dead mice. It had ended with a shouting match about bedtime the night before and a guilt-induced promise from Jay the next morning that she would be sure to be home before Kate finished school. Flexible hours had been one of the perks she had insisted on when she had been interviewed for the job, on the grounds that much of the work could be done at home, and the trustees' agreement had been one of the factors which had persuaded her to accept the job. But she was beginning to realise that Kate's reaction to the recent months of upheaval in her life was not going to be as sunny as it had seemed to her at first. Jay was not sure Kate liked her new home or her new school and she had come back from her sleep-over with her cousins on Saturday morning pale and taciturn, so she guessed that potential lifeline had not proved as soothing as she had hoped. Dead mice, she thought, were the last thing Kate needed just now.

Jay had found her new assistant Pam Bentley walking up and down in front of Pendle House looking slightly agitated when she pulled up outside the front door.

'Good morning,' she said, more brightly than she felt.

'It's still all locked up around the back,' Pam said, with a note of accusation in her voice.

'Sorry,' Jay said. 'Fred Marston's not here yet, then?'

'Not that I can see.'

'Don't worry, I've got a set of keys,' Jay said. The other woman did not reply and Jay wondered whether she was always so uncommunicative or whether this was a bad case of Monday morning syndrome. Whatever the reason, Pam was certainly not making much effort to impress in a new job, she thought.

'How did you get up here?' she asked.

'Bus.'

'And that's OK, is it? Convenient from where you live?'

'It's fine,' Pam said and headed off in the direction of the offices at the back of the mansion. But by the end of the morning, Jay was satisfied that however taciturn Pam Bentley might turn out to be, she was prepared to work hard. By that time they had sorted out desks, computers and an embryonic filing system in one of the two rooms allocated to them and cleaned and prepared cupboards and shelves and a long trestle work table in the other which would be where Jay would examine and catalogue the chests of artefacts stored in the attics of the main house. She had taken ten minutes to go over to the house and retrieve a few of the masks which now took pride of place on the work table.

'You realise a lot of this stuff will be pretty dusty,' Jay said to Pam as they sat down with a cup of coffee towards the end of the morning. 'You might like to bring an overall in to help keep your clothes clean. That's what I wear when I'm fiddling about with messy stuff.'

Pam glanced down at her dark suit and smart shoes, which looked brand new, bought perhaps, Jay thought, to celebrate the new job.

'Perhaps I don't need to dress up...?' she asked tentatively.

'Not really, no,' Jay said. 'Not normally. There may be times we have visitors, I suppose. Then we'd better look a bit business-like. But generally I think there'll only be the two of us here. We can be as informal as we like.'

'Right,' Pam said, and Jay wondered if she had

155

imagined the slight note of disapproval in her voice. This was a bit different, she supposed, from the jobs she recalled from her assistant's CV: PA to various businessmen and even a lawyer. Not much space for informality there, she thought.

They were interrupted by Fred Marston, who marched into the room without knocking.

'They've been at it again,' he said, his face flushed.

'Sorry,' Jay said. 'Who's been at what?'

'Blasted kids,' Fred said. 'The back door to the house has been forced. I reckon someone's been up in t'attics an'all.'

'I didn't notice when I went up there,' Jay said, surprised. Her trip to the attics had been brief and obviously she had not paid much attention to anything except the masks she had gone to fetch. She had certainly seen nothing that indicated a break-in. But she recalled one thing which had surprised her slightly.

'The attic door was unlocked, though,' she said, careful to keep any accusation out of her voice although she was pretty sure that Fred must have left it that way.

'You didn't teck a close look at the footprints up them dusty stairs, did you?' Fred said. 'Are you wearing trainers?' He glanced down at both the women's feet. 'No, I didn't reckon so. Well, someone's bin up theer in trainers, or summat like them, with a pattern on t'soles. Plain as a pikestaff if you keep your eyes open.'

'I don't think anything up there's been touched,' Jay said cautiously, knowing that in her hurry to get her hands on some of the masks she

156

had not checked on the tea chests in the other rooms. Was anything missing? She didn't know.

'I couldn't see owt disturbed, except them things,' he nodded at the masks on Jay's work-table.

'They'd been interfered with the first time I went up there,' Jay said. 'I'd already put them back in the tea chest myself.'

'I can't see as how anyone would want to teck any of them home,' Fred said. 'It'd be like living with Old Nick on t'sitting room wall.'

Jay smiled.

'Not pretty, some of them,' she conceded. 'But as we don't know how many there were up there we've no way of knowing if your intruder in trainers took a shine to one of them. Can you lock the attic door again, Fred, so that at least we know if anyone else tries to get up there unannounced. That's the best we can do, I think.'

'They're coming to put an alarm system on this building tomorrow,' Fred said grudgingly. 'That should help.'

'It should,' Jay said, though she wondered who in the world would hear a burglar alarm going off at Pendle House.

By three o'clock that afternoon, Jay had begun to feel she was making inroads into the box of paperwork which, according to the town council, were the only records they had inherited with the Wright collections. It was obvious no one had made any attempt to collate them over the past thirty years that they had been in the council's nominal possession and her heart had sunk as she had tipped the jumble of papers, a few typed, but most handwritten and some of them obviously very old, onto her large work-table. Pam had looked over her shoulder in horror.

'What a mess,' she muttered.

'It's the only paperwork we've got to tell us what's stashed away up there,' Jay said. 'Don't worry. What I'm looking for is some sort of catalogue or inventory. Once we've got that we can get it into the computer and begin to make some progress.'

By three, the box's contents had been sorted into four rough heaps. One was for correspondence between the Wright family and various dealers and suppliers around the world, another for bills and invoices, a third for a jumbled set of notes in a fairly illegible script evidently compiled by an early twentieth century member of the family who had set him or herself the task of attempting to catalogue parts of the collection, and the last for a few more formal, typed lists of artefacts which were interesting enough to make Jay hope that they were all still safe in their tea-chests waiting for some long-delayed and much-needed attention. So far she had found nothing to indicate where the exceptional collection of masks had come from.

She glanced at her watch and realised that it was time to go home if she was to fulfil her promise to Kate to be there when school finished. She collected together all the pages of handwritten notes and her own notebooks and put them into a folder to take with her. But just as she finished and was about to fetch her coat she heard voices in the main office and her heart sank. The door opened quickly to admit two of her trustees, George Hateley and Bernard Grogan, followed by a flustered looking Pam Bentley. Jay gave the visitors no more than a tight-lipped smile.

'Good afternoon,' she said. 'This is a surprise.'

'Bernie thought we should come to see how you were getting on,' Hateley said. He looked older and more subdued than usual, Jay thought, and she wondered if there was something wrong. She hoped it was nothing to do with the museum. He glanced round the room, with a slight frown.

'We thought we'd better make sure you've got everything you need,' he said, slightly lamely.

'I'm fine thanks,' Jay said. She hesitated. She wanted to tell the two men that she had to leave, but did not think that was a politic move so soon in her new career. She spun round quickly and reopened the box of masks.

'I've been looking at some of the collection,' she said, unwrapping the bird mask again.

'You've been over to the house already, then?' Grogan sounded slightly surprised.

'Well, yes,' Jay said. 'I wanted to have a quick look at the state of things in the attics. I just brought these down as a sort of sample because they looked so interesting. I've read about them but I've never seen originals like these before.' Some instinct made her hold the malevolent bird's head in front of her face and she was gratified to see the look of horror on Hateley's face, although Grogan seemed to take the bizarre

159

sight in his stride.

'By God, that's a nasty looking beggar,' Hateley said. 'What the hell is it?'

Jay put the bird down on the table again with a faint smile and went through her best guess as to the mask's provenance.

'Red Indians?' Grogan said. 'I thought they went in for feathers and war dances and all that stuff.'

'Native Americans,' Jay said sharply. 'These are the tribes that also carve those elaborate totem poles. You get the same images. Their dances tell complicated stories, some of them pretty horrific. Hence the masks. There are masks from other cultures stashed away up there too, Japanese, Javanese I think, and some I simply don't recognise. I'll have to do some research on those. But masks are very common, you know, especially for use in dance and drama and religious rituals. You'll know the Greek masks for tragedy and comedy. Every theatre's got them somewhere or other, usually right up above the stage.'

'You'd not want to meet one o'them on a dark night,' Grogan said, apparently still transfixed by the bird mask. 'You're pleased with these, though, are you? Make summat out of them, can you, for the museum?'

'Oh yes,' Jay said, her enthusiasm genuine enough though she was slightly irritated by Grogan's patronising tone.

'So how soon do you reckon you'll be able to do an initial report for the trustees, Mrs. Morton?' he asked. 'Some sort of estimate of just what we've got and how attractive it might be for the punters, as it were?'

Jay bit back the answer which first sprang to mind and was saved from working out an alternative by George Hateley.

'Nay, Bernie, she's only been here five minutes...'

'Less than a day, actually,' Jay said.

'Give the lass a chance,' Hateley said. 'We weren't thinking of a progress report for months yet, were we?'

Grogan's colour rose and his bulging blue eyes became even more protuberant at this show of independence on Hateley's part.

'Well, I'm sure no one's going to be rushing you, Mrs. Morton,' he said.

'When is the next trustees' meeting?' Jay asked. 'The end of March, isn't it? I'll certainly be prepared to give you an interim report by then, but I doubt if I'll have made any serious progress on the catalogue. From what I've seen of the paperwork I've inherited, that's going to be a long job. It's all a terrible jumble, no system at all.'

'What we really came up for was to have a look round the house,' Hateley said. 'I hear there's been a break-in...'

'Maybe more than one,' Jay said. 'Fred Marston says someone's been in there this weekend, apparently. There's a real security problem to be solved before we can even think about laying out a museum there.'

'Aye, that's what we were told,' Grogan said. 'Fred's got all the keys, has he?'

'He's over there now, I think,' Jay said. 'He was

161

going to make sure the attics were locked up.'

'Come on then, George. We'll find him over there,' Grogan said, catching Jay's quick glance at her watch with a slight frown. 'You've your little lass to get home to, I expect,' he said and Jay wondered why his smile had all the sincerity of a hanging judge. He marched out of the room, pushing past Pam Bentley, who was hovering in the doorway. George Hateley hesitated for a moment, as if he wanted to linger, but then he apparently thought better of it and hurried after the MP with an apologetic look in Jay's direction. Pam Bentley raised her eyes to the sky but said nothing.

Jay knew as soon as she got into the car and glanced at her watch again that she was going to be late and her stomach tightened and gave a slight stab of pain. She must find a way of organising some sort of afterschool care for Kate, she thought as she waited patiently for a gap in the traffic so that she could turn out of the Pendle House gateway. Most days, she thought, she would be able to get home by three thirty by taking paperwork home with her, but there might be occasions when she couldn't. She needed someone to fall back on in an emergency and she wondered whether Sonja's mother might be persuaded to help. Perhaps if she paid her, she thought with a twinge of guilt this time: if the family were refugees she was sure that they would be glad of the money.

She took the steep hill back down towards the centre of the town far faster than she knew she should, cursing as the traffic lights changed to red at the junction where she had to turn into Victoria Street, the main artery through the small estate of former mill-workers' cottages. Nerves already frayed, her heart missed a beat as she turned into Adelaide Street and saw that half-way down, outside her own front door, a small knot of people had gathered. Surely, she thought, Kate had not thrown a tantrum on the doorstep and attracted an audience of sympathetic neighbours ready to inveigh against the crimes, real or imagined, of working mothers. She wrenched the car untidily into a parking space and marched up to the group of women, most of whom had half turned at the sound of the car door slamming.

'What's happened?' Jay demanded of no one in particular. 'Where's my daughter? Where's Kate? She should...' She broke off and heard herself make a noise which was half moan and half cry and came from somewhere inside her she barely knew existed as she caught sight of exactly what had caught the neighbours' attention. Fastened to a nail, which had been driven into the wooden door just below the decorative glass fanlight, was something she recognised: a malevolent human face decorated in green and red, with a row of sharply pointed teeth fixed in a rictus snarl and, attached to the top of its head, a perfectly formed human skull. It was one of the masks from Pendle House.

Mouth dry and almost unable to speak, she found herself the focus of half a dozen appalled middle-aged faces which looked almost as shocked as she felt herself.

'Where's Katie?' she asked again. 'Is she home

from school? Has she seen this?'

'Him next door took her in,' one of the women said, her lips pursed in disapproval. 'Screamed her head off, she did, your lass. Brought us all running. I thought there'd been an accident, someone killed, at least. Hysterical, she was.'

'Thank you, thank you,' Jay said. 'I should have been here fifteen minutes ago. Something was bound to go wrong on the first day at work, wasn't it?' The ring-fence of disapproval which surrounded her did not soften in any way, but she was saved by Kate herself, who suddenly flung herself out of the Booth front door and pushed her way through the onlookers to fling herself into Jay's arms.

'What is it, Mummy, what is it?' she gasped between sobs. 'It's horrible. It's the scariest thing I've ever seen.'

'I know, darling,' Jay said, burying her face in Kate's soft dark hair to hide her own tears. 'But it's only a silly old mask. Come on indoors and we'll sort ourselves out, shall we?'

'Mr. Booth gave me lemonade and mint humbugs,' Kate mumbled incoherently.

Somehow Jay bundled her daughter in through her own front door before coming back to detach the mask from its nail and offer a wan smile of thanks to the neighbours who were beginning to disperse. As she struggled to prise the nail out the woodwork, Mr. Booth himself appeared and offered her a pair of pliers.

'Looks like someone's got it in for you,' he said.

'Thanks for helping out, Mr. Booth,' Jay said through gritted teeth, as the nail suddenly jerked free. 'I'm very grateful.'

'You're all right,' he said. 'She's a bonny lass. She can come in any time she likes if you're not at home. She's very welcome. She can watch the telly with me.' Jay glanced at the old man sharply and shook her head.

'I was held up today. Normally I'll be here when she comes home,' she said.

'Aye, well, I'm just saying,' Booth muttered, rebuffed. 'I had a visit from the social today,' he said, obviously anxiously changing the subject. 'My own social worker, I've got, because I've been poorly. Nice young woman.'

'That's good,' Jay said absently. 'I must see to Kate now...' But as Booth closed his door and she stepped back inside her own house, one of the other neighbours who had been watching turned back, giving a cautious glance in the direction of Booth's front door.

'You want to watch him,' she said.

'What do you mean?' Jay asked, her mind still fuddled with shock.

'He's bin a bit peculiar since his wife went,' the woman whispered urgently. 'I'd not let a child of mine in there with him on her own.'

It was obvious what the woman meant and Jay felt slightly sick.

'He seems a nice old man,' she said.

'Aye, well, I'm just saying,' the woman said. 'That's all.'

Kate proved difficult to assuage. She showed no interest in Jay's careful explanation of what the mask was and where it came from. She refused to eat any supper and sat watching television

165

afterwards in a tight little huddle on the settee, arms clasped tightly round her knees, watching her mother more closely than she did the screen. In the end Jay switched the set off and sat down beside her daughter and took her hand.

'You mustn't get upset,' she said. 'It was just someone playing a silly joke on us. You know about masks. Didn't you make one when you were in Mrs. Miller's class in London? That was pretty scary, as I remember.'

At this Kate simply burst into tears again.

'It's not just the silly mask,' she said. 'It's everything. I hate it here. I don't like school. I don't like Miss Ashcroft and I don't really like Debbie. She's new and doesn't know anything much. I don't like Pendle Bridge. I want to go back to London and I want to see my Daddy.'

'Oh darling, I'm sorry,' Jay said, hugging Kate until her sweater was wet with her tears. 'We can't go back, you know that. But it'll be half-term soon and you're going to see Daddy then. You haven't forgotten, have you?'

'It's ages till half-term,' Kate said her face obstinate now.

'So what's so wrong with school?' Jay asked. 'How's Sonja? She seems a nice girl, a nice friend to have.'

'She wasn't there today,' Kate said. 'And no one else likes me. They say I talk funny and I'm posh and stuck up. I don't talk funny do I, Mum?'

'No, of course not,' Jay said. 'Anyway, I expect Sonja's just got a cold. I'll come in and have a chat with your Miss Ashcroft in the morning, if you like. They shouldn't be teasing you like that.'

'Oh Mu-u-um,' Kate moaned. But no reassurance really seemed to soothe her and Jay sat with her at bedtime until she fell asleep, only to be wakened in the small hours by a small figure which crept into her bed and wrapped its arms like vines around her.

'I want to go back home to London,' Kate whispered forlornly before she fell back to sleep. But Jay lay awake for a long time, rigid with anger. I'm being harrassed, if not terrorised, she thought. And it's bloody well got to be stopped.

10

Donna was jubilant. The job had been secured, her first day had come and gone without incident, she had bought new shoes and some Elastoplast to cover the blisters on her heels and she was determined to make this a serious run for the first time since she had arrived back in Pendle Bridge. And she had taken a significant step in her plan to prepare for Kenny's homecoming. In trainers and somewhat thread-bare track suit, she set off up the steep hill out of town at an easy pace, breathing steadily and shortening her stride as she felt the gradient pull at her calf muscles.

'Come on, Mags,' she said to her companion. 'You can do it. We can do it. We'll go right up to the top of the moors where we used to go with Kenny.' The presence at her shoulder did not answer, she seldom did, but she could hear her breathing in harmony with her own. She smiled. It was going to be all right, she thought. She could afford to stay here and complete what she had to do.

By the time she had climbed to the point where the last houses petered out in a jumble of allotments and dilapidated sheds and the road levelled off on the shoulder of the hill above the town she was overheating, and she stopped for a moment to take off her sweatshirt and tie it round her waist. She was breathing heavily now and she wiped a trickle of sweat from her eyes before setting off again through the wooden pedestrian gate alongside the cattle grid which, in theory, contained the sheep left to graze for most of the year on the open moorland beyond. There was no pavement here, just a rough track alongside the paved road and the ground felt soft and spongy underfoot, though not muddy enough to cling to her shoes. She breathed the cold peaty air more deeply as she followed the winding road, relatively level now, and took in the rolling expanse of heather and bracken, rust and dun-coloured at this time of the year, and still silvered with frost which had not thawed all day. Tears pricked her eyes. She had once been happy here.

'Do you remember, Mags?' she asked, the words coming out rythmically in time with her steps. 'Where was that place we used to have picnics, light a fire, roast potatoes? Do you remember?' Mags did not respond, but Donna's memories were flooding back now, drawing her to the place where the stream went under the road and they had turned off to follow it, jumping over the muddy bits, laughing hysterically when she had lost her shoe in a bog and they had known that Mrs. P would be furious.

'I remember,' Donna said dreamily. 'I do remember. I wish I could find Kenny. He should be here too. He can't have died in that place, can he? He's not old enough to have died. His mother didn't know me, you know. And she didn't know where Kenny is. She's old now and doesn't know anything.'

She ran for a while in silence with Mags still

169

close behind her until she reached the dark brown boggy stream which passed under the road through a culvert and she sat down, panting on the stone parapet above the gurgling flow which was pulling last year's yellowed grass like the hair of drowned water nymphs.

'This is the place,' she said softly. 'Up there where the gorse is, that's where we used to go. I do remember it now.' She scanned the darker green vegetation which followed the twisting course of the water but could see that the stream was full to overflowing and the path underwater in places and far too muddy to venture down. Instead she scrambled round the parapet and dropped down below the road on the far side of the culvert, pulled her sweatshirt back on and huddled against a clump of dry and crackling dead bracken with her arms round her knees, content to feel the wind rippling through her hair and listen to the faint, thin call of a bird she could not see as she got her breath back and the thumping of her heart slowed to normal. Mags was still there, still very quiet, although she could hear her heavy breathing, slightly out of sync with her own.

She closed her eyes for a second and found herself immediately spiralling away up a dark staircase and opening her mouth to scream although she knew no sound would come. She had never been able to scream during all those nights, although Mags had pierced the darkness with cries that no one seemed to hear. But all was silence now, no ingratiating voices, no muffled fumblings, no doors opening and closing as men came and went, no Mags protesting. But the masks were there, as the masks had always been there, once Laurie had begun to invite his friends in to share their midnight feasts: the bird with the great beak and flaring nostrils and piercing eyes, the white faced man with obscene red lips permanently puckered in a blubber-mouthed kiss, the snarling devil with white pointed teeth preferred by the fattest of the visitors, the one whose belly hung over the waistband of his underpants and whose flabby fingers were the cruellest of them all.

Donna found herself moaning and sobbing now simply because she could. Then she had remained dry-eyed and rigid, too small and slight to resist, limp and floppy after they had finished and gone away and left the girls alone in the attics to creep downstairs again later and clean themselves up and slip back into the bunk beds to sob themselves to sleep in each other's arms. If there was a hell, Donna thought, that had been it and Laurie had been the devil's master of ceremonies. Well, he should feel at home now.

It had all started so innocently. They had liked Laurie, although now of course she realised that he had probably gone out of his way to make sure they liked him. But he had been kind to the two of them, spared the extra minutes to chat to them at the end of tea and before bedtime, slipped them the odd packet of Rolos or a Mars bar – Mags's favourite, Donna thought with a faint smile – and tried to protect them from the irascibility of Mrs. P. and the indifference of the rest of the carers at the home. He'd been fun at first, had Laurie, had made them laugh, had turned a blind eye when he must have known very well they had not been to school when they came back muddy and scratched from their countryside escapades with Kenny. So when he suggested a midnight feast in the attic they had felt no intimation of danger. They had gone willingly up the narrow staircase and shared his crisps and sweets and fizzy pop in the furthest of the rooms where there were a couple of mattresses and duvets on the floor and fewer of the tea chests which packed the rest of the space.

Even now Donna could remember the tingle of excitement they had felt as they had crept along that dusty corridor on tiptoe so as not to wake the rest of the sleeping girls below. This was his den, Laurie had said. Come into my den. And, giggling, they did, and insidiously they were betrayed as cuddles turned to sex, invitations became threats and eventually Lawrence invited his 'friends' to the parties, heavy, silent men, threatening and half-naked apart from the bizarre and terrifying masks they were already wearing as they came into the room where the two girls cowered. Later, when men had used her the same way on the streets, it had somehow never been as bad as those months at Pendle House. She had known the worst that could happen and had begun to dull the pain with chemical crutches by the time she was fifteen. And human faces, however degenerate, and some were certainly that, had never held the power of those impassively malevolent carvings which had born down on them when they were far too slight to put up even a token resistance. It was always the masks which came back to madden and haunt and destroy long after she had escaped to seek a freedom she had never found.

Bastards, bastards, bastards, Donna sobbed, her head on her knees. You'll find them, Archie said. They're still here somewhere. A shudder shook the whole of her frame and she sat upright again. I'll find them, she said. For you, Mags, I'll find them.

Jay Morton hurried a reluctant daughter through the press of parents and children at the school gate and through the main doors.

'I don't want you to complain, Mum,' Kate insisted as she was whisked down the corridor to her classroom. 'I'll be all right. Really I will.'

'Well, let's just make sure, shall we?' But when she opened the classroom door it was not the young, blonde, self-contained Miss Ashworth who was sitting at the teacher's desk but a slightly older, darker-haired woman Jay did not recognise.

'I was looking for Miss. Ashworth...'

'Ah, she's going to be late this morning. Dentist's appointment. I'm Debbie Flint, her assistant. Can I help you?'

'Mum, it's all right. It's not important,' Kate whispered urgently but Jay looked at her pale closed face and hardened her heart.

'Well, you could have a word with Miss. Ashworth for me,' she said. 'Kate hasn't been here long and she's being upset by some of the other children teasing her. I know she has to learn to

173

take the rough with the smooth at school but she's had a bad time recently, family problems and a move here from London, she may need a bit of help to settle down and I certainly don't want her bullied.'

Debbie Flint glanced down at the register on the desk in front of her as if checking Kate's name and then nodded. She seemed unperturbed by Jay's breathless assault.

'What have they been doing to you, Kate?' she asked and when Kate glanced away, sulkily, and did not reply, her voice sharpened slightly. 'I've not been here long myself, Mrs. Morton, but she's got to learn to toughen up, you know. Nobody's going to be nice to her all of the time.'

Kate spun round at that, her cheeks flushed.

'Nobody's nice to me any of the time,' she said in a fierce whisper. 'Nor to Sonja. They're really mean to her, call her names all the time – call her a terrorist and stuff. Tell her to go back where she came from. Call her a smelly Muslim and she's not a Muslim anyway. But they hate her and they don't like me because I like her.'

'Sonja?' Debbie said, glancing at her register again. 'Sonja Kradic hasn't been at school for a couple of days...'

'Could that be because she's being bullied?' Jay asked, trying to control her temper. As her sister had been only too eager to tell her, this was not the liberal middle class primary school Kate had attended in London, where children of a dozen different races had been enthusiastically taught to celebrate their differences, but she found Debbie Flint's casual attitude insupportable.

174

'Is there a time I can have a word with Miss Ashworth?' she asked sharply, and Kate turned away, her face flushed and screwed up with fury.

'She's always here after school,' Debbie said, obviously offended now. 'You could catch her then.'

'Right,' Jay said slightly wearily, knowing that this meant another scramble to get back from work on time. 'Katie, wait in school for me this afternoon and I'll meet you here. OK?'

'All right,' Kate said without enthusiasm and with that Jay had to be content.

By the time Jay had driven to Pendle House she had calmed down slightly but she was not best pleased to find a dark blue Rover parked outside the main house. If the trustees of the new museum were going to distract her every day, she thought, she would never be able to get on with any concentrated work and the whole project would founder before it had even begun. She parked her own car and strode round the stable block, ready to do battle with Bernard Grogan or whichever of his over-enthusiastic colleagues had decided to interrupt her this morning, only to find herself face to face with two men in the outer office, neither of whom was a museum trustee and one of whom she recognised immediately.

'I'm sorry to bother you at work, Mrs. Morton,' DCI Peter Shipley said. He was wearing a somewhat crumpled trench-coat, the sort of detective gear that Jay thought had gone out of fashion with black and white movies. 'But I called round to your house and your neighbour

175

said you'd already left.'

'I took my daughter to school,' Jay said, glancing at the other man, older, running to fat, dressed in grey slacks and a dark blue anorak and with a face grey and creased as if by too much life.

'This is DS Jack Barraclough,' Shipley said, waving a hand at his colleague.

'This all sounds very official,' Jay said, glancing at Pam Bentley who was apparently making tea and studiously ignoring the proceedings. 'You'd better come into the other room.' She waved the two police officers into the work room, closed the door, took off her coat and hung it up before sitting down at the big table and giving them her full attention.

'How can I help you, gentlemen?' she asked.

'You don't know then?' Shipley said, a look of faint disbelief in his eyes.

'Know what?' Jay said, all the irritation of the unsatisfactory start to the day in her voice.

'I'm surprised you haven't heard. We found the body of Mary Petherbridge in her cottage yesterday morning. You seem to have been one of the last people to talk to her before she died.'

Jay swallowed hard and tried to digest this information carefully, recalling the woman to whom she had taken such an instinctive dislike when she had turned up at Pendle House. She had looked neither ill nor particularly fragile and she guessed that if two detectives, one of them a senior officer, had arrived to talk to her about Mary Petherbridge then her death must have been sudden and suspicious at the very least.

'How did she die?' she asked quietly.

'She was murdered,' Shipley said. 'Apparently by an intruder in her own home. Every woman's nightmare, I suppose.' He did not sound as if he really believed Jay might fall into the category of nervous householder, in spite of what she had told him about being harrassed.

'That's awful,' Jay said. 'I can't say I warmed to Mary Petherbridge but that's really dreadful. How was she killed?'

'She was stabbed,' Shipley said, his voice curt.

'Twenty-nine times,' Sergeant Barraclough added, close to relish until subdued by Shipley's angry glance.

'I want you to tell me everything you talked about that day when she came to see you,' Shipley said. 'Did she say why she came up here, for instance?'

'I was surprised to see her,' Jay said slowly. 'She'd walked straight in through the front door and I never really worked out why she had turned up like that. She said she was just passing. It seemed to be no more than idle curiosity about what we were going to do with the old place. And I think she wanted to make sure the stuff in the attics was still safe. She obviously felt guilty because the kids used to go up there when she was in charge. Although "in charge" is not a phrase which springs to mind when you think of Ms. Petherbridge and the kids at Pendle House. You'd have thought she'd have had enough of the place after everything that happened when she was here.'

'Tell me everything you can remember,' Shipley

insisted, so Jay tried to recall everything that Mary Petherbridge had said that day.

'I can't think of anything else,' she said when her memory finally failed her. 'I told you most of it the other night in the pub.' Barraclough raised an astonished eyebrow at that but was too wary to say anything.

'Aye, well, this is official, that was social,' Shipley said quickly. 'But you don't sound as if you liked her much.'

'No, I didn't,' Jay said. 'It seemed pretty clear to me that she knew that there was some sort of abuse going on in that children's home and she did nothing about it for fear of jeopardising her own position. Didn't you get any hint of that after the girl was murdered? Did you not have any other suspects apart from Kenny Bairstow?'

'We've been through all that, Mrs. Morton,' Shipley said flatly. 'We had no reason to suspect that there were any problems at Pendle House apart from two little tearaways running wild with Kenny Bairstow.'

'Ms. Petherbridge did say the children wouldn't have been believed if they'd complained,' Jay said, her renewed anger getting the better of her. But Shipley just nodded, evidently unsurprised.

'To some extent she was right,' he said. 'Kids like that lie, manipulate, try a bit of emotional blackmail if they think they can get away with it. I seem to remember that the one who disappeared had tried some sort of abuse allegation with a foster family that Petherbridge clearly thought was a pack of lies. As far as I know there'd been no complaint of anything amiss at

178

Pendle House.'

'And if you'd discovered that twelve or thirteen year old girls weren't virgins?'

'Well, these days a medical examination would be the first step, wouldn't it? But then?' He shrugged. 'It wasn't an issue, Mrs. Morton. No one ever made a complaint.'

Jay sighed in frustration and the sound seemed to infuriate Shipley.

'Look, Mrs. Morton, I don't know what your agenda is here, but I can assure you that you're barking up the wrong tree if you still think Kenny Bairstow didn't kill Margaret Emmet. It was an open and shut case.'

'I don't have an agenda, as you call it,' Jay snapped. 'I'd never heard of this case before I came back to Pendle Bridge. I found myself involved simply because I bought the wretched Bairstows' house and once Kate and I had moved in no one spared me the grisly details. It would have been much more helpful if they'd told me all about Kenny Bairstow before I signed the bloody contract. Now I'm stuck with a young child in a house where I'm being harrassed and working in a place which seems to have been the scene of all sorts of nastiness years ago. And now you come asking what Mary Petherbridge told me last week. Well, that's your answer. She was still obsessed with the murder of that child. If there's a problem here, Inspector Shipley, it's a Pendle Bridge problem, it's certainly not mine. I've not lived here for twenty years.'

But Shipley was not to be placated.

'Well, if you didn't come back with a mis-

179

conceived miscarriage of justice on your mind, what did bring you back?' he asked. 'Was it Chris Hateley? He told me he was an old flame.'

Jay drew a sharp breath.

'I came back because a good job cropped up and I thought it would be good for Kate to be close to my sister and her family,' she said angrily. 'Not that it's any of your business, Inspector Shipley. And I can't see that it's got anything to do with your investigation into Mary Petherbridge's murder.'

'Have you ever been to her house?' Shipley snapped back.

'Of course not. How would I even know where she lived? I've only ever met the woman once, for about ten minutes, max. She did seem anxious about something, very anxious, but apart from what I've told you I've no idea what. She made me pretty angry, if you must know, but that's it. As you know, I've got a lot of other things on my mind. I went home. I suppose she went home. End of story.'

'Well, I hope so, Mrs. Morton,' Shipley said. 'If you can remember anything else about Mary Petherbridge that you haven't already thought of, please let us know.'

'Of course,' Jay said, willing herself to stay calm. Apparently about to go, Shipley spotted one of the masks, half hidden in its box and pulled back the concealing wrappings to reveal a curved beak and staring eyes.

'My God, that's pretty fearsome,' he said.

'Even more fearsome if you find one like it hung on your front door,' Jay said sharply. 'I haven't even got around to telling you about the latest bit of harassment at my house. Kate was scared half to death by someone playing silly beggars...'

'The whole thing sounds to me like kids mucking about,' Shipley said, his tone dismissive. 'Probably someone from your daughter's school. If you tell my uniformed colleagues about it they'll ask the beat constable to keep an eye open...'

'Thanks very much,' Jay said, her voice heavy with irony. 'But I don't think primary school kids could have removed one of those masks from the attics at Pendle House and then got it down to my place. It takes a bit more organisation than ten year olds are capable of, don't you think?'

'Ah, she's only ten,' Shipley said, looking slightly abashed. 'I thought she was older than that. But the advice still stands. Ask uniform to keep an eye open for you. There's more than a few teenage tearaways down where you're living. I doubt you've got a serious stalker, Mrs. Morton, I really do.'

11

Jay found it almost impossible to concentrate after DCI Shipley had left. She was strangely unmoved by Mary Petherbridge's death: a lack of sympathy on her part which she felt only fleetingly guilty about. But her worries about Kate only seemed to intensify after Shipley's curt dismissal of her complaint. He just put me down as an over-anxious single mother, she thought angrily. How dare he? Three dead mice might be the work of mischievous kids but to lay hands on the bird mask, which had undoubtedly been taken from the attics of Pendle House, indicated an altogether higher level of premeditation, daring and, above all, a knowledge of the collection's existence.

And there was another worry which she had only half formulated and had not risked mentioning to Shipley. Twice now she had come home to the vague feeling that someone had been in the cottage while she was out. There was nothing to pin down except a feeling that she had not left her book in quite that spot on the coffee table, or her papers arranged quite so neatly on her desk. Even the previous evening, with Kate in near hysterics, something seemed not quite right in the kitchen when she opened the door and set about preparing supper. Yet there was no sign of a break-in, the doors were locked and the windows closed and latched, just as she had left them. But she was sure someone had been there. Either that, or the pressures of her new life were beginning to get to her in a thoroughly alarming way.

As far as the mask was concerned, she would happily have offered up Mary Petherbridge to the police as a likely suspect, although she could not imagine a motive for such harrassment, but it now appeared that the woman had already been dead when the mask was nailed to her front door. Which left Fred Marston, the caretaker, who had had free run of the premises for years, Pam Bentley, her assistant who was busy in her office inputting the first lists of data into her computer, but who had been shown over the entire complex of buildings before she started work, and, more disturbingly, whoever else had disturbed the collection of masks at any time over the last twenty years or so. And that, she thought, might be anyone in Pendle Bridge who had worked at or lived in the house or been responsible for its management – and she could not even begin to work out how many people that might be.

At twelve o'clock she pushed aside the piles of paper on her desk, grabbed her coat and went into the outer office.

'I'm going to take an early lunch, Pam,' she said. 'I need some fresh air. You can go when I get back, OK?' But it was not fresh air Jay really craved as much as a sympathetic ear, so she turned down the hill towards the town centre. At the *Advertiser* office Chris Hateley came down to reception when called, took one look at the strain on Jay's face and beckoned her up the stairs to his office.

'What's the problem? You look awful,' he said, waving her into the one comfortable chair amid the sea of paperwork.

'I think I'm going out of my mind,' Jay said, leaning back and closing her eyes for a second. 'I don't know what's happening or why. I've only been back here five minutes. How can anyone have any reason for harrassing me and Kate like this?'

'I can't imagine.'

'That's not the end of it,' Jay said, and told him about the mask and the horrified reaction of her neighbours in Adelaide Street. 'Kate was terrified,' she said.

'I can imagine,' Chris said. 'Abbie would have been too. But are you certain this mask came from Pendle House?'

'Absolutely certain,' Jay said. 'There couldn't be two sources of North American masks locally. It's just not possible.'

'But you're not sure? It wasn't one you'd already seen at the house?'

'No, it wasn't, though I hadn't unwrapped them all. But where else could it have come from, for God's sake? They're pretty unusual, these things. Not the sort of ethnic status symbol you can pick up in Harvey Nicks in Leeds, let alone the Pendle Bridge Woolworths.'

'Point taken,' Chris said. 'Have you told the police?'

'I was actually interviewed by your friend Peter Shipley this morning about Mary Petherbridge.'

'Ah, yes, the murder. That will be our front page this week. Very nasty, apparently.'

'I dare say,' Jay said. 'But what it's got to do with me I can't imagine. I only spoke to the woman for a couple of minutes when she gate-crashed Pendle House last week for no very obvious reason. Anyway, I went over all that with him again, but when I complained about my own problems he simply wasn't interested. Not a big enough crime for him to be bothered with, evidently.'

'Well, a very violent murder may be a bit of a preoccupation just now,' Chris objected. 'It's not as if Pendle Bridge produces that sort of mayhem very often. I don't think we've had more than a couple of murders in my time as a journalist – since Mags Emmett was killed, in fact. We're a pretty peaceful community, on the whole.'

'Peaceful but with a thoroughly nasty streak, if you ask me,' Jay said. 'I can't go on like this, Chris. I can't sleep, Kate is miserable and jumpy, I'm beginning to look behind me every time I go out in case anyone is following me. I'm beginning to think people have been into the house while we're out. It's all starting to get out of hand and I'm beginning to regret ever taking this job at Pendle House.'

'Come on, it's not as bad as all that,' Chris said, although his cheerfulness seemed slightly forced. 'I'll take you out for a bite of lunch. How about that?'

Jay shrugged wearily, too anxious to object to being patronised.

'OK,' she said. 'And I will talk to the community police, or whatever they call themselves. But will you talk to Peter Shipley for me? This is real and nasty, Chris, and I need someone to take it seriously, not just the local bobby driving past in his panda car now and again.'

'Yes, of course I will,' he said, ushering her out into the main newsroom where a couple of people were tapping keyboards in a fairly desultory fashion. To her surprise she recognised the woman sitting closest to Chris's office, an intense expression on her thin, pale face. Jay smiled and was answered with a hesitant smile in return.

'Do you two know each other?' Chris asked. 'This is Margaret Davies, my new PA.' Margaret glanced away, as if embarrassed by the introduction.

'She was very nearly my PA,' Jay said, thinking that the woman was more self-conscious than she had realised at the interview.

'Mrs. Morton,' Margaret Davies said, a faint flush on her pale cheeks. 'Of course, the Pendle House interview. I'd have really liked that job, you know. I thought it would be very interesting.' She glanced at Chris.

'Sorry,' she mumbled, obviously realising that this was not the most tactful admission she could have made in front of her new boss. 'How's it going? With the new museum, I mean.'

'It's early days,' Jay said. 'But there's some interesting stuff up there. A wonderful collection of North American Indian masks, for instance, that I'm really excited about. You should come up and have a look if you're interested in ethnographic stuff.'

186

'Maybe,' Margaret said. 'Or maybe I'll just wait for the new museum to open. That might be best.' She glanced away, obviously still embarrassed by the slip of the tongue which had let Chris know he was distinctly second best as a boss.

'Don't mind me,' Chris said. 'But there is one thing, Jay. Margaret is looking for somewhere to live, she's just in a temporary place at the moment. You don't know anywhere round you with a room or a flat to let, do you? Perhaps you and Kate need a lodger to keep you company?'

''Fraid not,' Jay said. 'We've only got the two bedrooms. But there are places advertised in the newsagents in Victoria Road. Worth a look, maybe. There's a lot of elderly people around that area who might be happy to let a spare room.'

'Thanks, I'll give it a try,' Margaret said, turning her attention back to her computer screen, evidently embarrassed by the turn the conversation had taken.

They had beer and sandwiches in the crowded bar of the Woolpack and Jay wondered why Chris seemed almost as twitchy as she felt herself.

'The other night,' she said eventually. 'I won't mention it to Sue, you know. But it didn't mean anything. It was just a mad moment on my part.'

'That's a pity,' Chris said, his voice harsh with suppressed emotion. 'Because it wasn't on mine.'

'Chris, you're my sister's husband,' Jay said quietly. 'I'm not going down that road.'

'You were always the one, Jay.' He put a hand over hers and she pulled away sharply. 'My father said the other day... Well, never mind. But I think Sue knows the truth as well. You should never have come back to Pendle Bridge if you didn't want this to happen.'

'You may find it hard to believe, but it never crossed my mind,' Jay said. 'And nothing is happening, or about to happen. Anyway, I must get back to work. You won't forget to talk to Peter Shipley for me, will you? That's something really useful you can do.' And with that she turned on her heel and left Chris Hateley brooding over his half finished pint glass, aware of a few mildly curious eyes watching their evidently acrimonious parting.

Kate came home from school that afternoon with Jay, saying nothing and looking pale and tense. Jay rooted around in her still disorganised stock of books to find a guide to the North American masks which had so frightened her daughter and when she had settled herself on the settee with milk and biscuits she handed her the book.

'Have a look at this,' she said. 'It explains all about the masks. If you read the stories you'll see that they're not all scary. Some of them are quite jolly. Some just represent the villages people come from. Look, this is a raven. That's the sacred bird of one of the families who live in the north west of the United States and Canada. It's like their flag, I suppose. And this is an eagle. It's the same sort of thing. They were used in ceremonies and in dances. Look, some of them are really quite beautiful.'

'The one on the door wasn't beautiful, it was horrible,' Kate objected, but she did begin to read and turn over the pages of illustrations with a semblance of interest. Jay sat on the arm of the settee behind her daughter, reading over her shoulder, and when Kate seemed to be absorbed she went back into the kitchen to start preparing their evening meal, checking carefully to see that everything in the room was exactly as she had left it that morning. This time nothing seemed to have been interfered with but her moment of relief did not last long. As she chopped chicken breasts for a stir-fry, one of Kate's favourites, she became aware of a low noise coming from the next room. She wiped her hands quickly and went next door to find Kate, head down over the book she had been reading, sobbing quietly.

'What is it, darling?' she asked, taking the child into her arms.

'Everything,' Kate said.

'Oh, come on, it can't be as bad as all that,' Jay said, although she knew that for her daughter, wrenched away so suddenly from everything and everyone she knew, it probably was, and she felt overwhelmed with anger not just at David, who had precipitated this calamity in Kate's life, but at herself for compounding it.

'Tell me,' she muttered into Kate's hair.

'This bird,' Kate said fiercely, pointing at a now tear-stained illustration in the book on her lap. 'This one's just like the one on the door. This one eats people, Mum. It's horrible. It's a cannibal bird.'

Jay quickly scanned the caption under the picture which did look remarkably like the mask which had been hung on the front door and flinched slightly. She had been careless, she thought, not to look through the book more carefully before giving it to Kate.

'It's only a fairy story they illustrate with the masks,' she said. 'A monster a bit like the giant in *Jack and the Beanstalk*. You remember? Fee, fie foe fum...'

'A monster and three cannibal birds,' Kate objected. She was a bright child and at the pedantic stage. 'Look it says so. I hate it, Mum, I really do.' She snapped the book shut and flung it to the floor.

'I'm sorry, Katie,' Jay said. 'I thought you'd be interested. I thought I could take you up to Pendle House to see the ones I've got up there. Some of them are really quite beautiful – and not scary at all.'

'Ugh,' Kate said, dismissively, wiping her eyes with the tissue Jay handed her. 'I hate masks. And I don't want to make one at school either. Debbie says we're all going to make masks in art. I don't want to.'

'I'll talk to Debbie if you're worried about it,' Jay said. 'I still want to see Miss Ashcroft anyway. How was school apart from that? Was Sonja there today?' Jay was desperate to change the subject.

Kate shook her head.

'No, and the boys were being minging as usual. I hate it there.'

'Oh, Katie,' Jay said, close to despair. 'Do you think you'd rather go to the school Ben goes to? Perhaps we could persuade Daddy to pay the fees.'

Jay was surprised when Kate's face clouded again and her mouth set in a small tight line.

'I don't think so,' she said. 'I don't think Ben and Abbie like me very much either. No one in Pendle Bridge seems to like me, except Sonja, and now she's off school. I don't have any other friends here at all.' Her eyes filled with tears again, and Jay put her arms round her, wondering desperately how to distract her.

'How about we go down to Sonja's house to see how she is? It's only round the corner. Would that help?'

Apparently that would help, and when Jay had put the supper in the oven she and Kate walked the short distance to Fanny Street, another narrow road of stone terraced cottages identical to their own.

'Do you know what number it is, darling?' Jay asked, but Kate just shrugged. A woman coming towards them with a heavy shopping basket looked at them with curiosity that turned to disdain when Jay told her who she was looking for.

'Them asylum seekers,' the woman said. 'Shouldn't be here, should they?' But when pressed she suggested that they should try number 15 and when the door opened quickly in response to Jay's knock the pale, slim woman in jeans and sweatshirt who stood on the threshold was instantly recognisable as Sonja's mother, though her eyes were red-rimmed and she had obviously been crying.

'Is Sonja better yet?' Kate said eagerly before Jay could introduce herself. The woman looked blank and Jay guessed that her English was not good. She was not old, considerably younger, Jay thought, than she was herself, but her skin had the transparent appearance of someone who was short of sleep and probably eating badly, and her hair hung in pale, unwashed straggles down to her bony shoulders.

'Kate and Sonja – at school together,' Jay said, pointing at her daughter and smiling hopefully. She was rewarded with a flicker of understanding.

'Kate,' the woman said. 'Yes, Kate and Sonja. Friends.'

'Is she here?' Kate said impatiently. 'Is she better? Is she coming back to school?'

The woman hesitated at this barrage of questions and then shrugged and held the door open, evidently wanting them to come into the house. In the small, untidy living room, which boasted only the barest of furnishing, she waved them into hard chairs at the table and took another chair herself.

'Sonja not here,' she said. 'Sonja not come home. Sonja gone.'

A cold hand seemed to seize Jay's stomach. She wracked her brains for simple questions which Mrs. Kradic would understand.

'Where is Sonja?' she asked. 'Is Sonja with friends?'

'Sonja not here,' Mrs. Kradic repeated and Jay could see the tears welling up in her eyes again.

'Is she with family? Has she gone back to Kosovo?'

At the mention of Kosovo the tears began to spill down Sonja's mother's cheeks.

'No Kosovo,' she said. 'No more Kosovo. My husband, he Serb, me Muslim, all hate us in

Kosovo. Sonja not in Kosovo. Never more.'

'So where is Sonja?' Jay persisted.

'Not know,' the child's mother said. 'Not come from school...' She counted quickly on her fingers. 'Monday not come from school.'

The cold hand tightened its grip on Jay's stomach and Kate seized her hand urgently. Monday was three days ago.

'Where is she, Mum?' she whispered. 'Where's Sonja?'

'Has there been an accident?' Jay asked, not sure Mrs. Kradic would understand the word.

'Accident? Nnah-nah, nnah-nah?' Kate imitated the sound of an ambulance, but Mrs. Kradic shook her head.

'She stay out before,' she said. 'She not happy here.'

'All night? Has she stayed out all night?' Jay asked.

'No, not at night,' Mrs. Kradic said miserably. 'Not at night.'

'Have you spoken to the police?' Jay asked. 'Polizie, polizia?' She tried as many pronunciations of what she thought must surely be as international a word as any, but Mrs. Kradic shook her head frantically at that.

'No police, no police,' she said, her dark eyes full of fear. Oh God, Jay thought, the family must be here illegally, or had become so afraid of the police back home that not even their daughter's disappearance would allow them to seek help.

'You must tell the police,' she said desperately, but Mrs. Kradic only wept more desperately at that.

'No police,' she said. 'Police hurt my husband. He still sick in bed.' She glanced at the stairs as she spoke and Jay guessed that her husband was probably listening from above. 'Police hate him because Muslim wife. Because of police we run to England. No police. Police send back.'

'But you must find Sonja,' Kate cried. 'Perhaps the man in the car took her.' And Jay recalled with horror the warning from the school that a suspicious car had been cruising around the neighbourhood.

'Sonja will come home. Sonja good girl,' Mrs. Kradic said desperately. But Jay felt sick, certain that she was wrong, and equally certain that however much Mrs Kradic protested, she would have to go to the police and report the child missing even if her mother would not. She put her hand over Sonja's mother's tightly clenched fists.

'I will bring you good police,' she said. 'I promise, no one will hurt you. But you must find Sonja or someone will certainly hurt her.' If they haven't done so already, she thought angrily, glancing at Kate, whose eyes were full of unshed tears.

Donna lay in bed that night well satisfied with the way things were going. The new job seemed to have begun well, and although she had made no progress in finding out where Kenny had been taken, she and Mags were beginning to get a feel for the new Pendle Bridge, not least by reading the local paper where one of her targets regularly featured. He, she firmly believed, would lead her to the rest of the bird men, the tormentors who had made their lives a hell for two whole years.

Bumping into Mary Petherbridge like that had been an unexpected slice of luck. With only a child's estimate of age to go on, she had imagined Mrs. P. long dead and brought to judgement for the misery she had caused her and Mags. Some vaguely remembered quotation from her fragmented and much delayed education floated into her mind, something about sins of commission and omission. Mrs. P. had been a constant tormentor in her own right, with her erratic rules and her random punishments, that was true. But it was her wilful blindness that Donna and Mags had come to detest, her refusal to notice what was going on under her nose, the failure of a protector to protect that put her up there in Donna's gallery of monsters and the damned.

And there she had been, still in Pendle, living in comfortable retirement, not even much aged, though smaller than Donna remembered, almost shrunken by the passage of time. She had seen her trotting out of the covered market with her laden shopping bag and an expression of discontent which transmuted into shocked surprise when Donna had stood deliberately in her way and greeted her by name. Donna had recognised her immediately, although it had taken the older woman a little while to perceive the face of the child she had known beneath Donna's older, thinner and more knowing features. Within days Donna found herself gloating over the newspaper pictures of Mrs. P., of her cottage, and of the comments of police baffled by a killing of a blameless old woman with no apparent motive.

'Good riddance,' Donna said as she snuggled into bed with Mags. 'Just shows God's on our side. Now if we can just find somewhere better to live, we can get on with finding the rest of them.' And she knew that Mags and Archie were as content as she was at Mary Petherbridge's death.

She snuggled down under the duvet, her body curled around Mags, one arm over her shoulder, and fell into a sort of sleep, a half dream where past and present and future, reality and fantasy, swirled in a clinging mist of semi-consciousness. Mrs. P.'s cat was there, struggling for its life in murky water, but Mrs. P. herself, with her once substantial balcony of a bosom and sagging, plump chins, had shrunk to little more than a wraith, her voice fading helplessly amongst the screams and shouts of the rampaging children of Pendle House.

Then suddenly Donna found herself a runaway again, arriving shivering and panting at Pendle Bridge railway station in the faint morning light and cajoling a man in jeans and a duffle coat to buy her a single ticket to Leeds. They had got onto the train together and he sat by her as the stopping service trundled down the valley, gaining early commuters at every stop, and only picking up speed on the last lap of the journey through the maze of curving tracks and acres of industrial buildings on the approach to the city. The man had put a hand on her thigh once but when she pushed him away he had asked how old she was, and when she told him, had drawn back as if stung.

'You look older,' he had said. 'What are you up to going to Leeds by thiself at this time in t'morning?' She had spun him some yarn about meeting her mother and losing her ticket and long before the train pulled slowly onto the long platform he had got up and walked quickly to the front carriage, ready to jump off at the first opportunity. She, on the other hand, had lingered, and when she finally got off the little local diesel train she had explored the huge station carefully, reading the indicators, and watching the powerful expresses slide away to London, Birmingham and Edinburgh. She knew she needed to get away from Yorkshire, as far away as possible, and London seemed to her, as to so many others, the obvious place to lose oneself for ever. She had chosen her moment to slip onto the express to Kings Cross and hidden in a lavatory with an out-of-order sign on its door until she felt the train shudder and begin to inch out of the station, when, for the first time since she had left Mags and her assailant in the park, she began to cry, hot tears of despair which flowed silently down her cheeks.

She moaned now in her semi-sleep, as the dark years which followed flickered through her mind, like a video, shuddering from frame to frame without ever quite shocking her back into consciousness. She had expected Archie to protect her in some way, but although he was more and more at her side, sometimes whispering in her ear, sometimes there, an almost solid presence, fleetingly within her vision, more often hovering just out of sight, it soon became

197

apparent he could not help her. As she slid into the chilly underworld of life on the streets, abused, half-starved, and increasingly out of her head on whatever chemicals she could obtain, Archie came and went, apparently oblivious to her plight. And when she emerged from the dark time into the cruel white light of the hospital for the first time, Archie disappeared, banished, she had always thought, because he would never submit to this new regime of regimented baths, and bed, and talking sessions where she barely opened her mouth if she could avoid it. She found herself totally alone, for the first time in her life, on an endlessly flat, featureless plain, where no pits of horror opened up to claim her, but there were no exhilarating leaps of excitement either, the monotone, monochrome world of normality where she discovered, to her mild surprise, that she could survive, at least for long periods of time.

She woke with a start, the voice of authority ringing in her ears.

'You must take your medication, Donna, or you'll relapse and have to come back in again.'

'Yes,' she had said, and for a long time she had done as she was told. But when she finally decided it was time to take the train back to the north she had emptied her pills down the lavatory and was soon comforted to find Archie at her side again, and then Mags, her precious Mags, ready and eager to explore their old places again. And how they laughed each night as they realised how easy it was to fool most of the people most of the time. It would not be so hard, she thought with satisfaction, to do what she had set out to do, even if they couldn't find Kenny Bairstow. She and Mags and Archie would make it happen. They could do it. 'Clever Donna,' Archie and Mags whispered in her ear. 'Clever, clever girl.'

12

The knot of anger which had been tightening in Jay Morton's stomach since the previous afternoon finally unravelled in DCI Peter Shipley's office the following morning, startling them both with the force of the explosion.

'I told you why she hasn't reported it,' Jay said, her face flushed with emotion. 'The woman's scared witless of the police. Don't you understand that? That's what being a refugee is all about. She's run away from police, soldiers, immigration officers and God knows who else, her husband's sick, and she's terrified of being sent back if she makes a fuss...'

'But this is her ten-year-old daughter, for Christ's sake,' Shipley protested, stung by Jay's vehemence.

'She asked me to come and see you. I went back to see her again after I dropped Kate at school and persuaded her to talk to you. But she's afraid to come to the police station. I don't know what happened if you went to a police station in Kosovo, but I imagine it might not have been very pleasant. Can you please, please get someone sympathetic down to see her and post this child as missing? She may be dead by now, for all I know. But it's urgent. Obviously it's urgent. She's only ten years old. She doesn't speak good English. She hasn't lived here long...'

'Well, it's not CID's responsibility,' Shipley objected. 'Not at this stage, any road. It's a missing person inquiry, especially if she's stayed out before. I'll talk to uniform and get them to send someone round. What language do they speak?'

'Serbo-Croat I imagine,' Jay said. 'Albanian maybe. I'm not sure.'

'I expect we have someone on tap. Perhaps from Bradfield University. But that'll take time.'

'Time's what you may not have,' Jay said. 'I can't believe this, you know? The school's made no inquiries about why the child's been away. I thought these days they were supposed to check.'

'I'll set the wheels in motion, Mrs. Morton,' Shipley said. 'Children of this age, we do have procedures. We don't take it lightly, but the chances are she's had a row at home and run off. Her mother did say she'd done it before...'

'Not overnight,' Jay snapped. 'And I'll talk to Chris about publicity, shall I? In the *Advertiser?*'

'Leave it to us, Mrs. Morton,' Shipley said, angry himself now. 'We've a Press office to handle all that sort of thing.'

And with that Jay had to be content, although she was in fact very far from that happy state. She had slept badly and woken with a start from a dream in which she was searching for Kate along a wide stretch of wet sandy beach and beneath the dark timbers of some sort of pier where black pools shimmered with a movement which seemed to come neither from wind or tide, an involuntary shuddering of water where, she feared, the drowned still struggled fathoms

201

down. She had not found Kate on the eerie monochrome beach, where the sand and the water shifted constantly in a kaleidoscope of greys and black, although she had hunted for what seemed like hours on end, and she had woken breathing hard with her heart thumping and fear forcing her from her bed in the pale dawn light to pad across the landing and stand shivering at her daughter's bedroom door where she could hear the child's steady breathing.

She had gone downstairs and made herself tea, sitting at the kitchen table with her hands around the warm mug, wondering how she could cope with her new situation. She felt intolerably alone and she missed David with a physical longing which she could explain to nobody, though she knew with absolute certainty that she did not want Chris Hateley in her bed in his place. Then suddenly the horror of Sonja's disappearance came flooding back and she guessed that was what had sparked the nightmare. She had roused Kate unusually early that morning and, in spite of her protestations, had walked to school with her well before nine and marched purposefully into her classroom where she found both teacher and assistant busy sorting books at the front of the class.

'Mrs. Morton,' Miss Ashcroft said, only the faintest note of surprise in her voice. 'Debbie told me you came in yesterday.' Debbie Flint glanced at Jay without enthusiasm while Kate ostentatiously walked to the back of the classroom, took a book from a shelf and buried her head in it. She had lost her battle to stop Jay making another foray to the school and was still sulking.

'I'm sorry Kate's not settling down,' the class teacher said. 'She's very bright and I thought she was beginning to enjoy school.'

'She's being teased,' Jay said. 'But that's not really why I came in again this morning. I spoke to Sonja Kradic's mother yesterday and was horrified to discover that Sonja seems to have disappeared.'

'Disappeared?' Miss. Ashcroft's voice and expression were incredulous. 'How can she have disappeared? We've not been told anything about that.'

'Have you been told she's ill?' Jay asked. 'Have you heard from her family this week?'

'Well, the office should have,' the teacher said. 'We expect parents to let us know...'

'But did they? And if they didn't, what does the school do next? Don't you make inquiries if a child just drops out of sight?'

'We do, we do, Mrs. Morton,' Miss Ashcroft said quickly. 'We have a truancy policy.'

'Well, it doesn't look as if your truancy policy is working,' Jay said. 'Mrs. Kradic says Sonja didn't come home from school as usual on Monday and she's been too terrified to seek any help. If you'd contacted the family something could have been done about it days ago. I simply can't believe this has happened.'

'She didn't like school, any more than...' Debbie Flint stopped in mid-sentence and glanced at Kate, still sitting at the back of the classroom and ignoring the proceedings. 'If she's run away, Kate might know where she's gone.'

'I don't know,' Kate said, raising her eyes from her book for a moment, with a fierce expression. 'She didn't tell me anything about running away.'

'I'll make sure the education department knows that something's wrong,' Miss Ashcroft said. 'Sometimes with these asylum families, people come and go...'

'Not ten-year-olds on their own,' Jay snapped. 'I'll go and see Mrs. Kradic again and if she won't come with me to the police, then I'll go myself. This is ridiculous.' And that, after another tearful confrontation with Sonja's mother, who still refused point blank to go to the police station, was what she had done.

Deflated by her inconclusive interview with DCI Shipley, about whose professional competence she now harboured serious doubts, Jay drove up to Pendle House to arrive at work an hour after she had intended only to find a strange car parked on the gravel forecourt which Fred Marston had begun to make a desultory attempt to clear of its littered leaves and mossy patches. In the office she found Pam Bentley deep in conversation with George Hateley.

'Ah, there you are,' Hateley said, not quite jovially enough to hide the note of criticism as he threw her a thin smile and glanced at the wall clock. 'We thought we'd lost you already.'

'I got slightly delayed, Mr. Hateley,' Jay offered, as she hung up her coat.

'Oh, George, please,' Hateley came back quickly. 'We're going to be working together for many years, I hope, Jay, and after all, we're near family.'

Jay nodded, wishing the relationship was not so close.

'How's that pretty little lass of yours? Settling down, is she?'

'Not really,' Jay said. 'It's been a big upheaval for her.'

'Aye, divorce can be hard on t'little ones,' Hateley said, and Jay could not be sure how barbed the comment was.

'What can I do for you this morning?' she asked, her voice as chilly as she dared let it be with one of the museum's trustees.

'Oh, I just popped in to see how it's all going,' Hateley said. 'And to let you know that there'll be a surveyor's team coming round to look at the state of all the property. We need to know where we are with the roof and the heating system and so on before we start commissioning building work. You and Pam here come off the revenue account, but we need to be making plans for capital spending an' all. That's where the big money will go.'

'Of course,' Jay said. 'They won't disturb us if they're in the house. Fred Marston's got a set of keys to all the doors. But perhaps they could let me or Pam know in advance if they want to come tramping round here. That could be disturbing.'

'Aye, I'll pass that on,' Hateley said. 'I'll catch Fred on the way out.'

'Could you ask him to come in to see me when you find him?' Jay asked, hoping the request would not sound too much like a dismissal. She felt she had wasted too much of the morning already and did not want to encourage George

Hateley, or any of the other trustees for that matter, to think that they could pop in for a chat any time it suited them. 'I want him to bring some more boxes down from the attics for me so I can have a look at the range of the collection. So far we've only unwrapped a few of the masks.'

'Aye, you showed us them last time,' Hateley said, glancing at Jay's work table with an expression of distaste. 'Not a pretty sight. Perhaps the rest will be a bit nicer.'

'I wouldn't bank on it,' Jay said. 'Most of the written material is about ethnographic stuff. Nice isn't what a lot of those cultures went in for.'

'It makes you wonder, doesn't it?' Hateley said.

'Wonder what?' Jay snapped.

'How many people will want to come and look at all this stuff,' Hateley said, and marched out without waiting for an answer.

Jay succeeded in reaching home before Kate came out of school that afternoon, and was surprised to discover her sister's Golf parked outside the house. She got out of the car as Jay squeezed into the space behind her, right outside Mr. Booth's front door, and she was conscious, as usual, of being watched from behind the twitching curtains.

'Hi,' she greeted her sister without much enthusiasm as she opened the front door. 'This is a surprise. I don't seem to be able to escape from your family today. Your father-in-law popped in to see me at work this morning. You don't think you could tactfully tell him and his mate Grogan

206

to leave me in peace to get on with my job, do you? They're in and out of Pendle House by the minutes.'

'I'll see what I can do,' Sue said more readily than Jay had anticipated. She dumped the case full of papers she had brought home with her to read later, slipped out of her coat and waved a hand towards the kitchen.

'It's nice to see you,' she said, hoping the sentiment did not seem too belated. 'Cup of tea?'

'Yes, that would be fine,' Sue said. 'What time's Kate due back?' Jay glanced at her watch.

'Soon,' she said. 'Is this just a social call or is there something I can do for you?'

To her surprise, Sue's eyes filled with tears that she dashed away irritably.

'Sorry,' she said, and as Jay looked at her more closely and realised that she appeared pale and drained, and dressed with far less care than normal, the blue shirt under her fleece slightly grubby and faded jeans and flat shoes replacing her normal smart skirt and snag free stockings.

'Problems?' she asked, knowing from long experience that if Sue was letting her emotions show as nakedly as this it must be serious. Jay abandoned the kettle and on impulse threw her arms round her sister, something she realised, as the embrace was returned, that she had not done for years.

'What is it?' she asked, terrified that Sue might have found out that Chris had been pestering her but conscious that in that case she would have been more likely to have stormed into her house in a rage rather than in her present frazzled state.

'It's Abbie,' Sue said at last. 'I'm worried to death about her. They sent her home from school yesterday, saying she'd fainted in her gym class. She's as thin as a lath and I'm pretty sure she's been throwing up without telling me. She says there's nothing wrong, but it's obvious there is. I don't know what to do, Jay, I really don't.'

'Not pregnant then?' Jay said. 'I must say she did look pretty pale and wan last time I saw her.'

'Good God, no.' Sue looked shocked. 'She's only thirteen, for goodness sake.'

'It happens,' Jay said.

'I think it's quite the opposite,' Sue said, desperation in her eyes now. 'I'm sure she's anorexic.'

'What does Chris think?' Jay asked cautiously.

'He thinks I'm being over-anxious,' Sue said. 'He says all girls of that age diet, it's just a teenage thing, getting rid of the puppy fat. But Abbie never had any puppy fat. She's always been skinny. She's absolutely no need to diet. It's ridiculous. I kept her at home today and I've spent hours trying to get some sense out of her. But all she says is that she's fine, she eats enough, and I'm not to worry.'

'She's certainly never been fat,' Jay said, thinking that her niece still looked remarkably child-like for a thirteen year old and realising that this family crisis simmering away beneath the surface, rather than ancient grudges, might be why her sister had been so unpredictable since she had arrived back in Pendle Bridge.

'Have you tried to get her to see a doctor?' Jay suggested tentatively.

'I've tried,' Sue said. 'But she won't hear of it.'

'Oh dear,' Jay said, conscious of how she had probably misread her sister's reaction to her own situation. 'And here was I thinking I was the one whose family was falling apart while yours looked so stable.'

'Well, of course that's what I wanted you to think,' Sue said, a touch of the familiar waspish sharpness back in her voice. 'You were always little Miss Glittering Prizes, weren't you? I didn't want you to know that getting Chris wasn't such a big deal in the end. And now Abbie's going off the rails...' She shrugged helplessly.

'What went wrong with Chris?' Jay asked quietly. 'You always seemed pretty good together when David and I came up to see Mum and Dad.'

'Well, that's what I wanted you to think, of course,' Sue said, her voice harsh. 'I got used to covering up the cracks, even with Mum and Dad. The truth is, he's always played the field. And I always took him back because of the kids. But now this, with Abbie. He's useless when it comes to dealing with things like this. He'd much rather just turn a blind eye. What am I going to do about her, Jay?'

'Sit down,' Jay said, slowly. 'I think maybe if we're going to work this out, we should work things out between ourselves first.' Sue glanced away, her cheeks reddening slightly.

'It's all water under the bridge,' she said. 'It's all so long ago.'

'Everything I touch in Pendle Bridge seems to be rooted in the past,' Jay said. 'It's as if the place has put on a bright new painted face, made itself over with bells on, but it's all on the surface, and beneath the mask everything is festering with resentment and hatred because of things which happened twenty odd years ago. The more I hear about Pendle House the more it seems that all sorts of nasties have gone on there over the years. I'm even beginning to wonder if the fact that Mrs. Pertherbridge has met a violent end is connected with what went on there years ago. Someone caught up with her, maybe. It's beginning to get quite creepy. And this house which I thought was going to be fun to renovate seems to have an unpleasant history which has attracted some sort of stalker who's beginning to terrify Kate. And I can't say I find it much fun either. My life seems to be going pear-shaped just as much as yours is. But surely you and I can sort ourselves out, because as sure as hell, we're not going to be able to sort anything else out if we don't.'

'Oh, you know what our problem is,' Sue said impatiently. 'It all comes down to the same old thing. I was jealous of you all the time we were kids. You were clever, attractive, out-going and popular when I was none of those things. You even had a boyfriend I fancied like crazy. I thought that when you dumped Chris and he asked me out I'd got what I wanted. But when even that turned sour – and it didn't take long – and your marriage seemed so successful, all the old resentments came flooding back. Why do you think I insisted we stay in Pendle Bridge? I was terrified that if Chris followed his career to London or somewhere bigger, I'd be abandoned in a strange place when he finally left me. And I was sure he'd do that in the end. You have no idea, no idea at all, how much I've disliked you over the years.'

'Oh, Sue,' Jay said. 'That's awful.'

'Mum knows,' Sue said. 'She always knew but nothing she tried to do about it made much difference. Dad thought you were the most wonderful thing that had ever happened to him and hardly even noticed I was there.'

Jay cast herself back to her schooldays and had to accept the truth of at least some of what Sue was saying. She and her father had been close, sharing a passion for history which had taken her to university and into the world of museums. She still missed him every day.

'I didn't realise how you were being hurt,' she said. 'Can you believe that?'

'Oh, yes,' Sue said. 'That was part of the problem. You and Dad didn't even notice.'

It was true, Jay thought. She was sparing with her emotional commitments but when she gave them she gave them totally. She had been wrapped in the warmth of her father's attention, then of Chris's, and then finally David's. She doubted whether she would ever be so bold again. All she had left to give would be given to Kate. She hesitated, wondering whether to tell Sue that Chris seemed to be hoping to pull her again, but the decision was taken for her by the raucous peal of the old front door-bell.

'That'll be Katie,' she said, getting up to open the door. 'We must talk again soon,' she said. 'You must do something about Abbie. You can't just let it drift on. If she's anorexic she needs help now.'

'I know,' Sue said. It was with a shock of recognition that Jay realised as she faced Kate on the doorstep just how pale and pinched she had become. The cousins, she thought guiltily, seemed to be heading in the same direction.

'No news of Sonja?' she asked quietly in the hallway as Kate dropped her bag and took her coat off. Kate shook her head miserably.

'A policeman came,' she whispered. 'He asked us all sorts of questions in class.'

'Good,' Jay said, pleased that something she had done that day seemed to have borne fruit. 'Your Auntie Sue's here, darling.' But when she ushered Kate into the living room with a protective arm round her shoulder, Kate's greeting to her aunt was distant and Sue flashed Jay a questioning glance.

'Would you like to come and stay with your cousins again at the weekend?' she asked. 'I could pick you up after school tomorrow.' Kate shrugged.

'Maybe,' she said, without enthusiasm.

'I'll talk to your mum on the telephone,' Sue said. 'I must go now. Ben will be home from school soon and I usually meet him off the bus.' When her aunt had gone, Kate glanced cautiously at the back door.

'Can I look at my frogspawn?' Kate asked. Jay unlocked it and went into the yard herself first, just to make sure that there were no unexpected surprises to freak Kate out again, but all was peaceful, the daffodils Jay had planted in pots

212

and carefully transported from London were tightly in bud in their sheltered corner and Kate rushed to survey her incipient tadpoles with something approaching pleasure.

But later that evening Kate threw down her book and snuggled up to her mother on the sofa in a way which was rare these days. Jay bent down to kiss the dark curls.

'Mum,' Kate said slowly. 'The policeman who came to school kept asking us if we thought Sonja had run away. But I don't think she's run away. She's not like that. She's very nervous because she doesn't know many people and because she can't talk good English.'

'Did she ever mention running away?' Jay asked.

'No, of course not,' Kate said. 'That's what the policeman asked, and I told him that she'd have told me about it if that's what she was going to do. I'm her friend. We tell each other things.'

'And do you think he believed you?'

'I don't know,' Kate said. 'He did ask about the man in the car, though, so perhaps he did.'

Jay's stomach tightened and she hugged Kate closer to her.

'Have you seen this man in the car?' she asked.

'I think so,' Kate said. 'And some of the others have too. He drives down Victoria Street at coming home time sometimes, very slowly. The policeman asked us all about him and about the colour of the car but some people said it was blue and I thought it was green, so it was all a bit muddly. And James O'Malley said he was wearing a hat and some other people said, no, he was in an anorak sort of thing with the hood up, and someone said he had a green face, but that's silly, isn't it. Some of the boys are very silly sometimes.'

'Well, maybe it's not the same man each time,' Jay said with as much certainty as she could muster. 'Maybe it is just different cars doing different things. But if anyone stops to talk to you...'

'Mum, I know, I know,' Kate said angrily. 'I can run very fast, you know.'

'I'm sure you can,' Jay said, but she wondered whether Sonja had tried to run and not been fast enough. She shivered and cuddled Kate closer.

'Come on,' she said. 'It's your bed time. Do you want cocoa?'

'I can make it,' Kate said, jumping up with her most grown-up face on.

'Do you want to go and stay with Ben and Abbie this weekend?' Jay asked, when Kate returned with a steaming mug and she was surprised to see her daughter's face fall again.

'I don't think so,' Kate said.

'I thought you got on well with Ben.'

'I do,' Kate said. 'But I don't think Abbie's very nice really. She teases Ben and me.'

'Her mum says she's not very happy at the moment,' Jay said. 'Perhaps you can cheer her up a bit.'

Kate looked doubtful at that.

'You don't have to go if you don't want to,' Jay said. 'Perhaps if the weather's good you and I can go somewhere together instead. How about that?'

'Yes, please,' Kate said. But after sipping for a while, she glanced at her mother again.

'I loved my granddad very much,' she said. 'I really miss him now he's not here any more.'

'So do I, sweetheart,' Jay said.

'It's funny, because I don't think Abbie likes her other granddad at all.'

'You mean Uncle Chris's dad?' Jay asked, surprised. 'I'm sure that's not true.'

'It is, you know,' Kate said, draining her mug and jumping to her feet again. 'I don't like him either. I think he's creepy.'

13

Jay sat at her work-table toying with a cup of coffee. She had slept badly, lying awake for hours listening to her daughter's regular breathing through the two doors which she now kept ajar at night. She no longer felt secure in the cottage and although there had been no further harassment since Kate had found the mask hanging on the front door, she jumped every time the phone rang and regularly woke during the night, her heart thumping with incipient panic. She had no idea what had prompted this malevolence against the two of them but it was vile and she knew they could not stay where they were. Kate was turning into a ghost of her former self. She was due to visit her father at half-term and Jay knew he would be horrified at the change in her. By then she would have to have decided what to do next. She could, she thought, just about reconcile herself to looking for another house but she was not at all sure that would be enough to stop whoever it was who was making their lives a misery. What she had so far found impossible to contemplate was giving up this new life completely, admitting that her move back to Pendle Bridge had been a mistake, and that she should go back to the south which was where, she was beginning to suspect, she belonged. She was not used to failing and this was turning into the biggest failure of her life.

Thoroughly dispirited, she turned back to the papers on the desk in front of her and began to sort through them again. Suddenly she realised that she had at last stumbled across a useful piece of the jigsaw she was laboriously trying to assemble. There, risen to the top of the pile as if by magic, in the neat handwriting which she knew belonged to a Wright family member who had travelled in the Americas in the 1930s, was a list of the native masks he had acquired in British Colombia, each described in detail, and attributed to its village and tribe.

'Eureka!' Jay said, so enthusiastically that Pam Bentley, who was working at the computer in the next room, glanced up.

'Something interesting?' she asked.

'You could say,' Jay said. 'I've actually discovered where the masks came from. And, incidentally, how many there should be in the collection.'

'Ugh, those awful things,' Pam muttered, and Jay wondered, not for the first time, exactly why Pam had been so anxious to obtain a job working with objects she obviously disliked so much.

'There's likely to be even more horrific things than this up there,' she said. 'Shrunken heads at the very least. They're the sort of things the Victorians loved.'

'Real heads?'

''Fraid so,' Jay said. 'Collectors thought nothing of stealing people's ancestors in the nineteenth century. Much more grisly than the masks, which are just art.'

'I suppose so,' Pam said, but she did not look thrilled.

'Have you seen Fred this morning?' Jay asked, but Pam just shrugged.

'He's over in the house, I think. He was mumbling something about looking at the boiler.'

'Right,' Jay said, pulling on her jacket. She strolled round to the front of Pendle House and up the steps to the front door, which she found unlocked. Inside, pale spring sunshine was filtering through the stained glass of the huge almost ecclesiastical landing windows and throwing patches of colour onto the tiled floor. The front of the house, where the main windows were still boarded up, was in semi-darkness and seemed quiet and deserted, but she could hear faint sounds from further back which she tracked to what had been the main servants' kitchen at the foot of the back stairs. There she found Fred, in blue overalls, on his knees beside the heavy old-fashioned radiator beneath the window. He glanced up as she came in without much enthusiasm.

'They're bloody barmy if they think they can get this system running again,' he said. 'It's all corroded. Put the pump on and you'll have a flood from t'attics to cellars.'

'They look like the original radiators,' Jay said.

'Aye, they put a new boiler in, oil instead of the great coke thing they used to have down below. That's out there in t'back yard with the oil tank. But they've replaced nowt else as far as I can see since about nineteen hundred. Bloody miracle it hasn't flooded the place already.'

Jay wandered into a further scullery where the

window gave only onto a small cobbled yard, green with moss and algae, which she had not known existed. Access was by a door which led down a flight of steps at the side of what was obviously a relatively new boiler house.

'So there are cellars as well,' she said. 'They didn't store any treasures down there, did they?'

'Nowt that I know of,' Marston said, getting back to his feet with something approaching a groan. 'They'll have rotted away by now if they did. It's damp since they disconnected the old boiler.' He nodded towards the painted panelling beneath the stairwell which, Jay could see when she looked closely, was relatively new. 'There used to be a door there, but they blocked it off to keep the kids out. There's a cellar door down there in t'yard, that's been kept locked for years, and the yard gate was always kept locked an' all to keep the little beggars away from t'boiler room.'

'Very wise, I should think,' Jay said. 'Now I've a job for you, Fred, if that's OK? I need all the boxes out of that farthest room in the attic, the ones with the masks in. I've found a proper inventory for those so I want them over in the work room to check over against the list.'

'Peculiar bloody things they are,' Marston grumbled. 'You reckon folk'll take time to come and look at them, do you?'

'I certainly hope so,' Jay said sharply, wondering quite how she had acquired two assistants with so little enthusiasm for the project she was engaged on. She was beginning to realise that one of the problems with setting up this museum might be professional isolation and it was far too early yet to encourage any of her London colleagues to come up and help evaluate the artefacts she was only beginning to sort out.

'When you're ready, Fred,' she said, slightly wearily, leaving the caretaker packing up his plumbing tools with ill grace.

It was lunchtime before Fred Marston eventually arrived with the tea chests on a trolley, and almost time to go home by the time Jay had carefully untangled every single mask from its protective paper wrapping, watched warily by Pam Bentley. Placing the last technicolor bird head on the table Jay counted them quickly, but she knew she was merely confirming her initial impression. Edmund Wright's meticulous list of his acquisitions in Canada included descriptions of thirty six masks. Arrayed on her work table in all their malevolent splendour, Jay found herself with only thirty. Six of the masks were missing, and one of them was the terrifying example of tribal art which Kate had come face-to-face with fastened to the Adelaide Street front door, and which was now carefully wrapped up in one of her kitchen cupboards.

'We've been robbed,' Jay said quietly.

'Who on earth would want to steal those horrible things?' Pam asked.

'I wish I knew,' Jay said. 'And I wish I knew just what they wanted them for.'

'Not exactly something you'd want to wake up to in the morning, are they?'

Jay shook her head, although she realised suddenly that waking up in the morning to a

220

vision of masks was exactly what she had been doing recently, and that possibly Kate was doing the same. She glanced at her watch and realised that it was time she left.

'Cover the whole lot up with the wrapping paper, could you, Pam?' she asked, as she took her coat off its hook. 'We don't want to frighten anyone looking in through the window.'

'I'll be having nightmares myself at this rate,' Pam said, picking up some of the discarded sheets of paper with a shudder. 'I didn't know what I was letting myself in for with this museum.'

Jay drove home thoughtfully, aware of her next door neighbour watching as usual as she manoeuvred her car into its parking space. The old man opened his front door and peered out as she put her key in the lock.

'All right, then?' he said. 'Not late today?' Jay nodded bleakly.

'She can always wait here wi' me if you're late again,' Booth said. 'It's no trouble. She's a bonny little lass.'

'Thank you Mr. Booth, but that won't be necessary,' Jay said, recalling what one of her neighbours had suggested about the old man, probably no more than a nasty malicious bit of speculation on the woman's part, but with Kate she would take no chances.

'Aye, well, you don't want her waiting for you out on t'street, do you?' Booth said sharply. 'There's all sorts about these days, you know.'

Jay went inside and shut her door firmly, before the anger which had threatened to overwhelm her made her say something to her neighbour

221

that she knew she would regret.

'Bloody, bloody hell,' she said to herself, flinging her briefcase onto the sofa and wrenching off her coat. 'What right's that nosy old bugger got to criticise.' But she knew exactly why she was so furious with Booth, and it was nothing to do with the loneliness of a probably harmless old man. Willing herself to calm down, she sat with a cup of tea waiting for Kate, constantly tempted to go to the door as the minutes ticked by to see if she was coming down the street but determined to resist her own paranoia. But when Kate finally rang the front door-bell and flung herself into the house, Jay found no respite from the horrors which seemed to be engulfing them. Kate was pink faced and breathless and took a moment or two to explain why she had been running so hard.

'There was a car, Mum,' she said at last. 'This man in a car stopped and asked me to get in.'

'When? Where?' Jay gasped, almost speechless herself with shock.

'Just now,' Kate said. 'And Mum, he was wearing a mask. Not like the coloured ones, the painted ones. A wooden mask, pale, just with holes for the eyes...'

'But with eyebrows?' Jay said, her mouth dry, recognising the description of one of the missing masks from Pendle House. 'Black eyebrows?'

'Yes, yes,' Kate said. 'How did you know? It had big black eyebrows. Scary eyebrows.'

'I think, darling, we must go to the police, so you can tell them all about this.'

Kate stared at her, her eyes reduced to dark

sockets in her pale face.

'Is it the man who's taken Sonja?' she asked, her voice small and thin.

'I really don't know, Katie,' Jay said. 'I don't think I know what's going on any more. But we need the police to help us. We really do.'

Donna hung her work skirt and jacket carefully in her new wardrobe, stripped off her tights and put on her faded tracksuit, socks and trainers ready for her evening run. She would have to find a new route tonight, she thought, now she was settled in her bed-sit much further up the hill and away from the road which had taken her regularly past Pendle House and onto the open moors. But from here, she thought, she ought to be able to find the footpaths which had led to one of her other favourite walks as a child. Kenny had led them this way from the park where they usually met, past his own house, which she knew was only a couple of streets away, and out past the cricket field and down to Threshfield woods. She was not sure of the route, but starting from Kenny's street, she was sure she could find it again. She generally avoided conversation with anyone she did not know so she was not going to ask. She would explore until she found a way which would allow her to jog for the regulation four miles she set herself, and as far away from other people as she could get.

The bedsit was shabby and the furniture minimal but it was on Victoria Road which was where she had decided she wanted to be. Now all her modest possessions were neatly put away she smoothed down the faded bedcover and felt almost content. If you have slept in freezing shop doorways, and beneath stinking railway arches, she thought, a comfortable bed was all you really needed to make life bearable. She half-smiled at Mags and Archie, who ran with her every evening now. 'We're getting there,' she said as she closed her door and locked it carefully behind her.

'Sorry?' a voice said close behind her, making her jump and her heart thud uncomfortably. She spun round and found herself face to face with a young man in a red anorak who was coming up the stairs she was about to descend. She muttered something under her breath and pushed roughly past the man who, off balance, grabbed the banister for support and watched the thin figure of the woman in the tracksuit hurry down the stairs and out of the front door, slamming it behind her.

'Charming,' he said as he opened his own door off the same landing as Donna's room. 'Nice to know you too.'

She jogged steadily to the corner of Adelaide Street where she turned, slowing only slightly as she passed Kenny's house. The curtains were not drawn at the living room window and Donna could see the child inside watching television. Lucky child, with a mother of her own and no father in sight, she thought. She must try harder to find Kenny, she decided, as she speeded up again. Perhaps the Morton woman knew something that she could be persuaded to reveal. But although she longed to see Kenny again, he was not her main priority. Tracing the birdmen had to take priority. And every time the high-pitched child's voice whispered in her ear, reminding her that she was to blame for everything that had happened, the more urgent her search became.

She jogged on and by a process of trial and error, deceived more than once by the rows of modern houses which had sprung up on the outskirts of the town over the previous twenty years, Donna eventually found the muddy path down to Threshfield woods. It was a cold evening, already getting dark by the time she reached the stream, and she passed no one on the way. Panting, she sat down on a rock close to the rushing water and hung her head for a moment between her knees. The air was sharp and fresh, lights and noise from Pendle Bridge reduced to no more than a background murmur and a misty yellow glow as the street lights came on. The faint noises behind her in the low bushes and amongst the scattered twigs and leaves were more real than anything else as the wood woke up to its nocturnal existence.

She felt Mags and Archie very close to her in the shadows. But she was agitated tonight, and their presence was not a comforting one. Buying her supper in the corner shop close to where she now lived, she had overheard people talking about a missing child, and a wave of nausea had seized her stomach, as it always did when such cases penetrated the cocoon within which she normally functioned. Earlier, when she had got back to the bedsit she had scanned the week's *Advertiser,* which she had brought home with her, but could find nothing about the girl. Perhaps she had imagined the whispers she had heard, but she thought not. It was close, local, and they would search for this child, she guessed, although no one had ever searched for her. Perhaps the same people were still doing the same things, the people she knew were still in Pendle Bridge. And this too, the thin little voice which lurked outside the window had insisted, was all her fault. She was to blame.

'It's time to finish it,' she whispered, feeling a pressure building inside her chest which was nothing to do with her run, but just as exhilarating. 'Soon, very soon,' she said. She did not believe in coincidence or fate or God, but she knew that so far she had been very lucky. Mags and Archie were with her and perhaps something else. She deserved it, she thought. Surely over all those hellish years she had earned some sort of justice, though she had never for a moment believed she would achieve it until she had bumped into Laurie Wishaw that one last time.

It was not long after she had come out of the hospital in London for the first time and had begun to try to build a normal life for herself that Donna had come across Laurie again. She had been going up the escalator at Tottenham Court Road tube station on her way to the college where she had begun to study when she caught a glimpse of a face she thought she recognised going the other way. She could not believe it and flung herself onto the down escalator in pursuit, pushing past travellers on her right as she tried to catch up with the man she thought she knew. He was older of course, she realised that as she caught another glimpse of him in the corridor leading to the Northern Line, just as she was older and probably unrecognisable too. She had grown from a skinny child into a tall slim woman. She had changed her hair colour as well as her name, and wore glasses which she had not needed when she was ten. But she knew that the man she was following was undoubtedly Lawrence Wishaw, with shorter hair, a classy jacket, an almost jaunty tread, and she knew immediately what she had to do, even without Archie's prompting, because she was dutifully taking her medication then and Archie was a rare visitor even when she needed him most.

And when it came to it, it turned out to be laughably simple: the crowded platform, the dim lighting close to the tunnel entrance where he had chosen quite unwittingly to stand, the rush of stale air and then the roar of the approaching train and then not his scream, but hers as he fell, arms flailing, eyes meeting the appalled stare of the driver as he slammed on the brakes. She had screamed and screamed until, still sobbing hysterically, she explained to anyone who would listen – horrified onlookers, the station staff and eventually the police – how she had thought she was going to be pulled under too. They believed her. Why would they not? She and the dead man were obviously strangers, one of a million couples who brushed casually against each other for a few seconds and then ricocheted away again into the anonymous dark of the city. No one in the crowd of tired commuters with their minds on work or lovers or children or the drink they would pour themselves when they got home had noticed Donna's boot connect hard with Lawrence Wishaw's ankle as the train approached nor how she had dodged the despairing hand he had reached out in her direction as he fell. No one had noticed and no one, she concluded, had really cared. Laurie had gone to hell where he belonged and even when she forgot to take her pills and the voices offered their litany of curses and accusations as they usually did, she always knew that she was not the guilty one at all. He was. And he had got what he deserved. So would all the rest – however long it took.

Donna got up quickly and stretched, realising that the darkness was overtaking her and that the jog back up the hill from the woods would be perilous if she did not hurry. Clever girl, Archie whispered, as she got back into her stride on the narrow path between the darkening fields. Not long now, clever girl.

Jay sat up late that night, her mind racing on an overdose of dread and bafflement. She had left the living room door ajar and every now and again she got up from her chair to stand at the bottom of the stairs. She had chased Kate to bed early but she could still hear her tossing around, not awake but evidently dreaming. Her one desire now was to get the child away from Adelaide Street but Kate had refused point blank to go to stay with Chris and Sue for the weekend, and even in extremis Jay was still reluctant to call her ex-husband and ask him to make space for his daughter a good two weeks before her planned half-term visit. He had adamantly opposed her move to Pendle Bridge and she did not think she could stand the humiliation of his 'I told you so' stare. In any case, she did not think that David would agree to having his newly minted coupledom disrupted by a sulky and semi-traumatised child.

Jay had not realised quite how awkward Kate had become until she sat with her at the police station, in the supposedly relaxing surroundings of the 'rape suite', opposite a sympathetic plainclothes officer who tried tactfully to prise out of Kate exactly what had happened on the way home from school. The haunted look never left Kate's eyes but she provided little in the way of hard facts and it was obvious that the policewoman found her frustrating to interview.

'Did you notice what the man was wearing?' she asked, but Kate simply shook her head again.

'So what about the car? Can you remember what colour it was, Kate? Try hard for me, sweetie. We need to find this man so he doesn't scare anyone else, don't we?'

'I think it was blue,' Kate had mumbled. 'Or maybe green.'

'Do you know about cars, Kate? Do you know what make it might have been?'

But Kate simply shook her head. She herself would be hard pushed to name the make of a strange car, Jay had thought. Attempts to draw the car and the mask had borne little fruit either and the policewoman had grown dispirited. She sent Kate outside into the corridor to get a packet of crisps from the vending machine.

'She may be willing to tell you more later on,' she said to Jay. 'She's obviously pretty upset by the incident.'

'She's very upset by the disappearance of her friend Sonja Kradic as well,' Jay said. 'Is there any news about her?'

'We've issued poster appeals, and done all the obvious searches – parks, waste ground, and so on,' the policewoman said. 'But I don't think there are any new leads. There's hundreds of square miles of open moorland out there, you know. She wouldn't be the first to be buried up there and never found. It's a pity her parents didn't report her missing much sooner.'

'It's a pity families like the Kradic's are so scared of the police,' Jay said sharply. 'But this could be the same man who stopped Katie, couldn't it?'

'Of course it could,' the policewoman agreed. 'But who is he? And why would he have one of the masks from your museum? It's very strange.'

'If I hadn't found the inventory today I wouldn't have known there was a definite connection,' Jay said. 'I've only just discovered that some of the masks are missing.'

'I'll pass all that on to the DCI. I'm sure he'll want to talk to you himself. In the meantime, if Kate comes up with any more details about the man in the car, please let me know. She may be so shocked at the moment that things have gone out of her mind but they'll come back to her with time.'

And with that Jay had to be content. On the way home Kate was silent and withdrawn until they turned into Adelaide Street.

'Can we go and see Sonja's mum?' she whispered then. Jay hesitated for a second and then shook her head. The police, she assumed, would tell Sonja's family about the new developments and she did not want Kate upset any further tonight.

'Tomorrow,' she promised, relieved that the next day was Saturday and Kate would not have to face school. 'It's too late for you now.'

But it wasn't over even when Jay had double locked the front door and rested her head against the wood briefly to hide her tears. She knew someone had been into the house again as soon as she switched on the living room light. She always left the place tidy before she went to work, but this evening it was even tidier than usual. Books had been straightened, newspapers pressed into creases far sharper than she normally made, the ornaments on the mantelpiece regimented into straight lines. It was almost as if whoever was coming into the house wanted her to know that they had been there. She glanced at Kate, who had switched on the TV and noticed nothing unusual, and gritted her teeth. She could not distress the child any more than she had already been distressed, and the police were as likely to laugh at her as take her seriously. But deep inside, where no one could hear, she screamed for help.

It was late by the time Jay had helped a semi-conscious ten-year-old from the sofa where she had almost drifted to sleep and persuaded her up the stairs, undressed her and tucked her up beneath the duvet.

'Don't leave me, Mum,' Kate whispered, and Jay sat by her bedside until she slipped away again into a restless sleep.

Downstairs again she poured herself a Scotch and flung herself into a chair, fighting back the first tears since Kate had come home from school.

'Who can hate us so much?' she asked herself. 'And why?' But she found no answer either in her glass or the unresponsive cottage in which she had invested such high hopes.

14

Saturday dawned wet and cold and Jay, exhausted by another bad night's sleep, and hung over from one Scotch too many, had no suggestions to distract Kate from children's television. Jay left her daughter curled up on the sofa in her pyjamas to walk down to the newsagents on the corner to buy a morning paper. By now she had been into the cramped little shop often enough to elicit a shy smile from Mr. Patel, the newsagent and all-hours grocer, who was pinning a poster to the noticeboard in his window. With a sharply indrawn breath, Jay recognised Sonja Kradic's face.

'You must see a lot of the school children in here,' she said. 'My daughter was stopped last night by a man in a car.'

Mr. Patel shook his head mournfully. He was a heavy man who had difficulty fitting into the narrow space behind his counter.

'It's a bad business,' he said. 'It reminds me of that little girl who was killed when I first came here. The boy who killed her lived quite close, you know?'

'In my house, as it happens,' Jay said wryly. 'Though there still seems to be some doubt that he really did it.'

Mr. Patel looked at her curiously.

'I had to answer a lot of questions about that

boy,' he said quietly. 'They said he read my adult magazines.' He glanced at his top shelf, where the usual pornography was wrapped in cellophane, with a slightly shamefaced expression.

'And did he?' Jay asked, her attention seized in spite of her more urgent preoccupations.

'I don't know what he read, but I know what he bought, and it was not those. He always came in with the exact money in an envelope with what he wanted written down. I think his mother did that for him. He was not a very bright boy.'

'Not bright enough to go wandering round the town looking for that sort of magazine?'

'I don't think so, no,' Mr. Patel said.

'Did you have to give evidence at the trial?' Jay asked.

'No, I never did. The police spoke to me but they never came back again, and the next thing I knew was that the boy was in court and they said he had confessed, so I thought no more about it. It was a dreadful thing to do to a child.'

'It was, but some people still think Kenny Bairstow was innocent,' Jay said.

'So maybe he was,' Mr. Patel said. 'To me here he was just a big boy with a small mind. He bought comics and sweets like a younger child. Nothing more. But it's all a long time ago. Too late to change anything now.'

'Perhaps you're right,' Jay said, and as she walked slowly back home up Adelaide Street she found she could no longer summon up any indignation on Kenny Bairstow's behalf. She had too many more urgent things on her mind.

It was almost noon and she was beginning to

prepare vegetables to make soup when the front door-bell rang, making her start in a reaction out of all proportion to the sound.

'Mu-u-um,' Kate wailed from the sitting room. 'There's a man at the door.' Jay glanced out of the window and recognised DCI Peter Shipley trying in vain to find a little shelter from the relentless rain. She let him in in a state of mixed irritation and relief.

'Sorry to bother you on a Saturday morning,' Shipley said. 'But we're working all the hours God sends...'

'Come in,' Jay said, thinking the policeman looked like a more than usually crumpled Columbo with his soaking wet mac and sodden hair. He was, she thought, a curiously old-fashioned man that modern high tech policing seemed to have passed by, although she guessed that appearances might be deceptive. 'Let me hang your coat up somewhere to dry. It's a filthy morning. Come into the kitchen and I'll make some coffee. Kate's watching television and I don't want to disturb her. She's had enough to put up with just recently.'

Shipley followed her through without comment, and took a seat at the kitchen table as Jay put on the kettle and assembled coffee. The policeman looked tired and dispirited, she thought as she took in the dark circles under his eyes and the skin which looked even greyer than the last time she had seen him. That makes two of us, she thought, as she brushed her hair away from her face wearily. She took the chair opposite him when she had passed him a mug and pushed the sugar basin in his direction. He took two large spoonfuls and a grateful sip of the hot liquid before he spoke.

'These masks,' he said. 'Uniform tell me that some of the collection's missing. Is that right?'

'The inventories are a complete mess, but on Friday I found a detailed list of the mask collection and checked it against what we had. Six are missing. One of those described matches the one someone hung on the front door here. And from what Kate says the man – person, I suppose – who stopped her in a car on the way home from school was wearing one of the others. Something very nasty and very odd is going on here, Inspector Shipley, and what really scares me is that it might be connected with Sonja's disappearance.'

'Tell me about the masks,' Shipley said, ignoring Jay's speculation completely. 'Where were they kept?'

'Up in the attics with the rest of the stuff. There are eight rooms up there, with all the artefacts packed in tea chests and boxes. It's been like that since the house was converted into a children's home in the late 1970s, apparently. All the Wright family treasures were packed away and stored up there, and a door was put on the bottom of the attic stairs so that in theory the kids couldn't get access. It seems to have worked reasonably well. Most of the boxes are intact. But at the far end of the attic corridor there's a room where the masks were stored and that had been disturbed. Some of the masks had been taken out and were left lying around, and now I have a list of what's supposed to be there, I know that half a dozen of them are actually missing.'

'Are they valuable, these things?'

'Not intrinsically,' Jay said. 'They're not decorated with anything precious. They're basically painted wooden carvings with a few bits of hair or straw attached. As a collection dating back to the early twentieth century they have some value, I suppose, but I'd have to ask an expert to put a price on them.'

'So you wouldn't steal them to make money?' Shipley persisted.

'No way,' Jay said. 'And if you did you'd steal the lot, not just a few of them. They're more valuable as a collection than separately.'

'So why would anyone take them?'

'I'd have thought that was pretty obvious,' Jay said dryly. 'You saw one of them in my office. Look at this. It's even more scary.' She went to the cupboard where she had put the mask which had been attached to the front door and unwrapped it from its protective newspaper. She held it up in front of her face for a moment until Shipley recoiled slightly.

'This one was used to frighten us,' Jay said. 'If the man in the car was wearing another it would serve the same purpose, with the added advantage of providing a perfect disguise.'

'That's a pretty scary item,' Shipley said.

'Most of them are intended to be,' Jay said. 'They're part of the myths and legends of the tribes, used for acting out some fairly grim stories. This one's a cannibal bird. It eats its own young and, some myths say, human young as well.'

237

'So who could have got access to these things at Pendle House?'

'Anybody who was in the house over the last thirty years,' Jay said flatly. 'I don't know when they were taken. No one does. We might never have known they'd gone if I hadn't unearthed the inventory. But whoever has them has decided to use them to terrorise me and Kate, so perhaps the theft is recent. And I'm quite sure that someone is coming into this house while we're out, but I can't actually give you anything to prove it. All I want is for you to find whoever's doing this and get them to stop.'

'I'll get someone to look into it,' Shipley said. He glanced at Jay curiously.

'You sound as if you're beginning to regret coming back to Yorkshire,' he said. Jay shrugged slightly.

'It's not turning out to be a breeze,' she said. 'Are you any closer to finding Sonja?'

'We're going to launch a major search on the moors,' Shipley said, his face grim. 'But you know the history of looking for bodies up there. And after all this time, it's probably a body we're looking for.'

Jay glanced towards the living room but the television sound was still turned up high and Kate evidently oblivious.

'She was an unhappy little girl,' she said. 'I think she and Kate were the odd ones out at school. Friends in need, that sort of thing. I suppose she could have run away.'

'The family's here illegally. Immigration want them out, but I've persuaded them they can't move till we sort out the child, one way or another. Even if she's run away time's running out. You either find kids quickly or you find them dead. Sometimes you don't find them at all.'

'Oh God,' Jay said. 'That poor woman.'

'I must go, Mrs. Morton,' DCI Shipley said, getting to his feet, looking even more tired than when he arrived, if that were possible. 'I've a Press conference later about the Petherbridge case.'

'Of course,' Jay said, remembering Mary Petherbridge, whose violent death had slipped to the back of her mind. 'Are you making any progress on that?'

'Not a lot,' Shipley said, his creased face even more mournful. 'Some forensic leads maybe. Some hairs on her dressing gown which might give us DNA. We thought they might be animal hairs at first, but apparently not. But we need a suspect for that to be any use.'

'I suppose the Kenny Bairstow conviction was before you had DNA testing, was it?' Jay asked, knowing she was pushing her luck again with Shipley.

'Long before,' he snapped, unexpectedly reinvigorated by the obviously unwelcome question.

'And you won't have kept any samples to check against now?'

'You must be joking,' Shipley said, so dismissively that Jay knew she was wasting her time. 'But if we're talking forensics, can I take this mask for testing? It's a bit old-fashioned, maybe, but someone might have left a fingerprint on it. Would you be willing to give us your prints for comparison?'

239

'You'll certainly find mine and Kate's on there,' Jay said. 'But yes, of course you can have it, if it will help.'

'It might.'

'Quite honestly I'll be glad to have it out of the house. It's beginning to give me nightmares. I meant to take it back to Pendle House but I didn't want to get it out when Kate was around so it got left here.' She wrapped the mask up again and found a carrier bag large enough to contain it and handed it to Shipley. She glanced towards the living room again and lowered her voice.

'So you're not hopeful of finding Sonja?' she asked. 'The girl who disappeared from Pendle House was never found, was she? It can happen? I need to know what to tell Kate, you see?'

'We're pulling out all the stops,' Shipley said. 'But yes, it can happen. People vanish and are never found, even children. And it doesn't help that they're asylum seekers. People don't like them. They're less willing to help than they would be normally.'

'That's awful,' Jay said. 'A missing child is a missing child.'

'You'd think so, Mrs. Morton, but it isn't necessarily so. Blonde, blue-eyed and photogenic's best if you want help from the public, preferably with two parents in a nice semi-detached who'll look good on television.'

'Dear God,' Jay said, appalled as much by Shipley's matter-of-fact tone as by his analysis which she was sure was accurate enough. The tabloid newspapers, she thought, had spread their bile well.

'Which reminds me, there was something else I wanted to ask you,' Shipley said. 'When you saw Mary Petherbridge, did you get the impression she was anxious or frightened at all? Did she seem like a woman in fear of her life?'

'She was certainly tense,' Jay said thoughtfully, trying to recollect the detail of the single conversation she had had with the dead woman which had made her so angry at the time. 'A bit jumpy, maybe, but I just put that down to her being back at Pendle House and being reminded of what had happened there. Not what I would call frightened, no. She did get very angry when she talked about the dead girl, what was she called, Mags?'

'Mags Emmet,' Shipley said. 'You mean angry about the murder?'

'No, more angry about what Mags and her friend, the one who disappeared, got up to before the murder. They were obviously running wild and she couldn't control them. She said something about them killing her cat. It all sounded very odd.'

'Donna Latham,' Shipley said. 'There's another child no one made much effort to find when she disappeared. Family violence, in care, out-of-control, vanished. There's thousands of them out there, Mrs. Morton, believe me. We'd need three times as many officers to make even a tiny impact on the missing person problem. It's huge, and a lot of them are technically children, though I doubt they think of themselves that way. Bolshie teenagers most of them, like Mags and Donna –

into sex and drugs and rock and roll. Of course, we prioritise the younger ones, like your Sonja, but some of those we never find. It's a fact of life.'

'Have you told Mrs. Kradic that?' Jay asked sharply.

'I've told her,' Shipley said. 'And I've told her we'll do everything we can. Don't get me wrong. We're not giving up on Sonja. Not yet any road. We've another TV appeal tonight. We may strike lucky.'

'I hope so,' Jay said, glancing in at Kate as she handed DCI Shipley his sodden coat and saw him to the door. 'Kate will be devastated if she's not found soon. I'm not sure we'll be able to stay in Pendle Bridge if that happens.'

'Chris Hateley's not enough attraction then?' Shipley asked, glancing sideways at her as he pulled up his collar and stepped out into the rain again.

'What did you say?' Jay asked sharply. 'What the hell did you say?' But Shipley had turned towards his car and did not look back. Jay slammed the door hard and pressed her head against the woodwork to conceal her fury from Kate, who had glanced round at her raised voice. Just what, she wondered, did Chris think he was doing and how could he have the gall to discuss her with Shipley, who might be his friend but was to her a total stranger. Suddenly all the worries of the last few weeks seemed to rise around her like a tide and threaten to drown her. She felt a hand on her arm and turned to find Kate behind her, looking anxious.

'Mum, are you all right?' she asked.

Jay took a deep breath and kissed the top of her daughter's head.

'I'm fine,' she said, swallowing hard. 'The police have taken that awful mask away and are going to find the person who left it on the door. I'm fine. You're fine. Everything is going to be OK.'

She was becoming, she thought, an accomplished liar, and she hated it.

Donna and Mags. Mags and Donna. They ran, step for step and breath for breath, up the steep hill beyond Pendle House, past the allotments, over the cattle grid and out onto the open moorland road beyond. There was not much time for a serious run before the early spring twilight fell and they had begun taking their running kit to work with them so that they could get onto the road while it was still light. Saturday was an easier day and they had planned an early start after lunch, yet one distraction after another seemed to have slowed them down and by the time they reached the top of the steep climb out of town a steady stream of cars was passing them, some with headlights already on to light up the misty gloom, as they breasted the last rise before the summit where they usually rested for five minutes before turning back to town. Not commuters heading home to their suburban villages today, they thought. More likely shoppers jubilantly making off with their loot from one of the massive shopping centres which dotted the Pennine valleys these days. Living as she had lived, Donna had passed the shopping culture by, and resented the fact that even up here in the north there seemed to be no proper country any more. Everything was scrubbed and tended to within an inch of its life, even in what used to be the wild country she had roamed as a child. Barns had been converted and cottages restored with all mod cons, two bathrooms and a conservatory and not a hint of a muckheap in sight. Even Mrs. Cuddly Clough's place had evidently ceased to be a farm they had discovered, when out of curiosity they took a bus out to where Donna had so briefly lived. The five bar gate was painted white, the farm track gravelled, and the fields where the sheep had grazed were occupied by a couple of ponies and a set of modest jumps. Donna had smiled faintly, wondering what had become of the two heavy-limbed docile boys she had despised so thoroughly. Long gone, she thought, leaving the sheep in exchange for some factory job some-where else – long gone, unlike *him*.

They sat for a moment on a remnant of dilapi-dated dry stone wall at the crest of the moor, heads between knees, panting companionably.

'Come on,' Donna said to her companion at last. 'We need to get back in time to watch the news on the telly.' The fate of the little girl who had disappeared was beginning to obsess them and they glanced across the rolling expanse of heather and scrub in front of them, purple and violet now beneath the heavy cloud, wondering if Sonja had found her final resting place up here, buried forever among the low clumps of heather and spiky gorse or submerged in some black peat bog.

They got up and stepped back onto the road without noticing the 4x4, which came up the gradient fast with only sidelights on, until it was too late and it was almost on them. Jumping for their lives, they rolled across the margin of the road and crashed into what was left of the wall, and lay there dazed and winded. The dark vehicle did not stop or even seem to brake.

Donna sat up eventually, leaning back against the wall, trying out each limb in turn to estimate the damage. Her left arm hurt and she flexed the wrist tentatively, worried that it was broken but when she leaned her weight on it she decided that it probably wasn't. Mags, she realised, had gone. But this did not alarm her. Mags came and went to her own rhythms and she would be back when it suited her. It was another worry which flooded Donna's mind now. He knows I'm here, she thought. He knows and he's trying to kill me. Him – or his friends, and we know he has plenty of them – big men who hide their faces behind masks. He's found me, he's following me, he must have been driving that thing and be trying to kill me. She heard the small still voice then.

'It's your own fault,' it whispered. 'You know it is. You're too slow. You're too late. You always mess it up. You know you do. You never get it right. You destroyed your family. You destroyed Mags. You destroy everyone who has ever loved you. It's your fault, Donna, Donna, Donna...' The voice pierced her brain with its insidious message and she banged her head monotonously against the hard stone of the wall behind her as she wept.

15

Jay found herself facing an unusually acute case of the Monday-morning blues. Kate came downstairs reluctantly and sat poking her spoon disdainfully at her cornflakes rather than eating them.

'Come on, darling,' Jay said. 'You'll be late if you're not careful. Have you cleaned your teeth yet?'

'I don't want to go to school,' Kate mumbled, pushing her dish away with an expression of disgust. 'I hate school. I want to go back to my old school.'

Jay turned away to hide the despair which threatened to overwhelm her. Lack of sleep and increasing anxiety about Kate were beginning to get to her, though she could see no easy way of undoing the decisions she had taken so optimistically just a few months before when she had been offered the job in Pendle Bridge.

'You know we can't go back,' she said putting an arm round Kate's shoulders. 'Come on now. Changing schools is always hard. But it will get better. Really it will.'

'I hate it when you're not here when I get home,' Kate said.

'But I'll be here before you,' Jay said. 'I really will. I promise.'

'You weren't when someone left that mask.'

'No, I wasn't, and I'm really, really sorry about that,' Jay said.

'So I don't like going to school and I don't like coming home either,' Kate said with satisfaction. 'Not after seeing that man in the car. And Sonja's not there any more so I've no one to walk home with and no one to talk to. It's all horrible and I hate it.'

'Look, darling, you have to go to school. You know that. If you really hate St. Peter's we can look for somewhere else for next term but it won't be possible before that, I don't think. I tell you what. Until we know what's happened to Sonja I'll ask Miss Ashcroft if you can stay in school every afternoon until I pick you up. Then if I am late for any reason – and I'll really try not to be – you don't have to walk home alone. Will that help?'

Kate shrugged, still sulky, but got up from her chair and began to put her coat on. She said nothing on the short drive to school and followed her mother unenthusiastically across the crowded playground and into her classroom where they found Debbie Flint pinning work to the display at the back of the class.

'Hello Kate,' Debbie said with a cheerfulness that Jay did not think rang quite true. 'Did you have a good weekend?'

Kate shrugged and deliberately turned her back on the two adults, taking a book from the class library and going to sit in a corner. Debbie's smile faded and Jay realised how anxious she looked.

'Still no news about Sonja, according to the

radio,' she said. 'The whole class is upset.'

'No they're not.' Kate had turned round, her eyes full of tears. 'They're not upset at all. They don't care about Sonja.'

'That's not true, Katie,' Debbie said quickly, although Jay guessed that it probably was.

'What can I do for you, Mrs. Morton?' Debbie asked.

'In the circumstances, I wondered if Kate could stay in the classroom here until I fetch her every day. Just while this is going on? She's really worried about walking home on her own. She was really frightened last week when someone in a car stopped to talk to her.'

'Of course she can,' Debbie said. 'I live close by and I'm generally here until four, so I'll keep an eye on her. She's a great reader, isn't she, so I'm sure she can keep herself amused.'

'I'm sure I'll be here in time every day, but there's always the unexpected,' Jay said, wondering if she would ever escape the guilt which haunted her these days. 'My job is flexible...'

'It's fine, Mrs. Morton,' Debbie said. 'Really it is.'

'All right, Kate?' Jay asked her daughter who was ignoring them again. 'Stay here until I come?'

'I suppose,' Kate said, still not looking round. 'See you.'

Jay drove up to Pendle House faster than she should have done and slammed her car door in fury when she found George Hateley's car parked on the gravel in front of the house.

'What's Mr. Hateley doing here again?' she asked Pam Bentley when she got to the offices.

'The man's a menace.'

'He's going round the place with Mr. Grogan,' Pam said mildly. 'Something about getting the roof fixed and seeing if they can make the cellars usable for storage for the museum.'

'It might be sensible if they asked me what storage space is needed before they go planning extra renovations,' Jay said sourly. 'I don't think we'll need anything more than the attics once we've got the galleries arranged, and at least they're dry. Fred says the cellars are damp.'

'Well, they'll do their own thing, those two,' Pam said with unusual frankness. 'They're like a pair of kids with a new toy.'

'Silly me,' Jay said bitterly. 'I rather thought it was my new toy.'

'Then you don't know Pendle Bridge,' Pam said.

'No, I don't think I do,' Jay said. 'It seems an altogether more unpleasant place than it used to be.'

For an hour or so Jay tried to settle down again to her trawl though the Wright family paperwork, but her mind was not on it and she was not totally disconcerted when, as she had expected, the two trustees who had been inspecting the old house eventually put in an appearance, breezing through the office into her workroom without the courtesy of knocking.

'Now then, Jay,' George Hateley said, his expression cheerful. 'Bernie reckoned you might find us a coffee. It's bloody chilly down in that basement.'

'I'll see what Pam can do,' Jay conceded, passing

on the trustees' requirements to her assistant in the outer office who pulled a wry face in response.

'There's no biscuits left,' she said without apology and Jay flashed her a brief smile of complicity. She suspected that there were plenty of biscuits for guests Pam approved of.

Hateley and Grogan had made themselves at home at her big work table and she noticed with irritation that they had pushed some of her own papers to one side. She straightened them up ostentatiously and glanced over their shoulders at the plans they had spread out in front of them.

'I wasn't anticipating needing any more space than's available on the three floors we've got,' she said, conscious of tempering her scepticism slightly. The future of the museum depended on the support of these men, however insufferable she found them, just as much as on her efforts. 'What would we use the cellars for exactly?'

'It's more a question of making the whole building sound,' Grogan said and Jay could not fail to notice the condescension of the alpha male to the helpless little woman who might not understand such technical considerations. 'It's damp down there since they took the old boiler out. Some of the floors are lethal. Not good, that. And some of the ceilings don't look very safe either. I'll get our surveyor to give it a good going over. And he can have a look at the roof as well while he's at it. In the meantime we'll lock it up. You never know with these old places. Health and safety's always a problem. Maybe we should have gone for purpose-built.'

'I'm sure Pendle House will be just fine,' Jay

said, horrified at the casual suggestion.

'It's not as if we're short of a bob,' Grogan persisted. 'A bit of lobbying came good there, though I say it myself.'

George Hateley laughed as if on cue, though it had a hollow sound, and Jay wondered who owed who what in that relationship.

Hateley drained his coffee and began to pack away the paperwork while Grogan's sharp blue eyes roamed restlessly around the room.

'I see you've fetched all those masks down,' he said. 'Important, are they? The first thing you're looking at, as it were?'

'We were lucky with them, that's all,' Jay said. 'They're one of the few collections for which I've found a proper inventory. Though all that's told me so far is that some of them are missing.'

'Missing?' Grogan said, with an unexpected note of anger in his voice. 'What do you mean, missing? How can you possibly be sure of that?'

'The list is very detailed,' Jay said, her patience fraying. 'Detailed enough to match up with the collection. Six of them are missing.'

'It'll be those bloody kids who lived here,' Hateley said. 'I always knew they'd get their thieving little hands on some of the stuff. You'll not find them now, love, after all these years.'

'No, I think it was much more recent,' Jay said. 'If the Pendle House children had taken them they'd have been destroyed long ago. But one of them's already turned up and I've handed it over to the police. I reckon they've been stolen since the house was opened up again this month.'

'You should have told us you had a problem,'

Grogan said. 'We don't want any adverse publicity, you know. They're nasty looking things, those masks. They could frighten a child to death, don't you reckon, George? X certificate stuff?'

'I dare say you're right, Bernie,' George Hateley said, without his usual enthusiasm. Don't I know it, Jay thought, but she was not going to tell Grogan how Kate had been terrorised by the cannibal bird mask now in the possession of the police. That was a complication she thought the trustees did not need to know about.

'I would have told you, of course,' she said. 'But I only found the inventory on Friday and then I've had to check through each mask, matching it up with its description. Six have definitely gone. I've asked Fred Marston to make extra sure all the alarms are checked and in working order and turned on when we're not here. We don't want anything else to go walkabout. There may be much more valuable stuff up in the attics than the masks that I haven't started unpacking yet.'

'How long's it going to take you, then, to catalogue the lot?' Grogan asked, his eyes anxious.

'I'm really not sure, Mr. Grogan,' Jay said a touch wearily. 'Maybe a couple of months. Maybe six, depending on what I find amongst the papers. If I can't find details here I'm going to have to identify every piece and then try to prove that everything is genuine. There were lots of fakes floating about even in Victorian times. I can't rush it. It's detailed work and we need to get it right.'

'Aye, well, keep in touch and if you've any more problems contact me, or if I'm in London, George here will cope.'

Jay nodded and the two men got to their feet.

'Who did you talk to about the theft?' Grogan asked, one hand on the doorhandle.

'Peter Shipley,' Jay said.

'Oh aye, he's a good lad, is Peter,' Grogan said. And Jay wondered why she did not find that recommendation reassuring.

'He seems run off his feet with two major cases at once,' Jay said, surprised at the sympathy she suddenly felt for DCI Shipley. 'It's weird that the head of the children's home should be killed just as we reopened the old place. She still seemed very bitter about the murder of that little girl all those years ago, almost as if she blamed herself.'

'What makes you say that, Jay? Did you meet Mary Petherbridge somewhere?' George Hateley asked, evidently surprised.

'I did. Didn't I mention it? She came here one day when I was sorting out stuff in the attics.'

'I didn't even know she still lived in Pendle Bridge,' George said heavily.

'Mad as a box of frogs,' Grogan said dismissively. 'Gone completely ga-ga. She came to my constituency surgery just recently with some tale about the children's home. Said the police wouldn't listen to her but I wasn't surprised at that. She'd absolutely no evidence for anything she says, as far as I can make out. Sounded as if she thought she'd been seeing ghosts to me.'

'She was certainly pretty unhappy about what went on here when I met her,' Jay said. 'And still feeling guilty about it.'

'She was always a bit of a fantasist, that woman,' Grogan said. 'Though I dare say she'd good reason for blaming herself for what went on. Those kids were running wild wi' that lad who killed what-was-her-name? Margaret? Maggie?'

'Mags,' Jay said.

'She should have been on trial herself, if you ask me,' Grogan went on, his colour rising. 'Gross negligence, that was. I tried to get her sacked after, but the other governors wouldn't wear it. Gave her the benefit of the bloody doubt. Woolly liberals, all of them, except George here. I suppose she was trying to convince you that Kenny Bairstow didn't do it, was she?'

'She didn't seem very sure about that but she seemed convinced that there was more going on here than ever came out at the time. Suspected some member of staff was interfering with the girls.'

'So why the hell didn't she say summat to the governors then?' Grogan asked. 'It's a bit bloody late now.'

Jay sighed, not wanting to go over what she had told DCI Shipley with her trustees.

'I've really no idea, Mr. Grogan. I only spoke to the woman for five minutes or so. She didn't go into great detail about anything, but it was obvious she hadn't forgotten what went on that summer, and she wasn't convinced justice had been done. That's about it, really. She's not the only person I've met who thinks Kenny Bairstow was innocent, but as my brother-in-law says, there doesn't seem to be anything to prove the verdict was wrong. But I have to say, Mrs. Petherbridge didn't seem the least bit ga-ga to me. Quite the contrary. She seemed pretty sharp

254

for her age. And pretty unhappy about the way things turned out.'

Bernard Grogan shrugged massively.

'All water under the bridge now,' he said.

'Unless someone stirs things up again when Kenny comes out of gaol,' George Hateley said. 'Not that he'll be able to do much himself. He really is a bit doolally. He was when he went in and I don't suppose he'll be any better when he comes out.'

'Should have been hanged,' Grogan said, leading the way out without another glance in Jay's direction. 'Kinder all round,' she heard him add as George Hateley closed the door behind himself.

And more convenient for someone if he happened to be innocent after all, Jay thought. But with Laurie Wishaw and his accuser, Mary Petherbridge, both dead, she thought there was little chance of ever proving that to be the case. And she had more pressing problems on her mind.

Jay poured herself a large Scotch and slumped on the sofa, gazing sightlessly at the empty fireplace. It was ten o'clock and Kate had at last gone to sleep. She had gone to bed, looking pale and hollow-eyed, soon after eight but had then crept downstairs half a dozen times using one excuse after another not to return to her room. Jay was not really surprised. When she had arrived to collect Kate from school, dead on the stroke of three thirty, she had found dozens of other women standing outside the school gates and greeting even eleven-year-olds with smiles of relief and nervous hugs.

'You don't like them out of your sight, do you?' one woman had said to Jay as she pushed through the crowd.

'They're dragging the canal,' another said. 'It were on t'one o'clock news.'

She found Kate still in the classroom, with her coat on and a harassed-looking Debbie Flint tidying up a pile of worksheets. Kate, unusually, took hold of her hand as they walked back to the car.

'I'm glad you weren't late,' she said as she buckled her seatbelt. 'I don't like Debbie.'

'Oh, for goodness sake, Kate,' Jay snapped, and was instantly ashamed of losing control. Nothing, she thought, would be normal for her daughter or the rest of the school until Sonja was found – alive or dead.

'I know you're upset,' she said. 'But it's hardly Debbie Flint's fault. It's very kind of her to let you stay in until I arrive. I thought that's what you wanted.'

'I wish you didn't work,' Kate muttered and Jay bit her tongue, aware that this was not a good moment to run through the financial implications of divorce.

Once back at the cottage, Kate switched on the television, something which Jay's London child-minders had always been told not to allow her to do after school in the days that Jay was beginning to think of as PPB – pre-Pendle Bridge. She had been certain of what she was doing then, she thought. Now her whole existence seemed to be in a state of flux and more often than not laying down ground-rules for Kate began to seem like too much trouble. Once Sonja was found it would be different, she thought, but she feared it would not necessarily be better. And Kate's bedtime had brought no respite as the child padded up and down stairs in bare feet for a drink, another story, or just for a cuddle, until at last Jay found herself yelling at her to stay put and go to sleep on pain of not going to London at half-term, a threat she despised herself for using. She listened to her daughter sobbing under the duvet until finally silence fell and she crept up the stairs and into her room to tuck her up. Two bright eyes in a tear-stained face met hers as soon as she pushed open the door.

'You wouldn't really not let me go to see Daddy, would you?' Kate whispered. Jay sat down on the edge of the bed and gave her a hug.

'Of course not, darling,' she said. 'I'm sorry, I shouldn't have said that. We're both getting a bit upset with what's going on, aren't we, but you won't feel any better if you don't sleep. So please settle down now.'

She went downstairs and stood in the door to the sitting room gazing for a long moment at the bookcase to the left of the fireplace. She knew that she had arranged her reference books in order on the lowest shelf and that she had left the illustrated guide to North American masks tucked carelessly across the top of them. It now stood neatly upright alongside the rest. She knew, with every ounce of belief she could summon up that she had not moved it herself. There was no way Kate had touched the book which had disturbed her so much. Either someone had been into the house again, or she was going mad.

She jumped suddenly as the phone rang, but she made no attempt to pick up the receiver and when the answerphone clicked in she listened to the silence with her heart thumping uncomfortably. She shuddered as the caller eventually hung up. She did not think she could put up with much more of this. She went into the kitchen and poured herself a Scotch with shaking hands.

She heard no more from upstairs as she sipped her whiskey and felt the spirit work itself into her bones. She sat back with the TV turned on low and tried to relax. Kate's mention of David had reminded her of her sister's unexpected confession that her marriage too had turned out less well that she had expected and Jay had supposed. She had her own evidence for that, she thought, thinking of Chris Hateley's importunity.

She had almost begun to doze off under the influence of the Scotch when she was jerked awake by the rasp of her front door-bell and was surprised to find that it was still only half past ten. Cautiously she pulled back the curtains to see who was at the door and was surprised to see her brother-in-law standing with his coat collar turned up, though whether to protect himself from the spitting rain or to disguise himself she could not be sure. Damn and blast the man, she thought to herself and unbolted the door only reluctantly.

'Taking good care of security,' Chris said, stepping over the threshold without waiting to be invited. 'I was passing on my way home and thought I'd come to see how you were. Sue told me about Kate and the car. I hope she's not too upset.'

'It's not much fun when your best friend goes missing,' Jay said, her voice sharp with anxiety. 'Her only friend in Pendle Bridge as it happens.'

'Of course, she must be distraught,' Chris said, glancing around the living room until his eyes lighted on Jay's almost empty glass. 'A nightcap would be nice,' he said. 'I've just sat through an excessively boring meeting of the planning committee.'

With barely concealed resentment Jay poured him a Scotch and he settled down on the sofa with every appearance of a long stay.

'Daughters, hey?' he said. 'Who'd have 'em? Sue's convinced Abbie's anorexic, but I must say I think it's just puberty myself. You've that joy to come with Katie as well, of course.'

'I told Sue that I thought Abbie should see a doctor.'

'She's not keen on that idea,' Chris said, apparently unperturbed. He sipped his Scotch and raised an eyebrow when Jay half filled her own empty glass and took the armchair on the opposite side of the fireplace.

'Come on, Jay,' he said, patting the cushion beside him. 'I won't bite. You never used to be so stand-offish.'

'That was when we were both free agents,' Jay said tartly.

'Well, you're a free agent now, and I thought Sue would have told you that our marriage is not what

259

you might call a warm and loving relationship. I'm as free an agent as you need me to be, Jay, believe me.' He put his glass down on the coffee table and got to his feet, stood in front of her and pulled her out of her chair until they were standing close together. He put his arms round her and she could feel his erection against her stomach.

'No,' she said, trying to break free. 'This isn't what I want, Chris. No way.'

'You mean this isn't why you came back to Pendle Bridge?' he asked, as he attempted to kiss her. 'That's what everyone thinks. It's certainly what Sue thinks. David buggered off so you came back to see where we stood after all this time. The irritating thing is that I knew straight away that I stood where I always did, fancying you something rotten. Come on, Jay. No one will know and no one will care. You know how good we always were together.' His grip around her tightened and he forced her mouth open with his tongue and for a second the old magic reasserted itself and she began to respond.

'There. I knew you were gagging for it,' he whispered. 'How long has it been?'

Blind fury took hold of Jay then, and she kicked out wildly at his shins and wrested herself from his arms, before pushing him hard in the general direction of the front door. For a moment he lost his balance and she thought he would fall, but he clutched at the back of the sofa and leaned over it, panting, refusing to meet her eye.

'You bastard,' she said, trying to keep her voice low so that she did not waken Kate. 'Sue told me you'd turned into a promiscuous pig and she's not exaggerating, is she. Get out. Get out now before I call her and tell her what you've just said.'

'You're a tease, Jay. You always were a tease. How long did you keep me waiting before you finally condescended to open your legs all those years ago? My father was right. I got the more accommodating sister. It's just a pity *she* never learned to keep her legs closed.'

'Get out, get out, get out,' Jay said. 'I never want to see you again.'

'Getting too close to the truth now, are we?' Chris said as he picked up his glass and drained it in one. 'Well, if you don't want to see me again you'd better get yourself back down the M1 to London because Pendle Bridge is my town. You're the interloper here and if you didn't come back to see me, then there's nothing here for you. I can make life very uncomfortable for you and your tin-pot new museum, don't forget. I should get out before I find a good reason for the Pendle House trustees to throw you out.'

'You couldn't,' Jay said, her breath coming in painful gasps as she took in the full implications of Chris's threats.

'I could and I will, you supercilious cow,' he said. 'You've already annoyed people, raking over old ashes, asking questions, playing the amateur detective, wasting people's time. An editorial in the *Advertiser* questioning whether your museum is a good use of public money and you'll be heading back south sooner than you think.'

'Bastard,' Jay said again, her anger draining away to be replaced by a real fear. She had not seriously thought he would rape her but she could see from his eyes that the viciousness of a weak man might seriously damage her in other ways if he decided to take his revenge.

'Sleep tight,' he said, opening the front door, knowing as well as she did that was the last thing she was likely to do that night.

16

The two frogmen slipped into the dark waters of the canal again, disturbing the faint sheen of oil on the surface and fragmenting the reflections of the derelict mill on the far bank. Donna stood on the footbridge above them, her fist stuffed into her mouth to stifle the moans that she knew that the police team on the towpath must not hear. She had heard on the local radio news that morning that the police would search the canal for Sonja Kradic today and had been irresistibly drawn to the scene in her lunch-hour, unable to eat because her stomach was so clenched with fear. The towpath itself had been cordoned off with blue and white police tape but there was a handful of other spectators coming and going on the bridge. None of them watched for as long as Donna or with her fierce intensity. It's happening again, a small voice said inside her head, a child's voice she did not recognise. And she knew she should have tried to stop it.

Mags and Archie had kept up a long argument for as long as she had stood there, buzzing at the back of her head like angry wasps. Mags had been urging her ever since she had arrived in Pendle Bridge to carry the long knife with her at all times. She had bought the knife in London from a smart kitchen shop, a knife so sharp that it sliced through the steak she had bought to test it out on with so little effort that she had to look more than once before she could believe that the single steak was now two smaller steaks, and then four and eight and sixteen, until she laughed aloud at the simplicity of it all with a pile of bloodily minced meat on the chopping board in front of her.

Archie, dear Archie, who had been with her through it all for as long as she could remember, said no, leave it safely hidden until you're sure, until you've found him and discovered where you can reach him, until you're absolutely certain you can succeed. You don't want this to go off at half-cock.

On the whole Donna thought Archie was right. All that bothered her was success. She had made no plans to get away afterwards. She had no escape route mapped out. Finding him and his friends and doing it would be enough and that hidden knife would be her guarantee of success. Later could look after itself.

She was not discouraged that so far she had not tracked down her quarry. Now she had a job and somewhere to live, she knew she could bide her time. More discouraging was her failure so far to discover where Kenny Bairstow was being held. His mother had been no help there, ready enough to reminisce about the old days when she and Mags had almost become permanent fixtures in her house, stuffing themselves with biscuits and sweets, watching telly and listening to Blondie's hits over and over again. But when she had pressed Grace to tell her where Kenny was now, the old woman had become tearful and confused, refusing to answer her questions and eventually telling one of the care workers that she was tired and wanted to go back to bed. Donna had visited twice and both times stormed out of the home in a fury, her face pale and her lips tightly pursed to prevent herself hurling the abuse which welled up in her like bile. The old woman must know, she thought, but it was only by trawling through dusty old copies of the *Advertiser* that she finally discovered exactly what had happened to Kenny and had to accept that he was probably still in gaol and it would be very difficult to discover where without revealing why she wanted to know. She had found it very hard not to screw up the newspaper description of his trial and conviction. She had sat staring at the print, her eyes blurred with furious, frustrated tears, until she was able to compose herself enough to go back to work. Even Archie had seemed dumbfounded. Poor Kenny, he said. Poor, poor Kenny. Poor Donna, she'd muttered, still in shock, attracting odd glances from passers-by as she had walked through the shopping centre. She shook uncontrollably and had to sit down on a wooden bench outside the market when Mags joined in with unusual venom. Poor Mags, she had whispered over and over again. It was your fault. You knew who did it. You fix it. You don't need Kenny but you can help Kenny if you fix it. Fix it, Donna, fix it, fix it, fix it.

Even so, she was not completely convinced that she did not need Kenny, and she had taken to jogging past the Adelaide Street cottage with her tracksuit hood up, glancing in through the living room window to catch a glimpse of the woman she now knew was Jay Morton who lived there with her daughter Kate. She might know where he was, she told herself. Surely she must know. She wouldn't have bought the house without knowing where Kenny was, would she? She must know if he's still in gaol or if they've let him out. She needed to talk to Jay Morton, if only to check out that she knew nothing. And then there was the old man next door, watching them all the time, looking out through the net curtains at the girl. She knew only too well how watching could turn into touching and all the rest. They were all the same, men, wanting only one thing. Perhaps she should deal with him too.

Never mind him. He's not the one, Mags screamed with such force that she gasped out loud and an elderly woman pushing a shopping trolley paused to stare at her.

'Are you all right, love?' she asked.

'Yes, I'm fine,' Donna had muttered and jumped to her feet, walking off jerkily as Mags continued to harangue her. 'I'm fine, I'm fine,' she told herself as Mags's voice faded away. 'I'll find him, I promise. I'll find them all. I'll make everything all right.'

Jay had just settled down to do some of the work she had brought home from Pendle House with her that evening when the door-bell rang. She drew a sharp breath, hoping that Chris Hateley had not returned to renew his assault on her fragile defences, but when she drew back the curtain and looked out she was surprised to see not Chris but his daughter Abbie outside. She opened the door quickly and pulled her niece, who was shivering inside a flimsy jacket, into the warmth.

'Abbie, you look terrible. Whatever's the matter?'

The girl did not answer, pulling her jacket tightly around her slight frame and flinging herself onto the sofa, her eyes full of unshed tears. Jay went into the kitchen and made her a cup of hot chocolate which she accepted meekly, wrapping her hands around the mug for warmth. When she had sipped about half of it and pushed the rest away onto the coffee table, Jay sat down on the sofa beside her and decided it might be safe to start again.

'Can you tell me what's wrong?' she asked gently. 'What's happened?'

'I didn't have anywhere else to go,' Abbie muttered. 'I couldn't stay at home any longer and I didn't have anywhere else to go.'

'Is there a problem with your parents?' Jay asked, wondering if there had been some fall-out with Sue after Chris's visit to her the previous evening.

'Oh, they're just rowing, as usual. Ben and I are used to that,' said Abbie dismissively.

'But it's making you unhappy, Abbie, isn't it? Is that why you're not eating properly?'

'That's got nothing to do with anything. I just don't want to get fat. You must diet, Auntie Jay, don't you? You're much slimmer than my mum.'

'I always was,' Jay said. 'It's just the way we're built. But at your age you need to eat sensibly because you're growing so fast.' She took hold of Abbie's wrist and pushed the sleeve up, revealing a stick thin arm which shocked her. 'Look at you, darling,' she said. 'You're far too thin. It's dangerous for your health to go on like this.'

Abbie pulled away and pulled her sleeve back down to her wrist, hugging herself tightly again.

'I'm all right,' she said. 'Really I am.' But her voice trembled and her face seemed so pale that Jay was afraid that she would faint.

'No,' Jay said firmly. 'You're not all right. If you were you wouldn't be here at this time of night. The first thing we have to do is call your mum and tell her where you are. If she doesn't know she'll be frantic with worry by now.'

'No. I don't want to go home. I can't stay there any more. I thought maybe I could stay here with you and Katie.' And with that Abbie burst into floods of tears. Jay took her in her arms, feeling the bones beneath their frighteningly fragile covering of flesh even through Abbie's sweatshirt and jacket, and realising that this was not just a fit of teenage angst but something more serious. She let the girl sob herself into a breathless, shuddering silence, before offering her tissues to wipe her face.

'You must tell me, Abbie,' she said. 'I can't help you unless you tell me what's wrong. Is it a boy? Are you pregnant?'

'No,' Abbie said scornfully. 'I hate boys.'

Jay waited quietly as Abbie sat staring at the floor, still shuddering.

'My dad will be devastated,' she said at last. Jay suddenly felt very frightened.

'Not a boy,' she said, carefully. 'Is it a man, then? Has a man been persuading you to do things you don't want to do?'

Abbie nodded imperceptibly, and the tears began to flow again, silently this time as she stuffed the tissue into her mouth as if trying to choke herself. Jay took her in her arms again and held her close.

'That's wicked, Abbie,' she whispered. 'You're only thirteen. It's wicked and illegal and you have to tell me all about it so we can stop him.'

'I hate him,' Abbie said. 'I hate him so much I can't think any more. Everything's getting jumbled up in my head...' She trailed off miserably.

'Can you tell me who it is? Is it someone at school? A teacher?'

'No, of course not,' Abbie said, managing a tiny giggle between her hiccupping sobs. 'They're all women. There's only Mr. Giggs the computer nerd...'

She lapsed into silence again and Jay waited, her imagination rioting amongst malevolent possibilities until she too shuddered and let her anger take over.

'Who is it, Abbie?' she asked more sharply. 'We have to stop him, you know that, don't you? You wouldn't have run away like this if you didn't want him stopped. And if we don't stop him he might treat other girls the same way. You don't want that, do you?'

Abbie moaned and shook her head slightly.

'It's my grandfather,' she said flatly, all emotion drained.

Jay froze, her mouth dry. Whatever she had expected, it had not been that.

'How long ago did this start?' she whispered, a vision of George Hateley presiding apparently benevolently over her sister's family lunch party leaping into her mind and making her feel sick.

'A long time ago,' Abbie said. 'I can't remember. He was always cuddling me when I was little. And then it got to be more than cuddling.'

'Dear God,' Jay said, wondering how the child's parents had failed to notice. 'How much more than cuddling?'

'Kissing, stroking...' Abbie whispered.

'Did he force you to have sex? Did he rape you?'

Abbie shook her head frantically.

'No, no, not that. But will he go to prison, Auntie Jay?' Abbie asked, her eyes terrified now. 'He always said if I told anyone he'd go to prison and me and Ben would be taken away to a home... But I can't go on like this, can I? I thought of killing him. Or myself. I can't bear it any more, I really can't. So you see why I can't go home. He's always there, talking to Dad, having meals with us.' And paying the school fees, Jay thought bitterly, guaranteeing blind-eyed gratitude from his son and his wife.

'I hate him so much I'm nearly sick all the time,' Abbie whispered. 'It's not that I don't want to eat. I just can't. Please, please can I stay with you and Kate?'

'Yes, yes, perhaps,' Jay said distractedly. 'But I must talk to your mother. We have to tell her about this, Abbie. There really is no choice.'

Jay went into the kitchen to phone her sister, hoping against hope that Chris did not pick up

270

the phone. She was so relieved when she heard Sue's voice that found it difficult to speak at all.

'Abbie's here,' she said at last. 'Can you come round and talk to her? She's very upset about something.'

'Chris is out at some meeting,' Sue said, her tone offhand. 'I'll ask him to pick her up on his way back. I don't know what she's playing at. She's supposed to be doing homework at her friend's house.'

'No, I think you should come here yourself, Sue,' Jay said. 'There's something we need to discuss.'

The silence at the other end was so long that Jay began to think her sister had hung up.

'Is she pregnant?' Sue said at last.

'No,' Jay said. 'She says not. It's much worse than that.'

'I'll be ten minutes,' Sue said.

Jay lay in her bed at two o'clock that morning, rigid with anger. Sue had eventually recovered from her own near-hysterical reaction to what Abbie had disclosed and had persuaded her daughter to go home with her with a promise that George Hateley would not be allowed into the house again. When Jay had tried to persuade her that she must go to the police she had hedged and equivocated, saying that she and Chris must talk over the situation before any decision like that could be taken. And the longer Abbie listened to the adults' conversation the more it became clear that it would be extremely difficult to persuade the child to talk to anyone outside the family about what had happened. She sat and shivered and sobbed, adamant only that she never wanted to see George Hateley again.

And Jay was left to wonder where this catastrophe left her. Out in the everyday world, she herself had to deal with Hateley who was effectively one of her employers. How she could possibly bring herself to speak to him again, or be civil if she had to, she could not imagine. Waves of grief and anger for Abbie swept over her long after Sue had bundled the shivering child up in her own coat and into the car to take her home.

'Call me tomorrow,' Jay had said to her sister.

'Of course,' Sue had said, but her manner was distant and Jay wondered if she had found some way of blaming her for the evening's devastating disclosure. Abbie's confession was something Jay suspected that Sue did not want to hear and had no idea how to deal with. She hoped that Chris would be more decisive, but she doubted it.

Sleep refused to come however long Jay tried to read her book with drooping eyes, or lie with the bedclothes over her head attempting to relax. In the end she crept downstairs and made herself a cup of hot chocolate and sat in the untidy living room listening to the creaking of the old house and gazing sightlessly at the flowers in the empty fireplace. The move to Pendle Bridge which had promised so much, she thought, was turning more sour with every day that passed. She had thought, above all, that it would be good for Kate, the only child she and David had carefully planned, to be close to her cousins. But that relationship would be almost impossible to sustain in the fallout from Abbie's revelations. Nothing between herself and the Hateley family could ever be the same again. She leaned back and closed her eyes to try to still the horrors which would not go away. Was George Hateley, she wondered, responsible for the harassment she had suffered herself since she arrived back in Pendle Bridge. Had he determined to drive her away to keep his secret safe within the family he seemed to dominate? Then why help appoint her to the job in the first place, she wondered. She was quite sure that he was sufficiently influential to have prevented her getting her job if he had really wanted to. Perhaps he had thought he could suck her into his circle or worse – and she sat bolt upright, horrified – that he could add Kate to what might be his collection of little girls. Kate had said she didn't like George, hadn't she? She had said he was creepy. Had he laid a finger on her? The thought sent icicles of horror down her spine and she felt like rushing upstairs to wake her sleeping daughter and ask her. But she restrained the impulse. It would do no good, she thought, to worry the child more than she was worried already by what was happening in Pendle Bridge. She would choose her moment carefully to question her about Abbie's grandfather, if possible without alarming her.

She was wide awake now and felt little more than surprise when the front door-bell shrieked into arthritic life. She went to the window, pulled back the curtain to look out, half expecting it to be Sue or Chris. But she did not recognise the figure standing outside with a hood pulled up. She knocked on the glass, unwilling to open the door to a stranger, and the figure turned in her direction, the face still shadowed and unrecognisable.

'I'm looking for Kenny. Kenny Bairstow,' a voice, muffled by the glass, said.

Jay shook her head sharply.

'He doesn't live here any more,' she said. 'He hasn't lived here for years.' She felt overwhelmed by anger.

'Where is he?' the voice demanded. 'Tell me where he is.'

'I've no idea,' Jay said, her voice rising. 'Go away. Kenny's not here. I don't know where the hell he is. Go away!'

The figure turned away, shoulders slumped, and Jay heard another sound, probably a window being thrown up, and another voice.

'Bugger off, you silly bat,' it shouted, and even through the glass she recognised her neighbour, Mr. Booth. 'I've seen you before, you know. I'll call the bloody police if you don't bugger off.'

'Oh no,' Jay groaned to herself. 'It's nearly three in the morning. That's the last thing we need. We'll have the whole street awake next.' But the moment passed as the figure broke into a jog down the narrow street without looking back and eventually she heard Booth's window slammed shut again. As she slowly made her way back to bed she conceded for the first time that maybe she was defeated by Pendle Bridge and its horrors, past and present, that maybe the best thing to do now, for her own sake as well as Kate's, was to cut her losses and begin to look for a new job somewhere else.

17

Jay arrived at work the next morning late, tired and fractious. Pam Bentley glanced at her curiously as she hung up her coat and inspected the dark circles under her eyes in the mirror.

'You look a bit frazzled,' Pam said, the question implicit in her voice.

'Couldn't sleep last night,' Jay said shortly. 'Something I ate, I think. A cup of coffee would be good.' While Pam busied herself with the kettle, Jay glanced at the post on her desk, finding little of interest apart from a sticky note with a name and a phone number on it.

'When did Granville Stott call?' she asked as Pam put a steaming mug in front of her.

'Just before I left yesterday afternoon,' Pam said. 'Actually it was his wife. She didn't say what it was about but wanted you to call him today if possible. Isn't he the solicitor?'

'Used to be,' Jay said grudgingly. She sighed. Her interest in Kenny Bairstow had dissipated in the face of more urgent problems but it seemed that there were people still keen to remind her of the boy at all hours of the day and night. She dialled Stott's number reluctantly and it was answered by a female voice which identified itself as Joan Stott, Granville's wife.

'Oh, yes, Mrs. Morton,' she said. 'I did ring because Granville wanted to speak to you again urgently. Unfortunately he was taken into hospital again last night. He's taken a turn for the worse. I'm only at home now to collect some of his things and then I must get back...'

'I'm very sorry to hear that,' Jay said. 'Do give him my best wishes. I don't suppose he'll want to be worried with visitors so I won't bother him now...'

'He was very keen to see you, you know,' Mrs. Stott said hesitantly. 'He said it was important. Perhaps you could pop in?'

Reluctantly Jay made a note of the ward Granville Stott was in and promised to try to find the time to visit, but without much conviction.

'It's very important to him, you know,' Mrs. Stott said. 'I think he doesn't want to leave loose ends, and he hasn't got long.' Jay took a sharp breath.

'I'll do my best,' she said, and inevitably, for the whole morning, the thought of Granville Stott's need to tell her something before he died niggled at the back of her mind until, as it got close to lunchtime, she gave in to it, knowing that she would always have regrets if the solicitor died and she had not found the time to speak to him again. Pam looked at her again quizzically as Jay put on her coat and announced that she would be out for a long lunch.

'Don't mind me,' she said. 'But what'll I tell your friends Hateley and Grogan if they pop in again?' Jay choked back a sharp retort.

'Tell them I've gone to do some research,' she said. 'And don't let them touch anything on my work-table. They think they own the place,

276

those two.'

Pam looked grim.

'That's not all they think they own,' she said. 'There's the whole town – and that's just for starters.'

Half an hour later Jay had parked at the district hospital and walked through the swing doors with an uncomfortably thumping heart as she absorbed the familiar sounds and smells. It had been here that her father had died, hooked up to so many machines as he lay unconscious for three days after his car accident that he looked more like a puppet than a man. His brain injuries had been severe and he had never regained consciousness and in the end she and Sue and their mother had reluctantly agreed that the life-support systems should be switched off. Sue and her mother had wept, but Jay's tears had obstinately refused to come then, locked up within the cavern which seemed to have opened up inside her at the loss of her first friend and mentor, the inspiration for much of her life. She had not known then, and still occasionally wondered, how she could survive without him.

Finding her way to Granville Stott's ward, she found death staring her in the face again and she hoped that he did not see her flinch. As she approached his bed, where he lay prone and grey faced with his wife holding his hand, he managed a thin smile.

'I'm glad you could come,' he whispered very slowly, as if each word had to be weighed before it could be uttered.

'Your wife said it was important,' Jay said. 'But

if it's too much...'

'No,' Stott said. 'I wanted you to know this.' He squeezed his wife's hand and turned away slightly towards Jay, who had to lean close to hear what he was saying.

'Mary Petherbridge rang me,' he said. 'Dreadful woman. Should have been sacked after what happened. But no matter. Told me she'd seen Donna Latham – the other girl – the one who ran away – here in the town. She'd seen Donna. Donna recognised her. She said she recognised the girl – woman now of course – after all this time ... small world.'

He paused, evidently exhausted by the effort he was making. His wife gave him a sip of water from the glass beside the bed and he nodded urgently, wanting to continue before his strength failed.

'She said Donna knows who killed Mags Emmett. It wasn't Kenny...'

'Did she say who it was?' Jay asked.

'No, no, that's the point. Mary was going to come out to see me, give me all the details, a written statement, so we could think about another appeal, even after all this time, but then she was killed. I couldn't believe it, Mrs. Morton. I really couldn't believe it. But you see, Donna's here, back in Pendle Bridge, so you must find her. She's the key to it all. She's the one who was there that night. She's the one who knows what really happened.'

'Shouldn't you be telling the police this, not me?' Jay asked. 'After all, Donna could be the person who murdered Mary Petherbridge.'

'Could be,' Stott said faintly. 'Could be. But I don't trust the police. Les Green was a bully, a deeply unpleasant man, and Peter Shipley was on that case. Junior maybe, but still on the case. Not to be trusted, any of them. You need to find Donna yourself, Mrs. Morton, and see what she has to say. I can't do it now. You must. For Kenny and poor old Gracie, you need to find out the truth.'

Stott fell back onto the pillows and closed his eyes, evidently exhausted.

'My husband was never happy about the outcome of that case,' Joan Stott said bitterly. 'It's always worried him.' Jay nodded and took the old man's other hand.

'I'll do my best, Mr. Stott,' she said and was rewarded with a flicker of an acknowledgement.

'Your father would have been proud of you,' Stott whispered and Jay smiled slightly grimly. Maybe, she thought. But she doubted it. She was making too much of a mess of her life for that, and she was glad her father was not here to see it.

Later Sue and Jay sat shoulder-to-shoulder, facing Chris Hateley across his own kitchen table. Sue had summoned Jay on her mobile and sounded so distraught that she had found it impossible to refuse to call in at the Hateleys on her way back to Pendle House. Chris looked almost as grey as Granville Stott had done and refused to look either his wife or his sister-in-law in the eye.

'You must have known,' Jay said, her voice as hard as iron.

'No,' Chris said.

'But you were making light of Abbie's situation all the time,' Sue said. 'Telling me she'd grow out of it, it was just a teenage thing. I knew it bloody wasn't. I knew it was serious. You decided to protect your wretched father instead of your daughter.'

'No, I honestly didn't think it was serious,' Chris said. 'I just thought she was fed up because we were rowing even more than usual. I thought she was just getting her own back by being difficult. That's what adolescents do.'

'You must have known,' Jay repeated.

'No,' Chris said. 'I'd no idea. You have to believe me.'

'I'd like to believe you,' Jay said. 'I really would, Chris. Because if you did know what was going on, you've done one of the worst things you could possibly do to your daughter. You've failed to protect her from abuse and for that you're as guilty as your father is. You should go to jail too.'

'No,' Chris said, his voice rising. 'You can't say that. You don't know it's true. You're just going on the word of a hysterical teenager who's got her own agenda for making these vile accusations. I don't believe my father would do that. Even she says it all happened ages ago – if it happened at all. Abbie's lying. She's disturbed. She's trying to get her own back because she's pissed off with me and her mother...'

'I saw her last night,' Jay said. 'I don't believe she was lying.'

'Where is she?' Chris said. 'Get her down here. Let me talk to her. Let's go through it again. I simply don't believe it.'

'No,' Sue said, suddenly decisive, her hands clenched into fists on the table in front of her. 'I've had enough of this. I never want to see your father again, Chris. If I see him, I'll kill him. And I want you out of this house. Pack your bags and get out. If you don't, I'll go to the police and we'll have all this out in the open, in court if need be. I'm making an appointment to see a solicitor. Abbie will need professional help over this, and I'll be looking for a divorce.'

'Sue...' Chris began but he got no further.

'Get out,' his wife said vehemently. 'I mean it. Get out before I phone the police.'

White-faced, Chris shrugged and staggered to his feet and walked slowly to the door. Suddenly he turned and looked at Jay directly for the first time.

'This is all your fault, you interfering bitch,' he said. 'You should never have come back to Pendle Bridge. My father thought he was doing me a favour by giving you that job, the bloody old fool. Now look where it's got us.'

When he had slammed the door behind him Sue took Jay's hand and squeezed it, her eyes full of tears.

'Thank you,' she said. 'I couldn't have done that on my own. I should have thrown him out years back. He turned into a waste of space long ago. Though what Mum is going to say with two of us suddenly single again I can't imagine.'

'You said you were always trying to keep up,' Jay said with a grim smile, giving her sister a peck on the cheek. 'Are you sure you can't persuade

Abbie to tell the police about George? I'd feel much better if she did.'

Sue shook her head.

'Let it rest,' Sue said. 'She says it was all over a long time ago. I can't make her go through all that if she doesn't want to – questions, a trial, cross-examination – it's too much.'

'That's all very well,' Jay said fiercely. 'But you don't know how far back this goes with George. Or what he's up to now. Don't forget he was a governor at Pendle House when that child was murdered. He could have been involved in that, for all we know. Abbie might not have been the first – or the last.' She thought of Kate, safely at school and oblivious, and then of Sonja Kradic, still unaccounted for, and she knew that regardless of Sue's wishes she would have to point Peter Shipley in the direction of George Hateley. If she didn't, she thought, she would be as compromised as the rest of them.

'Leave Abbie out of it,' Sue said, as if reading her sister's thoughts. And reluctantly Jay agreed.

Jay spent the afternoon trying to concentrate on work and failing utterly. The cramped hand-writing of the Wright documents swam in front of her eyes, giving her a headache, and she could not find the remotest enthusiasm for the obsessions of Victorian collectors. She needed to talk to someone, but after the seeds of doubt Granville Stott had sown around Peter Shipley, was reluctant to approach the DCI. On top of everything else, she thought, Shipley was a friend of Chris Hateley's and she had no idea whether

Chris would pass on any sort of version of his family situation to the policeman. Whatever Chris said, she had no doubt his father's role would be severely edited. Half way through the afternoon she closed up her files.

'I need a breath of fresh air,' she told Pam Bentley as she slipped her coat on. Pam looked at her curiously.

'You're not going down with something, are you?' she asked. 'There's some nasty bug going round.'

'Hope not,' Jay said, thinking that the bug which seemed to be going round Pendle Bridge was far nastier than Pam could imagine. 'I'll just have a stroll round the garden for ten minutes.' Outside she could see Fred Marston talking earnestly to a tall man in overalls by the front door of the main house, no doubt one of the workmen who had begun to make repairs, and she resolutely headed off in the opposite direction. It was a damp, grey afternoon, threatening rain, and the rhododendron walks at the back of the house dripped mournfully and offered little inspiration. She supposed she could try to contact an even more senior policeman than Shipley but she wondered what guarantee there was that anyone in the town had not been a friend or acquaintance of George Hateley's over the years. Was there anyone who would be willing to take the dying Granville Stott's revelations seriously? At least she had some sort of a relationship with Shipley, if a prickly one.

Heading back towards the house from the rear she was surprised to hear voices, this time coming from the small cobbled yard from which steps led up to the kitchens and down to the cellars. The heavy wooden gate was ajar and she peered inside to see a different pair of workmen busy inside the boiler house. One of them spotted her.

'You want the offices at the back, love,' he said. 'There's nowt round here except a right cock-up of a boiler and some bad drains.'

'No, it's all right,' she said. 'I work here.'

'Just out for a fag, is it?' The men laughed and turned back to the boiler leaving Jay feeling depressed and wondering whether she would ever see this old mausoleum of a place restored.

When she finally left Pendle House for the day she knew she would be late collecting Kate, although she was not anxious about the fact as Debbie Flint had promised to keep Kate in school until she arrived. Still uncertain about what to do next, she slowed down slightly as she passed the central police station, hesitated, and then put her foot down on the accelerator again. Stopping to talk to DCI Shipley now would make her even later, she reasoned, and in any case she was not entirely sure how she could expose George Hateley without being forced to admit that the allegations had come from Abbie. Perhaps, she thought, a more informal approach to Peter Shipley would be better, although what assumptions he would make if she called him and suggested they meet for a drink she could not imagine. Maybe asking him round to the cottage where the presence of Kate would neutralise the situation would be best.

She pulled up outside St. Peter's and strolled

towards Kate's classroom. But to her surprise the lights were out and the classroom door was locked. Neither Kate nor Debbie Flint was there. Nonplussed, Jay looked up and down the long school corridor. At the far end a cleaner was mopping the floor.

'Have you seen Debbie?' Jay asked. 'She was supposed to wait for me to collect my daughter.'

'Oh, aye?' the woman said.

'My daughter, Kate Morton? Debbie keeps an eye on her after school if I get held up on the way home from work?' A tiny niggle of anxiety was beginning to worm its way into Jay's mind.

'Oh, aye? That's Kate, is it?' the cleaner conceded slowly. 'Debbie were in a state about her. Said she had an appointment to keep and she couldn't get hold of Kate's mother.'

Jay pulled her mobile phone out of her bag and realised that she had switched it off at Sue's house at lunchtime and not switched it back on again. With no landlines fixed yet in her office, she had been out of touch with the world for hours.

'Damn and blast,' she said under her breath, glancing into the accusing eyes of the cleaner again. 'Did she take Kate home or something, d'you know?'

'Said she'd take her up to wherever it is you work,' the cleaner said, offhand now. 'Didn't know what else to do by the sound of it.' The woman swung her mop round and narrowly missed Jay's ankles. She ran back to her car, panic at her heels now, and drove back up the hill to Pendle House, cursing every innocent motorist who held her up, however briefly. She pulled up outside the house in a spray of disturbed gravel and was surprised to see that there were no longer any cars or vans parked there. When the cat's away, she thought grimly glancing at her watch. It was barely four-thirty, the time at which Pam Bentley was supposed to finish work.

Increasingly alarmed, she ran up the steps to the front door and found it locked. The offices at the back were similarly secure, and in desperation, running now and feeling an ominous tightness in her chest, she continued a complete circuit of the house until she came to the back yard where men had been working on the boiler only an hour earlier. The gate was still ajar but the men and their tools had gone and the boilerhouse appeared to be locked up. She took a gulp of air and was immediately aware of why the men had been complaining about the drains. A sweet musty smell pervaded the whole area and Jay suddenly felt cold and very afraid. She glanced over her shoulder before walking across the slippery green cobbles to the steps in the corner. She tried the kitchen door first, and found it securely locked, but when she went down the stone flight to the cellar door the smell was distinctly stronger. She pulled out the bunch of keys that Fred Marston had reluctantly handed over to her when she told him that she needed access to her office at all times. Most were unfamiliar and newly cut and she had to try several before she found one that fitted the cellar door. The smell was strong enough to make her gag as she swung the door open.

She knew by now instinctively what she had found, but she had to make sure. She could never remember afterwards how she steeled herself to make her way through the cellars, from room to cobwebbed room, most of them empty, one with a couple of dirty mattresses on the floor, until she found herself at the back of the house, in a tiny space dimly lit by the grey light from the area window high up on the grimy wall. There was a bundle on the filthy floor in one corner and flies rose angrily from it and whirled around her head as she approached. Sonja Kradic's face had been covered by the sacking in which she was wrapped, but when Jay pulled it back her fair hair and pale grey eyes gazed at her almost as if she was alive. Jay was aware of making some sort of anguished animal sound over the child's body, and then she was out in the almost fresh air again, icy cold and sweating and vomiting helplessly in the corner of the yard. Hauling herself from her knees eventually, still shivering violently, her face wet with tears, she pulled out her mobile phone and dialled 999. When the operator answered she could barely speak.

'Can you put me through to DCI Shipley,' she said hoarsely. 'Tell him I've found the missing child.' And through her sobs, she told the operator exactly where she was.

18

An hour later Jay was sitting in her own office, still shaking although she had her coat round her shoulders and her hands around a cup of hot sweet tea. A sympathetic young woman PC who had introduced herself as Sandra Peel sat beside her, talking quietly into her mobile phone.

'Mr. Shipley says he'll be here in about ten minutes,' the officer said.

'My daughter?' Jay said faintly, fears for Kate overwhelming even the shock of finding her school-friend's body.

'We've launched a full-scale search for her and Debbie Flint,' Sandra Peel said. 'I'm sure it's just a muddle rather than anything more sinister, Mrs. Morton. If your phone was switched off all afternoon...'

'Maybe,' Jay said, unconvinced and almost overwhelmed with the terror which had seized her in an iron grip and made her incapable of coherent thought. The girl, and she looked no more than a girl in spite of the uniform, was doing what everyone did, overtly or covertly: blaming the mother for anything which went wrong with the child, as if mothers were not more than capable of blaming themselves. She sipped her tea and tried to persuade her brain to function properly. The school cleaner had mentioned Debbie worrying about an appointment. She glanced at her watch to discover to her surprise that it was still only just five-thirty. Aeons seemed to have elapsed since she had failed to find Kate waiting for her at St. Peter's. If Debbie Flint had kept an appointment after school and taken Kate with her, it must surely be completed by now: doctor, dentist, hospital even, all their staff would be coming to the end of the day's appointments and going home themselves. She checked her mobile again for the tenth time in as many minutes but there were no messages.

'Why didn't she text me?' she asked, her anger and fear welling up again.

'We don't know she had a mobile. She was probably using the school phone,' Sandra countered, reasonably enough.

'But if they went somewhere after leaving the school Debbie should have taken her home by now,' she said angrily. 'I should be there, not hanging around here.'

'We've got an officer in a car outside your house,' the young PC said. 'Honestly, we're doing everything that can be done.'

'Does Debbie have a car?' Jay asked, not believing the girl.

'Apparently not, so she can't have gone far.'

You don't need to take a child far to do her harm, Jay thought desperately, fighting back hysteria and thinking of the short distance between Sonja Kradic's home and her final resting place in the cellar not much more than a mile and a half away. Some kids vanish on their way to the corner shop. She tried to push the thought out of her head. Kate was somewhere with a responsible adult, she told herself. She was perfectly safe. Debbie must have been vetted before being allowed to work in a school, mustn't she? Although she knew even that was not necessarily certain.

But then her mind veered off down another terrifying track. What if Debbie was in fact Donna, the runaway who had been seen back in Pendle Bridge by Mary Petherbridge, who had been startled enough by her reappearance to tell Granville Stott about it. What if, having been recognised, Donna, who might be Debbie, had gone on to stab her old antagonist from the children's home to death? If Donna was back, who knew what resentments she was harbouring after all this time. Was she the hooded figure who had come banging on the cottage door the previous night demanding to see Kenny Bairstow? Or the person who drowned mice and nailed masks to the door to terrify Kate? Or the person who made those endless silent phone-calls and got into the house, moving things just enough to make her think someone had been there but not enough to be totally sure? And if Donna was Debbie what might she now do to Kate? Jay groaned in frustration and put her head in her hands.

At that moment the door opened and DCI Peter Shipley came in, looking grim. He had abandoned his crumpled trenchcoat but his suit looked as if he had slept in it and he had evidently drawn dusty hands through his hair, leaving smudges on his forehead. He was not, Jay thought, someone who inspired much confidence.

'Have you found Kate?' she demanded before he could even draw breath to speak.

'Not yet,' he said. 'We're doing all we can but I'm sure it will turn out to be a simple misunderstanding, Mrs. Morton. There's no evidence that she's been abducted.'

'I think I should be at home, not here,' Jay said.

Shipley hesitated for a moment.

'I need ten minutes of your time now,' he said eventually. 'Then, if you like, Sandra here can drive you home and wait with you there. I'll need to talk to you again later about Sonja.'

Jay nodded, feeling numb and disoriented and hating the fact that her autonomy was being stripped away by the effects of shock and the demands of this uncertain ally of a policeman. Of course she should be helping with the search for Sonja's killers, she thought. Sonja was dead. But even that appalling fact seemed to fade into insignificance in the face of her overwhelming fear for Kate.

'All right,' she mumbled.

Shipley sat down across the table from her and gazed at his grubby hands for a moment, as if not sure that they belonged to him.

'Right,' he said. 'For now, just run through the events of this afternoon for me. Up to the point when you found Sonja.' Slowly, finding words hard to come by, Jay recounted everything that had happened since she had foolishly switched off her mobile phone at lunchtime, leaving out the fact that she had wanted to talk to her sister and brother-in-law without interruption. That can of worms would have to wait, she thought.

'Who had access to the cellar apart from you?' Shipley asked when she had finished.

'Fred Marston did have a complete set of keys,' she said. 'Although Bernard Grogan said he'd locked the cellars up himself some time ago because they were dangerous so he may have borrowed Fred's, or maybe he has his own. He didn't say. I'd never actually been down there until today but the key was on the ring Fred gave me. The men working in the yard earlier were complaining about the smell. They thought it was the drains. But for some reason I knew it wasn't.' She looked at Shipley, her face ashen and completely desolate. 'How do you recognise a smell you've never experienced before?' she asked. 'I knew, I absolutely knew, what it was. I thought of Kate and I knew what it was, though I knew in my mind it couldn't be her. But I was still terrified it might be. I had to look, even though I knew I wouldn't be able to bear it.'

Shipley looked at her for a long moment and Jay thought she saw a flash of sympathy in the blue eyes, which usually gave so little away.

'I'm sorry. You never get used to it,' he said, but he moved on quickly, as if embarrassed to reveal even this much of his own response to the unthinkable. 'Has anyone else been down there recently that you know of?' he asked.

'Yes, yes, the trustees, Mr Grogan and Mr Hateley. They went down there when they were assessing the house for repairs and, as I say, they said they'd locked everything up again securely. That was when they said it wasn't safe.' She hesitated, appalled.

'Sonja couldn't have been there then, could she?' she whispered.

'Can you remember what day that was?' Shipley asked, making a note of her answer without appearing even to have heard Jay's own question.

'Not exactly. I'll have to ask Pam, my assistant. She'll remember.'

'We'll need to talk to her, and to what's-his-name? Fred?'

'Fred Marston,' Jay said automatically, taking on board the appalling possibility that anyone she knew could now be a suspect.

'And the men who were working here today?'

'Fred will know where they came from,' Jay said. 'I'm not responsible for the house, just for the contents.'

Shipley made another note, and then nodded, apparently satisfied.

'It's best if you go home now, Mrs. Morton,' he said. 'I've a lot to organise here. But at some point I'll have to come and see Sonja's parents, so perhaps I can call on you after that?'

Jay nodded, knowing that she needed to tell Peter Shipley something else but for a moment her brain refused to recall what it was. She was overwhelmed by the idea of the pain which was about to be inflicted on Sonja's parents and the fear that it might be her turn next.

'There's something else,' she said, trying to put her whirling thoughts in order. 'Donna Latham, it's about Donna Latham.'

Shipley looked blank for a moment, then incredulous, then annoyed.

'You mean the girl who disappeared? You're not still harping on about that old case, are you?'

'You don't understand,' Jay said urgently. 'She's back in Pendle Bridge. She's not dead, she's alive, and she's back here and I had this awful feeling that maybe she's using the name Debbie Flint, that maybe she's the one who's been pestering me at the cottage, and now she's taken Kate for some reason.' Her voice trailed away helplessly.

'Mrs. Morton, you're not making much sense,' Shipley said, though not unkindly. 'You've had a terrible shock and you're naturally worried about your daughter, although my feeling is that she's perfectly safe with Debbie. The school seems quite sure she will be. Let Sandra take you home now and we'll talk later.'

'No, you don't get it, do you?' Jay shouted suddenly. 'Why don't you listen to me? Mary Petherbridge saw Donna, she recognised her – well, she would, wouldn't she? Mary Petherbridge saw her and told Granville Stott, and he told me.'

At Mary Petherbridge's name Shipley became very still, all the irritation draining from his face.

'Do you know when this was?' he asked.

Jay shook her head helplessly, unable to go on now that she had got the policeman's full attention.

'You'll have to ask Granville Stott, but he's very sick...'

'Yes, I heard he was,' Shipley said. He reached out a hand tentatively and touched Jay's.

'Go home,' he said quietly. 'Kate's probably

there by now. We'll talk again later when you feel better.'

'Right,' Jay said, feeling like a child, putting on her coat obediently. She thought she might vomit again as she followed the young PC to her car and handed over the keys to let her drive, but in the fresh air from the car window she began to feel her stomach settle. But there was not air fresh enough to eliminate the memory of the thick sweet stench of the Pendle House cellar or the image of a child's clear grey eyes looking up at her in mute reproach. Why? she thought. Why, why, why? And as she wept silently she also begged some higher power not to let her precious Kate be the next.

Still numb, Jay allowed the police officer called Sandra to take her home to the cottage, where another uniformed policeman was sitting in a Panda car outside and the curtains next door were already twitching. Mr. Booth put his head out of his front door as soon as Sandra had put on the handbrake and Jay had opened the passenger door.

'Nah then, is there owt I can do?' the old man asked. 'Nowt's happened to your little lass, an' all, has it?' He seemed genuinely concerned but it was all Jay could do not to scream at her neighbour as some sort of surrogate for all the adults who had let children down so unmercifully that day.

'Everything's under control, sir,' Sandra said, opening the front door with Jay's keys and almost pushing her inside.

'Well, not according to yon bobby there it's not,' Booth grumbled, waving at the Panda car. 'Sounds as if nowt's under control at all, wi' kids going missing all round t'bloody houses.'

Sandra closed the front door on Booth's curiosity with a bang and marched straight into the kitchen where she put the kettle on.

'You sit and relax and we'll have a nice cup of tea,' she said.

'Relax? You must be joking,' Jay snapped, but she felt so exhausted that she threw herself down on the settee in the living room and closed her eyes, close to despair.

And through the dark jumble of her thoughts floated the faces of David, her ex-husband, and her mother, both with accusation in their eyes. What have I done? she thought. They'll never forgive me. I'll never forgive myself.

Jay had no idea how long she and Sandra had been sitting sipping their tea in awkward silence, Jay deep in her own dark thoughts and Sandra evidently with no more comfort to offer, before the arthritic ring of the door-bell made them both visibly start.

'You stay there. I'll go,' Sandra said sharply and Jay knew without asking that she feared bad news. But when she felt a swirl of damp evening air as the door opened she also heard what she feared she might never hear again, Kate's voice, tired and querulous, as she marched into the house and dropped her schoolbag onto the floor.

'We're very, very late,' she said. Then, puzzled, as she took in the uniformed figure who had opened the door to her. 'Where's my mum?'

296

'I'm here, darling,' Jay said, striving to keep her own voice steady. 'Wherever have you been? We were so worried about you.'

Dodging Jay's outstretched arms with a look of contempt, Kate stomped into the kitchen, flung open the fridge and poured herself a glass of milk, grabbed a handful of biscuits and went into the living room where she turned on the TV. She flung herself into an armchair without giving her mother another glance. Jay turned away with her eyes full of tears. Outside on the doorstep, Sandra and the constable who had been sitting in the Panda car were deep in conversation with Debbie Flint. Jay joined them.

'Mrs. Morton, I'm so, so sorry,' Debbie said, her face flushed and her eyes flashing frantically between the two police officers and Jay herself. 'I tried and tried to get hold of you at work. I had this late appointment at the hospital. I've been waiting six weeks to see the consultant and I simply couldn't cancel it. So in the end I thought the best thing was to take Katie with me. I'd no idea I'd be so long, or that you'd call the police... Oh, my God.' And she burst into tears.

Jay stared at her, not wanting to believe such a simple explanation but knowing that it would be easy enough for the police to check the truth of it. She was panicked and paranoid, she thought, but she felt overwhelmed by everything that had happened and in no mood to make life easy for Debbie Flint. She turned away and went back into the house and heard Sandra tell the school assistant that taking a child away without a parent's consent was a serious matter and that

297

they would want a statement from her. She pushed the front door to as Debbie was ushered into the Panda car still in tears. In the living room Kate was absorbed in *Neighbours*. Jay went into the kitchen, her mind made up. She called a London number and it was answered almost immediately by her ex-husband who, as she had hoped, must have been working at home that day. He sounded surprised to hear from her, and slightly defensive.

'You're not going to cancel the half term visit, are you, Jay?' he asked. 'We're looking forward to having her.'

'No,' Jay said, fighting back tears. 'What I'd like you to do is have her next week as well.' And she told him what had happened to Sonja Kradic.

'Good God,' David said.

'She was her best friend at school,' Jay said. 'She doesn't know yet but she's going to be devastated. I'd like her away from all the disturbance there's going to be round here. She's had enough to put up with...' She glanced at the closed kitchen door warily, afraid Kate might hear the conversation, but the TV volume was high enough, she thought, to give them privacy.

'Can we bring the arrangements forward a week?' she asked, afraid that David might have other plans, but he didn't hesitate.

'Of course,' he said. 'No problem.' He hesitated then for a second. 'I miss her dreadfully, you know.'

'Can you come up by car and fetch her?' she asked and realised from the silence at the other end that she had been too peremptory.

'I can't take the time off work,' David said, his voice colder now. 'Why don't you bring her down?'

Jay bit back a sharp retort and hesitated for a second or two, thinking of her own job, the demands the police would be making, Sue and Abbie's desperation.

'Kate really, really wants to see you,' she said. 'How about if I put her on a train in Leeds and ask the guard to look after her. Could you pick her up at Kings' Cross? She'd think that was a great adventure.'

'Are you sure?' David asked. 'Will they do that on the train? Like an air steward would?'

'I'll check it out,' Jay said. 'I'll call you back. I just think it's so important to get her away from here quickly. But it's difficult for me to come too.' As she hung up the door opened and Sandra came into the kitchen, closing the door behind her again.

'She's OK,' she said. 'She confirms what Debbie Flint said, they went to the hospital and had to wait ages. I think it was all quite innocent.'

'And bloody irresponsible,' Jay said, her voice sharp.

'Kate says Debbie tried to phone you several times.' Sandra's voice was neutral but Jay knew that she was thinking of the switched off mobile. She suddenly felt overwhelmed with tiredness.

'Whatever,' she said. 'And now I have to tell her that her best friend's dead.'

Jay felt completely wrung out by the time DCI Peter Shipley fulfilled his promise to call round to see her later. He had already phoned to give Sandra Peel permission to end her shift and after she had left, Jay had persuaded Kate to go to bed. She had taken the news of Sonja's death quietly enough at first.

'I thought she must be dead,' was all she had said as she sipped a mug of drinking chocolate. But as she pulled the duvet up to her chin she had grabbed her mother's hand and the tears had come.

'I thought she might have fallen into the canal,' she said through her sobs. 'I thought she might have got lost on the moors. Ben said people do get lost on the moors sometimes. But someone killed her, didn't they? The man in the car got her, didn't he? She was murdered.'

'We don't know that yet,' Jay had said, stroking the dark curls away from Kate's damp forehead. 'The police have to ask a lot of questions to find out what happened. That's why I want you to go and stay with Daddy for a bit, until all the unpleasantness is over.'

'Why can't you come too?' Kate asked. 'I want to go back to London and stay there.' And her sobs intensified.

'You know that's not possible while I'm working here, darling,' Jay said.

'So get another job in London.'

It was, Jay thought wryly, the best idea she had heard all day but she did not want to raise Kate's hopes. What was to happen to them both next needed some very careful thought.

'We'll see,' she said, giving Kate a hug, as the storm of sobbing passed. 'I promise I'll think about it. In the meantime you can have a ride on a train tomorrow. You'll enjoy that. The guard will look after you and Daddy will meet you. Do you think you can cope with that?'

'I want to see my Daddy,' Kate had whispered and eventually she had fallen asleep, her tear-stained face hot and rosy against the white pillow, and Jay had crept back downstairs exhausted to find Peter Shipley, as grey faced as she felt herself, standing again in pouring rain on her doorstep.

'How can I help you?' she asked wearily when they were settled at the kitchen table and he had accepted a cup of coffee.

'I've just come from the Kradic's,' he said. 'They've identified the body. They're devastated, of course.'

'Of course,' Jay said. 'I was that close to being there a few hours ago myself.'

'I was relieved that turned out well,' Shipley said. 'That's something. Is she OK?'

'Not really,' Jay said. 'Her trip with Debbie Flint may not have perturbed her at all, but she was very fond of Sonja. I'm sending her to her father's for a couple of weeks.'

'Sounds like a good idea.' The policeman sipped his coffee and Jay wondered if he had a family. She had never heard one mentioned and she shied away from an exhibition of the family snapshot in the wallet as her own relationships fell apart.

'I suppose they'll still try to send the Kradic family back, even after this?'

'I suppose they will,' Shipley agreed. 'They think Kosovo's safe now.'

'Not if you're a Serb married to an Albanian it's not,' Jay said. 'It's not safe at all.'

'Not my responsibility, thank God,' Shipley said. 'But Sonja's death is, so let's concentrate on that, shall we? Start at the beginning and tell me everything you know about Sonja and Kate, and what's been happening at the school.'

Jay wracked her brain for every detail of the two girls' brief time together and the threat from someone driving by in a car which all the children had been warned about.

'You need to talk to the school staff,' she said. 'They'll probably know more than I do, more than they put in the letter to parents, perhaps.'

'That's top of the tasks for tomorrow,' Shipley said. 'But you say Kate was sure the man in the car who frightened her was wearing a mask.'

'Quite sure,' Jay said. 'And it sounded like one of those I reckon is missing from Pendle House. And the one nailed to our door certainly was.'

'So when do you think they were stolen? Do you think it was recent?'

'Fred Marston reckoned that someone had been up in the attics fairly recently. There were footprints on the top corridor that he said were from trainers, but I honestly wouldn't know. They've all been scuffed away by now, of course. We never thought they were particularly significant.'

'But the masks could conceivably have been taken years ago? When the kids were living there, for instance?'

'They could, I suppose,' Jay said. 'But the one hung on my door, as you know, that was in good

302

condition. Not scuffed or damaged in any way. I'd guess it had been wrapped up safely until quite recently. It wasn't chipped or scratched at all.'

Shipley nodded, pulling a wry face at the thought of the cannibal bird again.

'There were prints on it, by the way, but no one we've got on record,' he said.

'What makes you think they might have been taken years ago?' Jay asked.

Shipley shrugged, looking uncomfortable.

'Just something I recalled from way back,' he said. 'Something I should have thought of earlier. A connection I should have made. There was a case about fifteen years ago, some little tarts from the Bradfield Road flats had set themselves up in what amounted to a brothel in an empty flat. There wasn't much to it. They were taking a couple of quid from the local lads most of the time. But when we finally jumped on them one of the lasses complained about a man who went up there by car and wore some sort of mask to disguise himself. She was obviously scared stiff of him, said he'd hurt her. We didn't take it very seriously at the time. The DCI reckoned she was trying to make excuses, making out she'd been coerced, when in fact the whole sordid little enterprise had been dreamed up by the girls themselves. But when you started talking about masks I looked up the records. The mask was a scary bird, she said. A brightly coloured scary bird.'

'How old was the girl?' Jay asked, with a feeling of foreboding.

'Thirteen,' Shipley said. 'And small for her age.'

'So what you're saying is that child abuse has been going on for fifteen years at least,' Jay said, the anger of the last few weeks suddenly exploding. 'Or could it be twenty? And you've done damn all about it? If you've got records of that case, what about Margaret Emmet? Could the person who killed Sonja have hurt your little tart and killed Mags too? How many sadistic child molesters can there be in one small town? Or is that a jump too far because you got the first case terribly wrong? Was it you personally? Or your precious DCI that Kenny Bairstow's solicitor still believes bullied him into confessing.'

Peter Shipley did not reply. He sat gazing into his coffee cup, his mind evidently a long way away.

'You don't have a very high opinion of the police, do you?' he eventually asked, surprisingly mildly.

'Not in Pendle Bridge, no,' Jay said, still furious. 'These are children we're talking about, twelve, thirteen-year-olds. All these girls were victims, not just Sonja. They weren't to blame for their own exploitation.'

Shipley nodded.

'It's not confirmed but it looks as if Sonja was raped,' he said slowly. 'There'll be forensic evidence. But I'd be very surprised if there were still forensic samples from the Emmet case. I was a junior DC then, as it goes. I wasn't involved in Kenny Bairstow's interrogation and as far as I'm concerned Les Green was an honest copper. He taught me most of what I know.'

304

Jay sighed and Shipley straightened up and met her disappointment head on.

'I'll see what the forensic labs can dig up on the Emmet case,' he said. 'I think I need to do that for my own satisfaction as well as yours.' And Jay realised that at last she had made a tiny dent in the monument of denial which had surrounded Kenny Bairstow since she had first heard the boy's name.

'There's something else you need to know,' Jay said slowly. 'As we're talking about child molesters. I can't tell you who's made the accusation at the moment, though I hope I can persuade her, or her parents, to make a complaint. But the person accused is George Hateley. And the victim is a girl of thirteen.'

'That's a very serious allegation, Mrs. Morton,' Shipley said, his face frozen in shock.

'I know that,' Jay said quietly. 'And I wouldn't be making it against a man who's effectively my boss if I didn't believe it was true.'

19

When Donna heard the news of Sonja Kradic's death on the local radio news the next morning she thought her heart had stopped beating. She put down her coffee cup because her hand shook so much and took deep, slow breaths to steady herself. But there was nothing she could do to quiet the voices which broke into a cacophonous babble in her head, all of them shouting to be heard. Even Archie, beloved Archie, who had been with her from the beginning, who had kept her safe from her father all those years ago, seemed to have given up on her now. It was her fault, he said, echoing Mags and the small child who only usually spoke when the rest of them were quiet. And whatever she said was repeated by a whole chorus of childish voices. Your fault, your fault, they screamed, children turning into demons and beginning to materialise in front of her eyes. Your fault, your fault.

It was happening again, Mags repeated faintly, her whole body shaking, as the children danced jerkily away. Her own voice grew more strident as the minutes ticked by. Then Archie broke in, but an Archie she no longer recognised as her long time friend. You heard what they said on the news. A man with a mask in a car. A man with a mask. He's still here. You know he's still here. And you've done nothing about him. Well, it's over with you, Donna Latham. I'm finished with you. You're too slow. Too cautious. If you won't finish the job I'll do it for you. Too slow, too slow, Archie parrotted, his voice growing harsh with excitement. Mags will do the job.

She pushed her coffee to one side and finished dressing in her tracksuit and trainers. Then she pulled her suitcase out from under the bed and unzipped one of the compartments and pulled out the knife she had bought in London all those months ago. She had kept it in its original cardboard sheath and padded bag and it gleamed in the dim light of her bedroom where the curtains were still half closed. It was heavy in her hand, but comfortable and she ran her finger down the blade and winced slightly as she drew a bead of bright blood. She was satisfied. It was more than adequate for what she had to do. She sheathed the blade up again and replaced it in the bag, and pinned the whole thing inside her sweat pants against her flat stomach. It felt comfortably at home there.

She tidied up the flat meticulously, washing up the breakfast dishes and putting them away in the cupboard, wiping down the sink and the surfaces, washing out the small rubbish bin under the sink with disinfectant and finally folding the teatowel over the radiator. Then she made the bed, plumping up the duvet and the pillows, opening the curtains wide and glancing without any interest at the damp grey morning outside. She took the rubbish bag down to the dustbin in its cupboard outside the front door and put the lid back on firmly before going back upstairs. She glanced around the flat for one last time. Mags had always been tidy. She did not imagine that she would be coming back but as she closed the door she slipped the key into her pocket just in case.

She had discovered where to find her quarry at last from a small item in the *Advertiser*. It looked as if it was a fixture, appearing every week, but she had not noticed it before. It was early yet and she decided to jog, setting off at a gentle pace down the hill towards the Saturday morning bustle of the town centre. There was no hurry. She knew he would be there at the time stated and she knew he would see her. He would have no reason not to. He would not remember her face. Mags was confident, buoyed up by the thought of resolution at last. She breathed easily as she ran. She did not want to get overheated this morning by pushing herself too hard. And Donna and Archie and the small child who had failed to kill her father and watched her mother do it instead trailed along behind her without a word.

Jay Morton braked with a heart-stopping screech of tyres at a zebra crossing. In front of her a woman with a pushchair glared angrily at her and Jay mouthed an apology through the windscreen. She had lost concentration for a second and she knew she must control her inner fury if she was to get back to Pendle Bridge without damage to herself or anyone else. She and Kate had got up at six that morning to drive to Leeds to catch the London train, after checking that the conductor

– not the guard these days, she was told loftily – would keep an eye on Kate during the two-and-a-half hour journey. Kate had been surprisingly cheerful after the previous evening's tears, her grief for Sonja evidently assuaged by the prospect of seeing her father.

'Will you come as well, Mummy?' she had asked more than once, though with decreasing hope as Jay said she could not, though promising that she would try to collect her at the end of her stay. In the end she had been overwhelmed by the excitement of a train trip, dancing down the broad platform, dodging abstracted travellers, to where the throbbing red express waited, rushing up and down the almost empty carriage to find exactly the right seat, arranging her soft drink and her crisps, her Harry Potter book and Jay's mobile phone carefully on the table in front of her, and flashing a brilliant smile at the female conductor when Jay explained to her that Kate would be travelling alone.

'I'll check her out after Doncaster,' the woman said. 'We don't stop again after that. Don't you worry. We'll get her there safe and sound. And I'll hang on to her until her father finds her at the other end.'

'Daddy will be waiting for you at Kings Cross,' Jay said. 'And he'll ring you if he's delayed for any reason. And you ring him if you have any problems. Ring me after the train gets going again after Doncaster. Keep in touch, darling. And this lady will help you if you're worried about anything at all. All right?'

'Yes, Mum, I know, Mum,' Kate said, putting

on her most grown-up face now. 'Don't worry, I'll be fine.'

But as the long train snaked out of the station with Kate waving cheerfully from the window, Jay felt far from fine. She would be anxious, she knew, until she heard that David had safely collected Kate, as arranged. It was, she thought, an unforgivable imposition, driven by desperation, to send the child so far on her own, although Kate herself had shown not the slightest sign of nerves, regarding the whole thing as an adventure. But quite apart from that, she was almost overwhelmed by a mixture of sadness and rage at what had happened to Sonja and Abbie. More than once on the winding drive back to Pendle Bridge she had to shake her attention back onto the road until the near miss on the zebra crossing concentrated her mind for the final few miles.

When she got home the phone was ringing and she was only faintly surprised to hear her assistant Pam Bentley's voice or the note of outrage in it.

'That poor child,' Pam said. 'What is it with these men? They should be castrated. You must be devastated, finding her like that.'

'It's public knowledge now, is it?' Jay said, slightly wearily.

'Well, it was on the radio news that they'd found a body, but then the police called me. They'd been trying to get hold of you, apparently, and then tried me. They wanted me to go up to the office to give them the inventory of those horrible masks. I hope you don't mind. So they told me

310

what had happened yesterday.'

'Right,' Jay said automatically wondering why Peter Shipley wanted the inventory so urgently.

'Anyway, when I got there I couldn't find it.' Pam had gone on with her story without apparently taking breath.

'What?' Jay said sharply. 'It was in with my notes...'

'Yes, yes, I know that, but your notes weren't there either so I thought you'd taken the whole lot home and you still weren't answering your mobile...'

'I gave it to Kate for the train,' Jay said, causing Pam to hesitate, though only for a second.

'Well, fortunately I finished putting the whole list onto the computer yesterday afternoon after you left so I could print it out for them.'

'I didn't bring anything home yesterday,' Jay said sharply, reducing Pam to silence.

'Oh,' Pam said at last. 'So where has that file gone?'

Jay didn't answer directly.

'Who asked you for the inventory? Was it DCI Shipley?'

'Yes, yes, he was there. They're using the office as a – what did he call it? Command centre, I think, until they've finished their searches up there.'

'So you gave him a copy? You didn't give him the floppy disk?'

'No,' Pam said, obviously puzzled now. 'I put it in my handbag, as it happens, and brought it away with me. They were making such a muddle up there, messing about with the computers even, and your file was missing, I thought I'd better keep it safe. I backed it up onto a floppy – I always do – and I thought that might be the only version we have now.'

'Well done,' Jay said, thinking she was getting more and more paranoid. 'I'll find out from the police when they think we'll be able to use the offices again. If you'll feel comfortable going back there, Pam.'

'Oh, yes, I'll be all right,' Pam Bentley said with surprising cheerfulness. 'It's quite exciting really, isn't it? It's funny, I was at school with that girl that got murdered all those years ago, Margaret Emmet, she was called. Or Margaret Davies, was it? Mags, anyway. But there was something odd about her name: she wanted to be called Emmet after her mother because her father had been such a bastard, but the school had her down as Davies and she wouldn't answer to it. Caused a fuss every day at registration. The father must have been a Davies, I suppose. She didn't talk about it much. In fact those kids from Pendle House didn't mix much at all. They clung together. But there'd been a lot of violence, one way or another, I remember that much. Anyway, whatever, she ended up dead, did Mags, murdered by her boyfriend.'

Jay swallowed hard.

'You were at school with her – and Donna Latham?' she asked.

'That's right,' Pam said. 'They were at Pendle House when it was the children's home. You must remember. You lived in Pendle Bridge then as well, didn't you?'

'I'd gone away to university by then,' Jay said automatically.

'Of course, they didn't come to school that often. They were always bunking off, those two. And then Mags got killed and Donna disappeared. I wonder what happened to her? I began to think this Sonja child wasn't going to be found, didn't you? It went on so long. How's your Kate taken it? She knew her, didn't she?'

'I've sent her to London to stay with her father for a bit,' Jay said. 'I have to go now, Pam. There's something urgent I have to do. Thanks for standing in for me with the police. That was very good of you.' And to her relief Pam said goodbye and hung up.

Margaret Davies was a common enough name, she thought. But the Margaret Davies she had met had come to Pendle Bridge from London and where else would a child run to twenty years ago but the anonymous capital, and what other name might she adopt if she wanted to hide her identity than that of her dead best friend. Her hands trembled slightly as she dialled the police. But the murder team, it appeared, was having a briefing and the operator agreed merely to pass a message to Peter Shipley to call her as soon as it was over.

Frustrated, Jay slammed the rest up and down and dialled her sister. The phone, rang for some time before Sue answered, sounding deeply depressed.

'How's Abbie?' Jay asked.

'She's been awake most of the night, crying,' Sue said. 'She's asleep now but I can hardly keep

313

my eyes open.'

'I'm sorry. Have you decided what to do about it all?'

'I haven't spoken to Chris since he left,' Sue mumbled.

'I think you should decide yourself,' Jay said. 'Chris is obviously reluctant to put in a complaint against his own father. Go to the police, for God's sake. You owe it to other children George might have interfered with – or might in the future. He should be locked up.'

'Abbie says she won't talk about it to anyone else. I can't force her. She says they didn't have sex, didn't go all the way, for what that's worth. She's so knowledgeable, Jay, so experienced. It's horrible.'

'They went far enough – and it's not they, it's he, for God's sake. He took advantage of her, and it's illegal and he's a bloody child molester, Sue. Even if he didn't rape Abbie there's no knowing who he did rape. You have to do something about it.'

'I can't if Abbie won't,' Sue said hopelessly. 'She won't go to the doctor, she won't go to the police, she's curled up in bed in a knot, crying and dozing and then crying again...'

'She needs help,' Jay said, growing more and more desperate. At the other end of the line she realised that her sister was crying too. 'Well, I've already told Inspector Shipley that I've heard allegations about George. They can make what they like of that but with a child dead it's the least I can do.'

'You don't think he killed that girl?' Sue sounded close to hysteria herself now.

314

'I've no idea, but if he's a paedophile the police need to know that. He's in and out of Pendle House all the time with his mate Grogan. George certainly had the opportunity to hide her body up there.'

'Oh God,' Sue said. 'I can't believe this is happening.'

'You'd better believe it because it can only get worse,' Jay said without much sympathy. 'Where is Chris, by the way? I need to talk to him.'

'Not about Abbie? Leave it alone, Jay. It's our problem.'

'No, not about Abbie as it happens.'

'He's staying with his father,' Sue said slowly.

'Wonderful,' Jay said. 'I'll meet him somewhere else, then. I'm not sure I can control myself if I see George Hateley this morning.'

Jay caught up with Chris on his mobile and he reluctantly agreed to meet her for a coffee in the town centre. But just as she was about to set off the phone in the house rang again and she found herself connected to DCI Shipley.

'You called,' he said, obviously not in a mood to waste words.

'Donna Latham,' Jay said, responding in kind. 'I've been told her friend Mags Emmett was officially Margaret Davies, her father's name. Did you know that a Margaret Davies has recently arrived in Pendle Bridge from London? She applied for the job Pam Bentley's doing and didn't get it, but she did get a job with Chris Hateley at the *Advertiser*. And I know she was looking around this area for somewhere to live.'

Shipley was very quiet for a moment.

'The girl's name was Davies, though most people called her Emmett because that's what she preferred and that's the name we used with the Press. I do remember that. Are you suggesting Donna could have taken over her identity?'

'It's not that difficult to do if someone's dead, is it? I've read about it happening to get false passports and so on,' Jay said.

'It's a possible line of inquiry,' Shipley conceded.

'At the very least, she could be the person who's been harrassing me and Kate,' Jay insisted. 'You know Donna Latham's in Pendle Bridge. She's been seen, according to Granville Stott. But would she use her real name if she came back to cause trouble? Surely not?'

'We'll check it out, Mrs. Morton,' Shipley said. 'Thanks for your help.'

Feeling dismissed and dissatisfied, Jay put her coat on and drove into the town centre where the Saturday morning shoppers had reduced many of the narrow streets to a no-go zone for cars. Finally easing into a parking space, she walked the short distance to the town's first, and so far only, American coffee shop where Chris was wrapped defensively around a cappuccino and barely looked up as she walked in. Jay waved the list away impatiently.

'I need to see your father,' she said. 'I've told the police that I think he's a paedophile. I didn't offer them any victims' names but I guess Peter Shipley'll be arriving to talk to him pretty soon. The least I can do is tell him to his face what I've done.'

316

Chris said nothing for a moment, his face grey and haggard, his eyes refusing to meet Jay's. He seemed to have aged ten years overnight.

'I had no idea,' he said. 'Not at first. You have to believe that.'

'I don't know what I believe any more, Chris,' Jay said. 'Nothing in Pendle Bridge is quite what it seems.' She glanced at the new Pay as you Talk mobile she had bought as soon as the shops opened and then at her watch. She had given Kate and David the number but she knew that the train was not due into Kings Cross for another half hour. She wondered if Kate was still as cheerful as she had been when she set off, and her heart ached. Wearily she turned her attention back to her brother-in-law.

'You must understand. The Kenny Bairstow thing was so open and shut, over so quickly, that no one dreamed it might not have been him. But later, when he launched an appeal and I began to look into it in more detail, I began to have my doubts.'

'But you didn't follow them up.' It was a statement not a question and Jay's voice was full of contempt.

'My father said that someone he knew had got too close to those girls and people might jump to the wrong conclusion. He asked me to leave it alone.'

'It didn't cross your mind that it might have been him who'd got too close?'

'I thought he was covering up for a friend, probably for Les Green.' Chris stared fixedly into the froth in his cup.

317

'The policeman who put Kenny away?' Jay said, astonished. 'You mean he might have killed Mags himself and then set Kenny up?' The enormity of what Chris was suggesting almost took her breath away.

'They were mates, those three, always had been from way back, my father, Bernie Grogan and Les Green. They drank together, played rugby together when they were younger, until the injuries got them, connived together politically to make sure their party ran the town. My father never went into detail, just suggested it would be better to leave the Kenny Bairstow case alone. It wouldn't do my career any good to embarrass people, he said.'

'And you went along with it? Even though you found out that Kenny was very unlikely to be into pornography, that he was very unlikely to be able to rape that girl, that according to his mother he was their best friend and loved them to bits? You left him to rot in jail for something he hadn't done? And left a child murderer free to carry on and do it again?'

Chris said nothing, still gazing into his empty coffee cup in silence and Jay saw a tear run down his cheek until he dashed it away angrily.

'You are disgusting. And you've wrecked your daughter's life,' Jay said.

'Rubbish,' Chris said, with a spark of anger. 'I still think she's probably making the whole thing up. My father wasn't involved in all this. No way. Abbie's never much liked her grandfather and she's getting her own back for some reason of her own. She's a malicious little cow.'

318

'I don't think so,' Jay snapped. People's capacity for self-deception never ceased to amaze her. Her heart ached for Abbie, curled up in bed like a wounded animal.

'Who stole the masks?' she asked. Chris shrugged.

'I think my father's friends did, years ago.'

'To terrorise young girls?'

'I've no idea.'

'And who hung one on my front door, to terrorise Kate?'

'That was me,' Chris said, and Jay wondered if she had imagined just the faintest hint of remorse in his voice. 'When my father said he didn't want you stirring up the Kenny Bairstow case, even after all this time, he asked if I could put you off somehow. At first I think he thought you and I could get it together again and I could persuade you to leave it alone. He always liked you, you know? Fancied you as a daughter-in-law.' Chris gave a hollow laugh. 'Anyway, that approach didn't get me far, did it?'

'Even that was smoke and mirrors, was it?' Jay asked bitterly. 'And there was I thinking it was something different.'

'You're much too prim to go down that road,' Chris snapped. 'I should have realised.'

'So you turned on Kate instead?'

'It was perfectly obvious Kate didn't want to stay in Pendle Bridge so we thought it would be easy to persuade you to go back where you came from if I unsettled her a bit more. He said he got hold of the mask from a friend. I didn't realise its significance, I promise you. I'd no idea it came

319

from Pendle House. I didn't do Kate any harm, Jay. It was just a couple of practical jokes.'

'You scared her half to death,' Jay said, her voice full of contempt. 'You never did know me very well, Chris, did you, if you thought you could get away with that? And the dead mice? The phone calls. The visits in the night? That was all you? And creeping around in my house, moving things, scaring the wits out of me? That was a joke?'

Chris looked puzzled.

'I never came into your house,' he said. 'How could I? I don't have a key.'

'So who...?' Jay hesitated. 'You're really asking me to believe I had two stalkers?'

He nodded slowly.

'Perhaps you did. You said you'd had some funny phone calls so I gave you a few more. And I wasn't the only person hanging around your cottage, you know. There was a woman looking through your front window one night. I don't know who she was.'

'I think I do,' Jay said slowly. 'I'm sure I had two stalkers, not just you.' She put her hands over her eyes and pressed hard for a second, gazing into the darkness. Betrayal came in all shapes and sizes, she thought, and she had had more than her share, more, surely, than she deserved. Then her anger for Kate and Abbie took hold again.

'You know I don't know which of you is the bigger bastard, your father doing what he did to Abbie and probably other girls as well, for all we know, or you for covering up for him and terrifying my daughter. Where's your father now? I want to tell him to his face exactly what I think of him before the police pick him up. That's the only satisfaction I'll get out of this mess, unless I see you all in court. You disgust me, Chris, utterly and completely. I never, never want to see or speak to you again.'

George Hateley sat behind a desk in the reception area of Bernard Grogan's constituency office sorting through the post which had accumulated since the MP's last Saturday morning voters' surgery. A couple of depressed-looking men sat on grey plastic chairs against the wall, reading the sports pages and waiting their turn to take their problems to the local representative of the power which they generally blamed for their desperate situation. No one so much as glanced up as Jay opened the door, the glass opaque with posters and the remnants of posters. She positioned herself in front of Hateley until she had his attention. His smile of recognition faltered as he took in her grim expression.

'I need to talk to you,' she said quietly. 'In private.'

Hateley's eyes flickered round the room.

'What's it about, Jay?' he asked.

'You don't want me to tell you here,' she said, glancing at the waiting clients. Hateley flushed and then turned very pale, his usual bluster draining away.

'I'll ask Bernie if we can borrow his office as soon as he's finished with the woman he's got in there now,' Hateley said, glancing at the door just behind him. 'He shouldn't be long. Kate's all right, is she?'

'Kate's gone to London to see her father,' Jay said, knowing now, to her immense relief, that Kate and David had actually found each other safely at Kate's journey's end. Ending the brief call from the noisy train terminal she had felt as if she had just received a reprieve from a death sentence. Now, she tapped her fingers on the desk, impatient to get this over and be rid of Hateley and his son, if possible for ever, so she and Kate could return to something approaching a normal life again.

Suddenly, from behind the closed door, there came a sound which was half a scream and half a groan, and then a man's voice calling quite distinctly for help.

'Jesus, what's that?' Hateley said, lumbering to his feet and opening the door into the other room. Jay followed him and faced a scene which paralysed her with shock.

'You'd better come in, Mr. Hateley,' the woman she knew as Margaret Davies said, glancing up from what appeared to be a body slumped on the floor and half concealed by the desk towards the back of the room. She held a long blood-stained kitchen knife in her right hand and her tracksuit was splattered with blood and more was oozing from beneath the desk and forming a crimson pool in a slight depression in the dirty floor tiles. A low moan came from behind the desk. Bernard Grogan was evidently still alive but as Jay stared in horror at the steadily moving flow of blood she wondered how long he could survive. Appalled, she spun round, hoping to get out of the room but Davies was too quick for her. She leapt across the small space and slammed the door with a strange high pitched cry, slashing the steel knife so close to Jay that she felt the air move against her cheek. Jay backed away sharply, colliding with George Hateley who was also attempting clumsily to get out of the office and they almost fell into each other. His face had gone the colour of putty and he was breathing heavily.

'Stay here or I'll finish him off. I want to talk to you, too,' the woman said to Hateley, her eyes shining with an unnatural glitter.

She jabbed her knife at Hateley's neck, slashing the hand he flung up to protect himself and drawing blood beneath his chin but evidently missing vital vessels. She waved them both further into the room.

'I recognised your voice,' she said as Hateley sank into the chair facing the desk, clutching his neck, shuddering with shock, his shirt collar soaked with blood. Jay stood stock still with her back to the wall trying to control her own breathing. Grogan was still moaning but more quietly now, his breath bubbling in his throat as his strength evidently ebbed and the viscous pool of blood grew larger and slithered round the leg of the chair in front of the desk and reached Hateley's shoes though, with his eyes fixed on the woman with the knife, he was unaware of anything else.

'Let me see if I can help Mr. Grogan,' Jay whispered, but Davies just laughed. For a split second she seemed to glance over Jay's shoulder at the wall with a distracted look in her eyes.

'Yes,' she said, just as if there were someone else in the room. Then, focusing on Jay again, she seemed to remind herself of Jay's question and become aware of Grogan's desperate struggle for air behind the desk.

'He's going to hell where he belongs,' she said in a matter of fact tone. 'And so is this one.' She nodded at Hateley who had further slumped down in the chair, his face chalk white now, his eyes bulging, his feet sliding in his friend's lifeblood.

'I don't know you,' he said faintly.

'Oh, yes you do,' the woman said. 'You've forgotten me but you know me. Even in the biblical sense you know me. You may have hidden behind a mask but you didn't bother to disguise your voice. I'm Mags. Mags Emmett. And you did things to me that no one should do to a child. You hurt me, over and over when I asked you to stop. And he...'

'You can't be Mags,' Hateley muttered, but Davies just laughed again, more wildly. She swept her knife perilously close to Hateley again, before pointing towards Grogan, whose breathing was growing fainter.

'He took his mask off and then he strangled me,' she said. She moved away from Hateley for a moment, pointed the knife menacingly at Jay and quickly turned the key in the lock, before putting the knife to Hateley's throat again.

'Now, we can all have a nice chat without being interrupted,' she said. 'It's been such a long time since I saw you. I've been really looking forward to it.'

324

Her mouth dry, Jay watched in silence, wondering if the two men in the outer office would have realised something was terribly wrong. She wondered if screaming would distract them from their newspapers or whether it would merely bring that lethal blade slicing in her direction. It was a small room and becoming desperately hot and thick with the smell of blood. She swallowed hard as she realised Bernard Grogan's laboured breathing had stopped and the pool of blood had ceased to move.

DCI Peter Shipley drove from the Pendle Bridge police station to Bernard Grogan's constituency office through the mid-morning Saturday traffic with some reluctance. He was going to talk to George Hateley because he had to, rather than because he wanted to. But he had recognised in Jay Morton an implacable quality which he knew would not let him rest until he had dealt with Hateley and her allegations against him, vague as they were. The trip, he thought, was almost certainly a distraction from the two murder inquiries which, if he did not make significant progress soon, threatened to provoke heavyweight intervention from county HQ. What he really should be doing was pushing the murder teams into frantic action and watching his back. But he reckoned he owed it to his friend Chris Hateley to deal with this personally.

At his side DS Jack Barraclough, always taciturn, was letting him know with every inch of his body hunched inside his duffle jacket that this was a Saturday morning's overtime too far. And away at the back of his mind was the destabilising knowledge that the absolute faith he had placed in his old boss Les Green might not have been remotely justified.

They parked a block away from the office where George Hateley's wife had told them he was working that morning and made their way to the shop-front which housed the constituency party HQ. A man in tracksuit bottoms and an England football shirt was coming out as they approached and almost bumped into Barraclough's burly form as he turned into the doorway.

'You'll wait all day, mate, if you go in theer,' the man said, scowling as he stood aside. 'I've been theer an hour and some bird swans in and gets to see Bernie ahead of the queue wi'out a please or bloody thank you. Bloody brilliant!'

Shipley hesitated for a moment.

'What did she look like, this woman?' he asked, putting a hand on the man's arm which was flung off as if he had been stung.

'Look like?' he said incredulously. 'She were just a middle-aged bird, weren't she? Nowt to write home about. George Hateley seemed to know her and took her in to see Grogan.'

'Blonde? Dark? Tall...?'

'Tall, dark hair, right curly, looked like she'd not combed it for a week, a brown leather jacket, quite nice that. A right posh bitch, though. Not from round here,' the man said and Shipley half-smiled, recognising a description of Jay Morton, whose accent would always give her away in this part of town. Although there was another woman from London in town, according to Jay herself, and he felt a slight niggle of anxiety at the back of his mind.

'What's it to you, any road?' the man continued belligerently. 'D'you know her or summat? You can tell her to bloody wait her turn next time, snotty cow, even if she is a mate o'Hateley's. I've not got all day to waste hanging around here.'

Barraclough pushed open the door, glanced at the second man in the waiting room and jerked his thumb over his shoulder.

'You may be in for a long wait, flower,' he said. 'I'd come back later if I was you.'

But when he eased himself round the back of Hateley's desk and tried the door to the inner office, he found it locked and rapped sharply on the wood.

'Mr. Hateley?' he said. 'Are you in there, Mr. Hateley? It's the police. We need a word.'

There was no response from the other side.

Shipley and Barraclough exchanged looks, faint alarm in both their eyes now. Shipley turned quickly to the waiting man who was still folding his newspaper with deliberation, on the point of leaving.

'How many people should be in there?' he asked. 'To your knowledge?'

Pale blue eyes in a stolid, pale square face gazed back at Shipley.

'Mr. Hateley and t'woman who came in late,' he said slowly, as if suspecting that Shipley couldn't count or that this was some elaborate quiz in which he stood to lose a large sum of money. 'Plus Mr. Grogan and whoever were in theer wi' Mr. Grogan when I came in. I don't know who that were, but I think Mr. Hateley said it were a woman. Another woman, that is. I mek that four.'

Shipley rapped on the door himself and this time there was an answer of sorts. A female voice Shipley did not recognise responded, shrill and very determined, like high tensile wire quivering with electricity.

'Fuck off or I'll kill them all,' the voice said. 'You're welcome to George when I've finished with the bastard.'

Shipley turned round as if galvanised by a cattle prod.

'Out!' he said and neither the waiting constituent nor Jack Barraclough wasted any time in obeying him. Once outside on the street where normal life was going on unperturbed, Shipley felt his knees buckle slightly and he leaned against the plate glass façade of the constituency office for support. He pulled out his mobile and got through to county HQ.

'I need armed backup,' he said. 'I've got a hostage situation here.'

Inside the steamy and increasingly foetid locked room, Jay's heart had leapt when she heard the police outside and had then contracted painfully when she heard Margaret Davies's response. She felt icy cold but could feel sweat running down her back beneath her shirt and her heavy leather jacket. George Hateley doubled up suddenly, narrowly avoiding impaling his own neck on Davies's hovering knife, and retched vainly, inches over the puddle of congealing blood at his feet.

'For God's sake,' he groaned as he recovered

himself. 'For God's sake.'

Davies's eyes roamed the room restlessly and Jay guessed that the slightest pressure might tip her over the edge and bring that knife plunging in her own direction as well as Hateley's. She recalled that Mary Petherbridge had been killed in a frenzy of knife blows. She had no doubt that the woman who believed herself to be the dead girl Mags, but was probably her friend Donna Latham, was in the grip of some sort of hallucination where action and reaction would be totally unpredictable and probably very violent. She had no idea of the best way to save her own life, still less how to protect Hateley's. But she knew that as the only person in the room who was not in the grip of overwhelming emotion, she had to try.

Unglueing her tongue from the roof of her mouth she tried to speak.

'Mags?' she said tentatively. 'I have a little girl called Kate.' Davies's eyes flickered momentarily in Jay's direction, but only momentarily.

'You were the man with the green face,' she said to Hateley, whose only response was a strangled groan.

'How many were there of you?' Jay found herself asking almost in spite of herself. 'Six? One for each mask?' But all she got in return from Hateley was a swift snarl of anger.

'Sometimes they swapped masks,' Davies said. 'Just to confuse us. But he...' and she nodded to where Bernard Grogan's body lay half concealed behind the desk. 'He was always the bird, the big ugly cannibal bird. It was so big, that mask, that the night we went to the park and his friends didn't turn up he sent Donna away and he took it off. But she hid in the bushes and watched. She saw him. She saw him take the mask off and put it down on the grass.'

'Too hot maybe,' Jay said, trying to keep the conversation as normal as she could, yet knowing that it would return with its full horror in her nightmares for years to come, if she was lucky enough to still have years ahead of her. 'They're very heavy, those masks.'

'His son put it on your front door, you know,' Davies said conversationally. 'I saw him. He was often around, in the dark, the son. Too young to be one of them, though I bet he'd have liked to have been.'

'Yes, too young,' Jay said quickly, though a new niggle of doubt insinuated itself immediately into her adrenaline-saturated brain.

'I think it's time to go now, Mags,' she said, her desperation growing as the silence outside the door lengthened.

'Not finished yet,' Davies said. 'Stand up,' she said to Hateley, who very slowly obeyed, needing his hand on the desk for support and shaking visibly.

'Pull your trousers down,' she instructed, waving the knife, and again Hateley obeyed, letting them fall to the floor to reveal grubby white Y-fronts where his genitals appeared to have shrivelled to almost nothing. He moaned faintly and again put his hand on the desk for support.

'Leave it, Mags,' Jay said desperately. 'Let him go to jail instead. There's plenty of evidence to get him convicted. He's even been interfering with his own grand-daughter.' Hateley half-turned in Jay's direction at that, his face full of fury until, with a sudden flashing movement, Davies stabbed down the knife hard, hitting Hateley's hand dead centre and pinning it to the desk, and Hateley's rage turned to a scream of agony. For just a moment Davies had to struggle to release the blade from the wood of the desk top where it had lodged itself firmly and Jay saw her chance. She leapt across the room, unlocked the door and almost fell into the outer office and over the outstretched gun of an armed policeman who had just taken up a crouching position outside. Davies screamed as she freed the knife and followed on Jay's heels with murderous intent and the marksman shot her at near point blank range, propelling her backwards into the inner room where she fell sprawling into the puddle of blood and urine at George Hateley's feet.

A couple of days later Jay was sitting opposite Peter Shipley over a drink in the Woolpack, close to the police station where she had just signed a long and detailed statement. He had been waiting for her when she had finished.

'I owe you a drink,' he said and Jay had not felt strong enough to argue. She took a serious draught of her vodka and tonic and glanced at the crumpled policeman as he gazed into his pint.

'Is that what you call a result?' she asked. Shipley shrugged.

'A spectacularly messy one,' he said. 'The Crown Prosecution Service is going spare. We've one murderer dead, and another in intensive care who's going straight to a secure mental hospital if she recovers. There'll be no trial to speak of.'

'And George Hateley?' Jay asked.

'Will probably get away with it because Donna Latham's the only witness we've got to the fact that he was involved in anything: a very sick woman who says she recognised a voice.' He shrugged dispiritedly.

'DNA?' Jay asked, feeling slightly sick.

'Grogan's, yes, Hateley's, no,' Shipley said. 'I was surprised to find that there were still samples from the Bairstow case and they link Grogan to Mags Emmett and Sonja Kradic and – and this was a surprise – to Mary Petherbridge. I think he got rid of her because he was afraid of what Donna Latham might have told her. And he tried to make it look like a random attack. A lot of the stab wounds were inflicted after Mary Petherbridge was dead – purely cosmetic, you might say. Ironic, really, that Donna chose a knife as well, but it definitely wasn't the same one. So we've nothing on Hateley, except what Donna Latham says, and I very much doubt the CPS will put her in the witness box against Hateley when she's been dealt with herself. It's not a credible option.'

'Poor Abbie,' Jay said without thinking.

'It was Abbie, was it?' Shipley said quickly.

'She won't talk to anyone about it,' Jay said.

'Well, I'm glad for your sake it wasn't Kate. When you sent her away, I wondered...'

'I'd have killed him,' Jay said quietly, meaning it and thinking how easy it would be to slip into the sort of desperate hatred that had driven Donna Latham. 'I shouldn't be saying that to a detective,' she said, smiling faintly.

'What do you want to do about Chris Hateley?' Shipley asked. 'Do you want to press charges over the harrassment?'

Jay shook her head wearily. She might comprehend the need for revenge but when it came to it she had not the stomach for it.

'I don't think so,' she said. 'My sister's family's got enough to put up with.' Restoring the three cousins damaged by what had happened might be a life's work, she thought. Shipley nodded and drained his pint, then reached into his pocket and pulled out a small plastic evidence bag.

'Have you got your house key with you?' Jay gave it to him and he compared it with the key in the bag.

'It's the same,' he said. 'Donna had it, of course, though I'm not sure where she got it from. I'm sorry I didn't take your stalkers more seriously.'

'Stalkers,' Jay said. 'As if one wasn't enough. You could ask my next-door neighbour if Grace Bairstow gave him a key to her house. He's a nosy old boy and lonely with it. If Donna was hanging around and she talked to him nicely he's quite capable of asking her in for a cup of tea.'

'And she was canny enough to turn the conversation to the odd goings on next door. I'll check him out,' Shipley said. 'Will you stay in Pendle Bridge after all this?' he asked.

Jay glanced at him and managed a wry smile.

'I don't know,' she said. 'Will the museum project survive now? I rather doubt it. And Kate certainly won't want to stay. But maybe what's left of my family need me up here. I just don't know.'

'Oh, there is one bit of good news,' Shipley said, although he looked less than delighted with it. 'They released Kenny Bairstow on bail yesterday. His conviction will be quashed.'

'So Grace will see Kenny again after all. But your old boss's reputation will go down the tubes with the rest?'

Shipley got to his feet and pulled on his crumpled mac.

'I wouldn't tell anyone else this, and I'm not going to follow it up, but I went to see Les's widow yesterday. She lives up the Dales now and she must be eighty odd, if she's a day. She found a mask in a box in Les's wardrobe when he died, a brightly coloured bird with feathers she'd never seen before. She's no idea where he got it from but she's put it up on the dining room wall.'

This Large Print Book for the partially sighted, who cannot read normal print, is published under the auspices of

THE ULVERSCROFT FOUNDATION